D1395266

EMMA'S HAVEN

EMMA'S HAVEN

Elizabeth Daish

This first world edition published in Great Britain 1995 by
SEVERN HOUSE PUBLISHERS LTD of
9–15 High Street, Sutton, Surrey SM1 1DF.
First published in the USA 1995 by
SEVERN HOUSE PUBLISHERS INC., of
595 Madison Avenue, New York, NY 10022.

British Library Cataloguing in Publication Data

Daish, Elizabeth
  Emma's Haven
  I. Title
  823.914 [F]

  ISBN 0-7278-4831-3

Typeset by Palimpsest Book Production Limited,
Polmont, Stirlingshire
Printed and bound in Great Britain by
Hartnolls Ltd, Bodmin, Cornwall.

Chapter 1

Emma Dewar pulled her fleecy dressing-gown closer and tied the thick beltcord tightly against the night chill of the hall, the soft green tassels heavy and silky against the darker green of the fabric. A narrow rod of light showed under the door and she tapped a gentle tattoo before she turned the handle and peeped into the living-room.

"You awake?" asked Emily Darwen, as if it wasn't obvious. "Couldn't you sleep either?" She regarded her niece with disapproval. "I expect to have bad nights at my age but a young thing like you should be fast asleep."

"It's warm in here," Emma said and came closer to the stove.

Emily eyed her with barely concealed concern, then opened the double doors of the stove and put four small logs of cherry wood onto the bed of red coals. "Things on your mind?" she asked and left the fire doors open so that they could watch the flames. "Have you enough room for all your stuff in that small room? There's the cupboard on the landing you can use too. You can make this house your base for the future as far as I'm concerned."

"It's fine," Emma said gratefully. "I am still officially on the staff of The Princess Beatrice but I'm not sure if I want to go back after my leave is up. If I can keep some things here until I decide what job I'll take, it will be a relief. After years of training and the place in Bristol before that, suddenly I'm free to make a choice from several ideas, and quite candidly, I'm at a loss."

"You make some tea and we can have a biscuit," Emily said. "I did put the kettle to boil."

Emma went through into the morning-room and fetched a large new tin of biscuits, then went further into the kitchen where the water was boiling and the brown teapot stood on the hob, warming. She put far more tea-leaves in the pot than she thought necessary, but knew her aunt's weakness. "Tea strong enough to stand a spoon in," she would say after the first sip.

As the water flowed into the pot, Emma smiled. It was so encrusted with brown tannin that she wondered if she need add the fresh tea-leaves as there must be enough brown crust to make a strong cup without any more, but her aunt refused to scrape it clear as she said it had weathered to her liking.

The tin tray was ready with two cups and saucers and a small jug of milk. The sugar was in the blue bowl that she had known since she was a child, when she visited her aunt and her grandmother in the big house on the Mall in Newport, Isle of Wight, about two miles from where Emily now lived.

Emily was picking at the sticking-plaster that sealed the tin and Emma took it from her arthritic hands. "Let me," she said. "My nails are longer than yours."

She left Emily inspecting the contents of the tin, her face alight with anticipation, while Emma poured the tea and added water to her own cup to make it drinkable. "Can I have first pick?" Emily asked, her fingers hovering over a chocolate covered wholemeal.

"Of course. Bea did send them for you, but I hope you'll spare me some of the ones you usually leave until last," teased Emma. She went to the cupboard in the corner and produced a bottle of whisky. "Bea sent this too. Purely therapeutic, but I think a tot in that tea might improve it."

"She's an angel," Emily said and chuckled as she added a generous slug of spirit to her tea.

"Bea, an angel? Don't make me laugh." But Emma didn't laugh, she just looked wistful.

"Dr Sutton says that whisky will do more for my arthritis than any of the medicine he can offer me, and it does ease the discomfort," Emily said.

"What it is to have a tame general practitioner," Emma said. "I hope he doesn't see you in that dressing-gown." She regarded the green-and-maroon-checked, masculine garment with amusement. "You've had that for ever! What happened to that nice gown I brought for you from America?"

"I save that for when I'm ill," Emily said. "I bought this before rationing in 1938, when they made really warm mens' clothes and it's done me well, so it will do until the end of rationing."

"What about Dr Sutton? He seems very fond of you, Aunt Emily."

"When I need him as a doctor, he'll see the other gown, until then he sees me fully dressed," Emily said. "He plays a good hand of bridge and we get along well," she added. "I was hoping that you and Paul could make up a table," she said hopefully.

"I doubt it." Emma's voice was flat. "Paul had to go to Southampton in a hurry. He rang me when you were at work yesterday. He decided to continue that course in neurology and has persuaded Dr Sutton to defer his appointment as his partner in the practice and employ a locum for six months until Paul has this extra qualification."

Emily Dewar raised her eyebrows. "So you feel deserted?"

"Of course not," Emma said sharply. "Just because Paul has been useful and was very kind when Guy died, it doesn't mean we have any permanent link."

"Early days," Emily said. "You're still too raw to think of any other man." She pushed the biscuit tin over towards Emma and spoke carefully. "It's no use anyone telling you that it will pass and you'll forget. I know that, and we have that in common." She glanced at the girl's frozen face. "Your Guy died of typhus in that terrible camp, Belsen, when he was helping the sick and dying, and my Arnold died of typhoid at the front in the First World War." She sighed. "Hardly heroic deaths, if you believe what people think, but they were heroes for all that. They both volunteered for something dangerous and must have known that they might not come back."

"I'd forgotten that you lost your man too," Emma said apologetically. She took a biscuit and crumbled it.

"That's no way to treat those good Swiss biscuits," her aunt scolded her. "If you don't want them, leave them for someone who does and I'd like another cup of tea, thank you."

"What would I do without you? It's so good to be here," Emma said impulsively. "I'll try not to be a misery and I will have to make up my mind soon about my future."

"Do nothing in a hurry. You can stay here as long as you like and welcome, but consider what is on offer and weigh it all up carefully."

"Paul suggested the casualty sister post on the Island, but I think he was just being polite and helpful. It hasn't even been advertised yet, so I have time to think about that. He's sure I would get it, with the name of The Princess Beatrice Hospital behind me."

"What else?"

Emma looked at her with a puzzled frown. "I thought you wanted me here."

4

"What I'd like and what's right for you might not be the same," Emily said. "Your mother bossed you about for years and made you feel guilty, and I think Guy did too, if you're honest enough to admit it. So now you can take a clear view and choose what you really want to do, without looking over your shoulder at any disapproving faces."

"I have a few weeks leave from Beatties that was due after qualifying for my State Registration and they want me back as a junior theatre sister for mainstream surgery. It would be in London, as they are thinking of closing the sector hospitals like Heath Cross as soon as the wards empty of doodle bomb casualties and all the wounded German prisoners of war have been taken away. The war in Europe is over except for a few patches that the Russians seem to be mopping up and the Japs can't bomb us here."

"Do you want to live in London again?"

"I didn't want to live in the cottage that Guy bought for us near Epsom," Emma said firmly. "Bea and her husband bought it and have had all sorts of things done to it, and I am relieved to see the back of it. I might visit them there when I can no longer remember what it was like, but, for now, I'd rather not go there."

"Any other ideas?" Emily stared into the fire. "You're restless and no wonder after all those years of training and nursing the wounded and then your fiancé's death. What does Bea say?"

"Bea?" Emma looked startled. "Dwight's fracture is nearly healed now and I suppose they'll be going to the States for good. She has a job back at Beatties in orthopaedics for a few months, or for as long as she needs it, but she could leave at any time, so we can't work together again, at least not on a permanent basis. Unless I follow them to the States, as Bea suggested." She wrinkled her nose. "I would want a holiday there first to test the climate and the people," she said cautiously. "Someone suggested midwifery. It would be a useful qualification for work in surgery when we have Caesarians but I can't say I'm attracted to bawling babies and women with breast and bowel fixations and all that bottle feeding."

"Why not visit Bea for a few days now, or, if she can spare the time, ask her here. I seem to know her even though we have never really met and I do have to thank her for her gifts over the last year or so. If she goes away, this might be the last time you can be together and I know you are close."

"What a wonderful idea. I'll telephone her tomorrow." Emma's smile had more warmth now and the fire had nothing to do with it. "Finished with these?" she asked and put the lid on the biscuit tin, sealing it again with the sticky tape.

"That's right. Make it tight." Emily laughed. "I hate a baggy biscuit as much as your Gran did. We had a shop near us where they sold broken biscuits, loose by the pound, and Mother would try one first in case they'd been left out and gone soft."

"You don't have to get up to go to work as it's Sunday, so I'll get you breakfast in bed," Emma promised.

"You'll make me lazy," Emily said, but her expression was softer than most people saw.

"You work too hard. When do you ever take a break and relax? Will they close the British Restaurant soon? You'd have to retire then."

"There are no plans to do away with them yet. Too many people depend on them to eke out their rations and some of the food is very good." Emily frowned. "It isn't only the food that's useful. If people living alone have to cook, it takes fuel, and an hour or so in a warm building where they can eat makes the coal last longer."

Emma gazed into the depths of the fire, a smile touching

her lips as she recalled doing this years ago, imagining that the red and black caves were the homes of gnomes and fairies. "You don't seem short of fuel," she said.

"I keep the fire banked up all the time and use a lot of wood that Bert Cooper gets for me." She shook her head in disbelief. "Sometimes I can't think he's the same man I remember when I was younger."

"My mother disliked him," Emma said, "But that's nothing to go by, as she hated most people and probably still does, including me," she added cheerfully.

"He and your grandfather were good friends and I think they got up to some fairly questionable deals, but, under it all, he was what they call a rough diamond with a heart somewhere. His first marriage was sour and they never had children. Annie Cooper was a bitter woman and I can't think how my mother ever put up with her, but she did a lot for her and even made ointment for her rheumatism." Emily too, gazed into the fire.

"He married again?" Emma mentally prodded her aunt while she was in this relaxed mood. It was seldom that she reminisced, and, as her own mother had not been willing to talk about the past, Emma listened eargerly to any snippets that her aunt would tell her.

"That was the talk of Newport! Maudie Dove was no better than she ought to be, or so they said, and your grandfather knew her better than he should, but after he died, Bert took her on and when Annie went soon after, she pretended that she was carrying Bert's child and they got married."

"Surely that was a recipe for disaster?" Emma was enthralled.

"Not at all. Poor Maudie! When she admitted that there was no baby, Bert was angry. He said that if she bore him a child she could have a good life with him, and if not, she could get out. By then she was quite fond

7

of him and knew which side her bread was buttered. He knew she was able to have a child, as she had a girl when she was hardly more than a child herself. At least the local tongues stopped wagging when the gossips added up dates and found that she didn't have to marry to make it respectable. They were very disappointed, I can tell you. Maudie Dove, suddenly dressed in a rabbit-fur coat and living like a lady! She did her duty and more, and made Bert the contented man he is today."

"All this is news to me," Emma said. "Mother would never discuss her early life. I do remember a bit, but vaguely. What happened to the girl?"

"Lucy was in love with your Uncle Sidney, whom you saw in America, and she followed him out there, thinking he loved her."

Emma pursed her mouth and tried to recall what he had said in the sanatorium. "They did get engaged and she was killed in a car accident, wasn't she?" She glanced at Emily. "You said she thought he loved her."

"I remember the message he gave you to tell me. He said that he did love Lucy – as much as he could ever love a woman." She sighed. "I think we all knew, all except your Gran that is, that he was queer. Being engaged to Lucy meant that he was acceptable out there in Hollywood and the Hearst circle, where, in spite of the things they showed on film, they were very strict about the public morals of their movie stars.

"I never saw his manager, but I gather that they were lovers and Ivor vetted all his mail. When he was dying, he made all his decisions for him. When I met Uncle Sidney, I felt a tremendous bond of family and I wish I could have got to know him." Emma's eyes were moist.

"It was important to Mother to know they were engaged."

"Why? Perhaps she suspected that he was that way inclined?"

"He was very handsome and that side of him was never shown until he went to America. Girls adored him. No, she was relieved when she heard of the engagement because she thought it broke the spell that had haunted her for years. An old Gypsy told her a lot that came true and said that one son would never marry but would be lost to her for ever. My other brothers were married young, so she knew it was Sidney that the Gypsy meant and she loved Sidney dearly. She thought that if this was not true, then some of the rest would not come true either, but it all came home to roost in the end."

"I suppose the Gypsy is dead now. I could do with a glance into the future," Emma said wistfully. "I can't seem to see what I must do."

"Go with the tide," Emily said firmly. "Fight, and you might land on the rocks as your mother did, but you could find a safe haven close to home if you drift. Take your time." She laughed to dispel the suddenly serious atmosphere. "I can't see you doing midwifery!"

"Nor can I or Bea. She said that she would get broody and Dwight would kill her if she became pregnant before they are settled in America."

"Ring her tomorrow, if you don't mind using that contraption." Emily was looking with a fearful dislike at the heavy black telephone lurking on the sofa table.

"I'll do that. Bed for us, if we can sleep after all that strong tea!" Emma said.

"My joints feel easier and I've enjoyed our chat," Emily said. She gave Emma a rare hug. "I've enjoyed it too much, so don't go away just yet."

Emma washed the cups and Emily piled coke on the fire before closing the doors tightly and pushing in the damper to keep the fire only just burning until morning. The hall

9

was cold after the warmth of the sitting-room and Emma hurried back to bed, first putting a stone hot-water bottle covered with a knitted slip-over into her aunt's bed.

It had been like looking into a distant generation of the Darwen family and Emma felt a sudden twinge of jealousy that Emily had been one of seven children and they had a loving mother watching over them.

But I would never have gone to The Princess Beatrice Hospital to train as a nurse, she told herself. I could not have taken Guy as a lover and would not have had as much freedom as I enjoyed in London and down at the sector hospital at Heath Cross. I would not know Bea and the others. She felt warmer under the blankets and knew that she had real friends.

For the first time since she heard of Guy's death she curled up and hugged her pillow, but felt no sadness. The house was quiet after the night-time hum of traffic in south-east London and the restless movement along the corridors of the nurses' home when night-duty girls, disregarding the rules, crept back to their rooms for books or clean uniform in their midnight break period.

She tried to remember the telephone number of the apartment in St James's where she thought that Bea might be staying if her father was away on his political duties, then decided she would ring the American Air Force base, as Bea spent a lot of time there with Dwight now that he was recovering from his badly fractured leg.

"Tomorrow," she murmured. "What's the rush?" As she drifted off to sleep she thought of what she had talked about with Aunt Emily. They had not mentioned the war as a threatening reality. Maybe it really was all over for her and for Aunt Emily, and Paul and Bea. No, not Bea, as the Pacific war had still to be won, but if Dwight was out of flying, it didn't matter.

10

Chapter 2

"Hold the line, caller," said the disembodied American voice and Emma heard the background of activity in the Airbase. The echoes of other voices on the switchboard came in a blur of sound with the schmaltzy music that sweetened the operators' working day.

"You're through now," the voice said and the line crackled.

"Emma!" Bea's shout of joy was heart-warming. "How are you, ducky? And how did you know I needed to hear from you?"

"I'm fine," Emma said. "I thought I was the one who needed to hear from you!"

"I wanted to ring, but Dwight, who seems to have developed second sight since his accident, said no!"

"I thought he liked me. He said I was next in line if you misbehaved."

"He told me to leave you to Aunt Emily and to let you make up your own mind for once about what you really want to do. He said I might try to influence you . . . as if I ever have!"

"He said that?" Emma gulped. "He was right, but how did he know? He hasn't met my aunt and neither have you."

"Come off it. We know almost as much about her as you do. I have been madly jealous for years after enduring my awful family, and Dwight nods his head and says she sounds like his granny in Ohio or somewhere rustic. So, have you made up your mind?"

"No. I can't say that any of my options appeal just yet. Aunt Emily says I must go with the tide, but I think she is a fatalist as well as being a bit fey."

"What about the job in Cas on the Island? Paul sounded keen that you should apply for it."

"It's possible, but I don't think I'd like it."

"How is Paul?"

"Paul who?"

"Ouch! I can feel the ice forming. Had a row?"

"Of course not. It's just that even Aunt Emily sees more than exists where Paul is concerned, and he might find it embarrassing. He was helpful in Bristol when I went to my father's funeral, and we had fun when he took you and me out a few times when Guy and Dwight were away and we needed an escort, but that's all there was to it, and now he's away doing that neurological course that he wanted, so he'll be in Southampton for ages."

"The London celebrations of VE day were fabulous and we would never have been there, but for Paul," Bea pointed out. "Dwight is still sulking that he wasn't there to see it all," she said, as if she knew that somehow Paul was not her friend's favourite man of the moment and thought that maybe Emma needed reminding of his finer points.

"It was wonderful, but I shall never be able to look back on the anniversary with pleasure, as it was after that I heard that Guy was dead."

"True," Bea replied. "Now listen. This call must be costing a lot. I have a car coming in half an hour to take me back to London, so I'll ring you from St James's as soon as I get there."

The line went dead, leaving Emma to wonder why Bea was going to the apartment and not staying at the base with Dwight or even going back to Beatties.

12

She put down the phone and went to make some coffee.

"I hope you didn't cut short your chat because of the cost," Aunt Emily said.

"It was Bea who cut me off, but she's ringing back later," Emma replied.

"Is he going away again?"

"Dwight? I doubt it." Emma bit her lip. "He's mobile, but the fracture must ache a lot now it's out of plaster and off traction. They couldn't expect him to go back on active service yet, and he has such a high rank now that he's more valuable in command from a base than flying a bomber."

"Dr Sutton listens to the wireless a lot," Emily said. "The Americans still have their hands full in the Pacific and they say that many of the planes they used in Europe are being sent back to the States and to other theatres of war."

Emma looked thoughtful. "At the beginning of the war Americans had no idea of what went on over here, and for them the war was such a long way away it was unreal and they didn't even want to know. I suppose the same thing is happening now in reverse. We have no idea about the war against Japan except where we have our troops, in Burma and a few other places in the British Empire. There are thousands of small islands in the Pacific about which we know nothing and yet they might make a lot of difference to the outcome of the Japanese war. Australia is more vulnerable than we are in Europe and we tend to forget the tremendous part that the Aussies and New Zealanders have taken and how they could be affected if they were overrun by Japs."

The telephone rang. Emily hastily picked up her coffee cup and went to the door. "I'll finish mine in the kitchen and knock up a sponge cake if she's coming here," she said.

"It won't bite you!" Emma lifted the receiver, still laughing.

"You sound happy."

"Paul? Sorry, I was expecting Bea to ring."

"And my voice doesn't make you glad?"

"Don't be silly. I was laughing at Aunt Emily. She is scared of the phone and doesn't even like to be in the room when it rings."

"I know. It's a disappointment to Dr Sutton. He was hoping she'd retire from the catering job and be a kind of receptionist at the surgery. She'd be great with giving advice before the doctor could get to a patient, but she'd never be happy on the phone."

"Your patients would never want your services if she was there," Emma said dryly.

"Lovely! I could write them all up for aspirin and go fishing."

"As yet we haven't seen your skills here," she said lightly.

"I'm going to be busy. I'm cramming in a years' work into six months before I take up the partnership with Sutton."

"So you will stay in Southampton all that time?" Emma was disappointed.

"Not all the time. I shall be at St Thomas's for a week or so."

"But not here?"

He hesitated. "Not for a while. I have to concentrate on one thing at a time, which is why I rang. The keys to my car are at the surgery along with a fair number of petrol coupons, and Dr Sutton doesn't want to use the car as he has a better one of his own. I know that Guy taught you to drive, so rather than let it rust away,

I hoped you'd look after it for me and take Aunt Emily for drives."

"That's kind," she said. "I know that you are fond of her."

He coughed. "I'm fond of her niece too." He seemed to be controlling his voice. "Are you applying for the casualty job?"

"As yet I don't know what to do, Paul."

"Good. Do nothing in a hurry. You have all the time in the world."

"I thought you were keen on me taking it?"

"I am, but what I want might not be right for you," he replied. "I'm selfishly biased."

"Go with the tide, is what Aunt Emily said."

"Wise woman. If only she was twenty years younger," he said cryptically. "Fetch the keys, and remember, if at any time you really need me, Emma, call me."

She replaced the phone and it rang again almost immediately.

"Aunt Emily talking to her lover?" asked Bea. "I tried to get you three times."

"That was Paul. He is lending me his car while he is away," Emma said.

Bea chuckled. "Artful!"

"What do you mean?"

"Nothing. Just that he will be away from your dreaded allure, yet keep tabs on you for the future when everything is calm again."

Emma felt her colour rising. "Sometimes you talk a lot of rot," she said dismissively. "Now what are *you* up to? Divorce or a tiff or is Dwight going back to the States?"

"I need you, Dewar."

Emma was immediately alert. After years of calling each other by surnames on duty, they had abandoned it off duty, but Bea reverted to that form of address in rare moments of tension or indecision.

"I'm here," she said.

"Thank God for that. All this so-called recuperative leisure after our exams is killing me. They work us to death for years and wonder why we get lost when we have spare time to think."

"You loved every minute," Emma said calmly. "Now tell me what is really wrong."

"My husband is a fool!"

"I'd never agree with that," Emma said warmly. "Apart from the fact that he married you, I'd say he was blissfully sane."

"Why do I think this woman can help me?" Bea asked the phone. "The fact is that he has volunteered to ferry planes back to the States."

"It wouldn't be combat," Emma said quickly. "The Atlantic is free from German ships and aircraft and he would be flying huge, safe planes."

"It does have certain advantages," Bea admitted. "He will be stationed here and brought back in a transporter each time he delivers a plane. Otherwise they are murmuring that he could be called back to Washington, possibly as an adviser to the Pentagon." She gave an explosive snort. "Can you see me there, with all those service and political wives, smiling and making small talk all day?"

"I wonder they haven't scooped you up earlier," Emma said heartlessly. "You have the background of politics from your father, you have been groped by fat Army Brigadiers and Rear Admirals . . . no pun intended, suffered the company of Dwight's godfather's crowd at Epsom, so you're a natural, as the Yanks say."

"But you wouldn't be there to share a giggle," Bea wailed. "I might even take them seriously after I'd been thoroughly brain-washed."

16

"Not you. It's much more likely that Washington would reel under the force of your zany personality and the fate of the world would be transformed."

"We're enjoying this! I wanted sympathy from you and here we are laughing about my poor husband's fate."

"That's better. It's 'my poor husband' now, is it? I'm sure that Dwight would not do anything dangerous now that he's not at the sharp end of the war."

"There was another alternative," Bea said seriously. "They use Catalina flying boats over the battle zones at sea, picking up the wounded and shipwrecked, and then flying them direct to emergency hospitals they set up as close as possible to the action. There have been several major losses at sea and the boys on that stint are kept very busy. They save an enormous number of lives and sometimes become casualties themselves under strafing fire."

"Could Dwight lift heavy men into a plane of that type? It's one thing to sit at the controls of a plane, but there would be other, very heavy duties on a flying boat. You said that he's not all that good on his feet yet, so how would he clamber in and out of small boats if the plane was anchored offshore?"

"I feel better! When Emma Dewar puts on her mother hen voice, I know the war is really over, or very nearly. Calm down, ducky. You are quoting what the medics told him and he is stuck with ferrying to fill the time before he is discharged. I was feeling blue this morning as he has left on the first trip and won't be back for a week or more."

"So, you are free? Aunt Emily thought you might be and she wants to know if you can come here for a break. I think the biscuits and whisky went to her head last night," she added dryly. "I know she's a bit psychic, but putting hot-water bottles in the spare bedroom as if she knew you'd come is a bit much. The room is all ready."

"Bless her." Bea sounded husky. "She'll let me call her Aunt Emily, won't she?"

"Come on the early ferry and I can meet you if I can get Paul's car to start."

"Does she like strawberry jam or lemon curd?" Emily Darwen regarded the perfect Victoria sponge cake with a critical eye. "And if she comes early there's some nice soup out there.

"What makes you think she'll be here to eat it?"

"If I didn't know already, one look at your face would have told me," Emily said and smiled. "What's that husband of hers done now?"

Emma told her about Dwight. "I hope he'll be all right. I suppose your Gypsy woman would have been able to tell us what to expect, but I don't think I'd want to know." She shivered. "I'm glad I knew nothing of Guy's death until after it happened."

"She'll want something hot for supper," Emily announced. "It may be so-called summer, but I've felt warmer in February, and last night was really cold."

"I wonder you felt it with all that whisky inside you," Emma teased her. "At least the sky's cleared and it's dry now. She might have a good crossing. Before I forget, I still have a few emergency ration cards that I didn't use on nights off. Dwight's godfather, the General, spoiled us and sent us lots of food parcels when we were at Heath Cross."

"I don't like American biscuits much," Emily said. These Swiss ones that Bea gets from her father are much better, but if I hadn't tasted them I'd be thankful for the Yankee ones, I suppose." She looked at the crumpled ration cards and put them behind the vase on the mantelpiece. "Leave them there until we need them. Sutton had a few nice rabbits left on his doorstep and he sent over a couple, so we can have a nice stew."

"A grateful patient?"

"Yes, but he never asks who leaves them, as they are probably poached," Emily said calmly. "My father used to say they were all the sweeter, taken like that."

"I'll do the vegetables for tonight before I go to fetch her," Emma said. She put on a frilly apron and peeled potatoes and carrots and a swede turnip, then sliced an onion ready to be browned with the rabbit pieces before they went into the casserole. A large fresh cabbage was washed and drained ready for cooking in boiling water and Emma tried not to see the piece of washing soda that Emily put on the raw leaves ready for cooking, as she knew the result would be very green cabbage with not a hint of vitamin C left in it, leached out by the soda.

Emily quickly and efficiently skinned the rabbits and gutted them, reserving the liver and the heads which would add flavour to the stew. She tossed a furry rabbit's foot over to Emma and then another. "If Dwight is superstitious, give him one of these to keep away evil."

"Two?"

"No, one is for you to fend off strange men," she said crisply.

"I can't wear it down my bra," Emma said. "It would tickle. What about Bea? Doesn't she get one?"

Emily severed another foot. "Might as well let her have one if she wants it, but she doesn't need one," she said, as if she really knew. "Put them to dry off on the shelf and fill the kettle ready."

"What do you do with the skins?"

"Sell them to Clancy, who collects junk and empty bottles down by the quay. I give the money to the Red Cross but it doesn't amount to much. He collects from the restaurant once a week and we are glad to get rid of the jars and bottles and any skins. The fur goes to make fur felt hats, although there is less call for that now."

Emma walked slowly down the lane behind the house. The air was full of early summer scents and sounds and the hedgerows were white with damp Queen Anne's Lace. The rain of the past few days had stopped and the sky promised a fine spell again.

She crossed the main road and opened the gate. The path up to the house and surgery was grassy between the paving slabs and the former tennis court was bereft of the net and marker lines. We could get it back into shape and play there, Emma thought with growing interest, then realised that she was thinking of playing tennis with Paul.

Almost angrily, she pressed the bell on the front door of the house. Paul would be away until winter, and that would waste an entire summer. I might be far away, too, she thought, with a sense of everything she held dear and solid drifting away.

Iris, the girl who "helped out" answering doors and cleaning the surgery, asked her in and Emma stepped into an old-fashioned hallway. "Dr Sutton is on his rounds but he said to give you the car keys and this envelope."

"Tell him that Miss Darwen was very pleased with the rabbits as we have a guest coming today."

"Who is that?" Iris asked with the curiosity and confidence of long and trusted service.

"A friend of mine from London. You haven't met her, Iris, but she's been anxious to come here for a long time."

"Then you'd better take some fruit," Iris said. "I picked lots of gooseberries and a few early strawberries that Dr Sutton tried to grow in a pot in the greenhouse. It does bring them on a bit in there, but hardly worth the trouble."

"Are you sure?"

"He doesn't eat much stewed fruit and likes to wait for the apples." Iris laughed. "He grumbles that we can't buy oranges and he pines for a few bananas. I gave him some that my sister's boy wouldn't eat when he was given a bunch at school as a treat, and you'd have thought they were the crown jewels. Most of the children didn't know what they were and one tried to eat one with the skin on!"

"I'll try to get some." Emma said, remembering the huge hand that Dwight brought back from America before his accident, and the piled glass bowls of fruit that decked the dinner tables when the General entertained in the house on Epsom Downs. If anyone could find bananas, it would be Dwight, and now Bea, who had access to the lavish American food at the Airbase.

"Is she posh, your friend?" asked Iris.

"She is, but it doesn't show very often," Emma replied, finding it difficult to describe the beautiful blonde woman with the deceptively haughty expression. "She does give that impression at times as she's always been used to the best of everything at home and she dresses very well, but she's a lovely person," Emma added warmly.

Iris tugged at her garishly patterned apron and smoothed back her untidy hair. "I could come and serve supper, I mean dinner," she offered wistfully. "When Mrs Sutton was alive I used to wear my cap and apron and looked very smart, and I have it all ready in my room, but the doctor won't let me wear it any more. She liked the coffee and cream colours and the apron has a nice little frill round it."

"Times are changing, Iris. Most people don't like the idea of having maids in uniform any more except in hospitals and very big houses. There aren't many women who want to do that sort of work after earning

21

lots of money in factories and wearing what everyone else wore."

"Some of them got their hands more dirty working in factories than in private service," Iris retorted, "But they think they're a cut above me. Just wait until they find they can't get work when the bombs have all been made!"

"I don't know what Sutton would do without you, Iris," Emma said tactfully. "But lots of people have the urge to do work of what they call 'national importance'. Even Princess Elizabeth is in the ATS, servicing huge trucks, and she can drive an armoured car. On VE night she was on the balcony of Buckingham Palace in uniform."

"Fancy!" Iris gave an envious sigh. "I'd like to have seen that." She picked up a basket. "I'll put the fruit in this and you can bring it back any time," she said and Emma followed her into the immaculate kitchen.

The basket went into the trunk of the car and Emma cautiously started the engine, relieved to find that the gear change was similar to the one on which she had learned to drive. With growing confidence, she drove slowly through Newport and on to the main road to Ryde and the pier.

On impulse, she parked at the town end and walked the full length of the long pier to meet the ferry from Portsmouth. She sat on a bollard, watching the sea. The rusting defences were still in place along the coast, but there were growing gaps where some of the jagged sheets of corrugated iron had been destroyed by storms and had not been replaced now that the secret building of parts of Mulberry Harbour was over. It had been towed out to Normandy to make an instant harbour for D-Day landings and almost forgotten now that people were once again allowed to travel freely between the Island and the mainland without showing passes.

The sun was warm on her face and arms. Her discarded blazer hung on a post that had been part of a barrier and she felt contented and sleepy. Why think of leaving the Island? The local hospital was big and very busy and the work would be familiar and varied. The department would be similar to the smaller of the casualty units at Heath Cross and she would have the Island waiting to explore when she was off duty.

A group of soldiers wandered out to the end of the pier to wait for the ferry and they eyed Emma with the interest that she expected now when servicemen in uniform passed by. In civilian clothes they might lose that almost aggressively bold stare, but she knew that they meant no harm and she could handle any approach that went beyond the bounds of courtesy.

The ship's siren announced the impending docking of the ferry with as much noise as the *Mauretania* might make, and minutes later, Bea almost ran down the gangway, followed by a young army officer carrying not only his own luggage but hers as well.

"Good old Bea," Emma whispered as she hugged her. "You can't move an inch without a retinue!"

"Isn't my husband here?" Bea asked in an offended tone.

"He couldn't make it," Emma said. "He'll see you later."

"What a pity." Bea turned to her escort. "Thank you, Captain. I'd like to invite you for drinks, but I am staying with stuffy relatives and my husband will be waiting." She gave him a devastating smile. "Good luck at the barracks and with your demobilisation."

He murmured his goodbyes, then realised that he had been dismissed, very gently, but very firmly. He saluted and walked down the pier, carrying his bag.

"Do we walk down there, too? If so, let's admire the seagulls until he's gone. He is expecting to be met at the town end of the pier and wanted to give me a lift, but he was getting a bit fraught and wanted to tell me his life story."

"We'll wait for the next train down the pier. That case looks heavy. Are you staying with your stuffy relatives for a month?" Emma asked dryly.

"A little train? How quaint." Bea sat on the hard seat and gazed out of the window at the wide sweep of sand by the eastern bandstand, her bright eyes full of interest. I'm going to love your Island, Emma."

"It won't like you if you call it quaint," Emma retorted. "We're fussy who we accept down here."

"I tried to get something to eat on the ferry, but it looked like Heath Cross night duty food on a bad night, so I'm hungry. Can we buy something here?" Bea glanced at the shuttered hotels along the sea front without much hope.

"Aunt Emily said you might need something so we'll get home quickly. It isn't far."

Chapter 3

The living-room fire burned brightly, although the day had blossomed and was now warm. Bea slipped off her pale yellow silk jacket and stretched like a contented cat. She ate her second slice of strawberry Victoria sponge cake and licked her fingers free of jam.

Emily Darwen laughed. "I'd have known you in a crowd," she said.

"Am I so unique?" Bea asked with satisfaction.

"One alone, I'd say, and I can't help thinking that your husband has married a handful."

"He does know," Bea replied. "As he's bigger than me, for the first time in my life I take orders from a man!" She laughed. "At least that's what he thinks."

"Go and unpack and have a rest on the bed," Emily suggested. "You didn't sleep last night, did you?"

"Do I look such a wreck?"

"You know how you look and you needn't come to me for compliments or sympathy. You need neither. I have some paperwork to do for my job tomorrow, and Emma can dish up a meal at seven if you can last out that long."

"Yes, Aunt Emily," Bea said meekly and dragged her case up the stairs to the chintzy, comfortable room with the far view across the wheatfields to the central chalk ridge of the Island. She opened the window to breathe in the soft air and suddenly felt exhausted.

Tears fell in unexpected relief and Bea felt the tensions slip away. Until now, she had thought she was in control and the efforts at being bright and cool over the past months had convinced her and everyone except Dwight that she was not suffering.

"Ease up, darling," he'd said.

"I went through hell when you were injured and I had to concentrate on my exams and, well you know, Emma and Guy and things," she said and tried to smile. "I'm fine now that you are well again," she'd assured him, but he kissed her closed eyelids over the brittle brightness and held her close.

"Honey, let go," he said and shook her gently. "I feel a heel, taking you away from everything that has been your life for several years, but it will be OK I promise."

"It's just anti-climax. For years, people, and women in particular, have trained me and bullied me into a certain very efficient mould. I welcomed it as I needed stability after my awful family gave me nothing. Without the friends I made at Beatties I know I could have gone the same way as them, taking lovers and never experiencing real love."

"They can't be as bad as that any more," he said.

Bea laughed. "Pa doesn't dare as his position in parliament would be on the line if they sniffed scandal, and my mother finds it difficult to attract the young men she needs to have following her around. As the song says, 'They're either too old or too grassy green, the pickings are poor and the crop is lean', and she finds the young officers boring. She was reduced to picking up a rather fat Dutch colonel during the VE celebrations and I think he must have been drunk at the time."

Dwight chuckled. "Not famous for humour, some of the Dutch guys, but solid soldiers."

"Who needs a solid soldier in bed? Or a present of a whole red Edam cheese when my Ma hates the stuff?"

"No wooden clogs?" They dissolved into laughter and Dwight was partly reassured, but he was still worried. "You'll miss Emma," he said bluntly.

"Don't," she said faintly.

"She's the sister you never had," he went on relentlessly. "She's your best friend and I know that some of the things you've endured and shared together are there and always will be, tucked away somewhere that I can't get to, just as I have experiences and memories of guys I shall miss every day of my life."

"You, too?" she asked as if this was a fresh idea.

He made her look at him directly. "I don't need to share those things and nor do you, but they'll never come between us. We are damned lucky to have found each other and Emma may be the one who needs help just now, not you."

"Emma is strong," Bea began.

"Maybe, but she hasn't had an easy time. Think about it. People who are relied on get no sympathy as we think they can cope, but under it they might be crying out."

"We support each other," Bea said defensively. "I was there when her best friend in Bristol was killed and I think I helped over Guy's death."

He smoothed her hair. "I know you did. But you are afraid that if you are on the other side of the pond, this won't happen any more for either of you."

"I feel so alone when you are away," she murmured. "You are a swine, making me love you as much as I do!"

"That's my girl," he said and grinned. "Sweet talk will get you everything."

"I hope we don't go to the States yet. I have to see that Emma has someone again." Bea wriggled down into his arms.

"Uhu?"

"Why 'uhu'? I think Paul will do nicely with a little encouragement. He's followed her to the Island and is playing it cool at present, but he's mad about her."

"So why not leave any encouragement to Emma when she's ready? You can't rush in bull-headed and make something happen. My worst enemies were made when my mother assured me that I'd like someone she'd lined up for me at a party, and I dug in my heels before I'd even met them and vowed that no way would I like them."

"Touché! But she does like him."

"Is that enough? I may not like you! I love you! There is a difference."

"You do like me," she replied complacently. "If not, you'd never put up with me."

"Leave Emma's love life alone. If she wants a social life we can arrange that, but she'll have to lick her wounds for a while longer I think."

"She'll have to make up her mind what to do next as far as work is concerned. The casualty job could be fun, but not if she doesn't want to marry Paul, as he will have a lot of contact there. She could come back to Beatties with me, but I think she dreads returning to Guy's old stamping grounds and if you and I suddenly disappear, she'll feel the break even more."

"What do you want to do? That's my concern. You could stay on at the Base. They like you and you can enjoy some leisure for a change. A bit easier than Beatties."

Bea wrinkled her nose and he kissed it. "I like most of them, but I feel in a vacuum," she said. "Most of them came over late and have no idea of what happened here. If I mention the wounded, their eyes glaze over, and if anyone wants to discuss the peace, they talk about the luxuries they are missing with rationing, even though the American Forces' wives have never lacked anything, and at home they have had a lot more than us."

"Come on, Bea, they aren't all the same. What about Mamie who was out in the Marianas when she met Duke and married him? She saw action and plenty of blood and guts, and works for the Red Cross over here as she still feels real commitment."

"She is different," Bea conceded. "She makes some of the others look like soft pink cushions."

"Maybe you should transfer to the US Nursing Service," he teased her.

"And wear ghastly white stockings and white uniform dresses that look like the ones the attendants wore in the mental hospital section of Heath Cross?"

Bea crossed her elegant silk-clad legs and he bent to kiss her knee. "I know that the nurses at Beatties have the sexiest uniform ever," he said. "It should never be allowed! Anyone who thinks that calf length dresses with wide skirts, cinched-in belts and black silk stockings, are sober and godly, must be mad. The first time I saw you in uniform my pants got too tight."

"I wonder if Florence Nightingale had the same affect on her wounded? That kind of uniform was good enough for her," Bea said and chuckled. "Even the girls who have no figures look good in the dresses and I think it does a lot for the morale and recovery of patients," she added piously.

"You kidding? It plays havoc with them. Men pay a fortune to have tarts dress like that!"

"Don't be coarse, darling . . . and how would you know?" she asked with a dangerous expression.

"Men talk," he said hastily. "I'd never touch them, especially when I have the real thing!" He grabbed her and kissed her. "You still drive me mad," he said.

"Good. Keep it that way," she replied calmly and began to undress.

The release of love-making made her sad with "la petite

tristesse" that many women feel, and long after Dwight was asleep, she lay awake and stared at the chink of moonlight through the gap in the curtain. His arm was heavy across her breasts and at last she turned carefully and slid from the bed.

The cottage near Epsom smelled of fresh distemper and paint and she lit a cigarette to dispel the sickly aroma. The light in the sitting-room showed pale walls and a brand-new, pale blue carpet that picked up the tones in the chintz-covered settee and armchairs. She huddled in the deep chair by the window, after hesitating and then pulling back the curtains, almost expecting a voice to say, "Put that light out", but of course the war in Europe was over and the blackout had become a thing of the past.

She remembered the black rep drapes over ward windows, curtains that had lost their dye as the war laboured on and they became grey with tinges of blue in the worn fabric where the light struck.

This is a mistake, she decided. It had seemed a good idea to buy the cottage from Emma and make it over to suit her and Dwight to use as a bolt-hole when they could be together, but now, she knew that it would take more than a coat of paint and fresh furnishings flown all the way across the Atlantic, to dispel the memories of Heath Cross and what had happened there; too many memories that she had shared with Emma when they had nursed the wounded of D-Day and later, the German prisoners of war. Even the fact that Guy and Emma had slept in the the double bed on which she now slept with Dwight made her uneasy as if she was encroaching on their private and tender territory.

She drowsed in the chair and woke to find Dwight with a coffee pot in his hand. "How does this thing work?" He turned the expensive Swiss percolator over. "My Granny makes real good coffee in a jug," he grumbled.

"And gives you deep orange pumpkin pie and blue, blue, blueberries."

"Don't you get sassy with me, Missee."

"I'll show you how it works," she said and reached up to kiss him.

"First, gimme my robe. I thought you had enough of your own without stealing mine." He handed her a thick, but pretty dressing-gown and took his own heavy woollen one away from her. He eyed her with a thoughtful expression. "When my father was injured in a riding accident, Ma wore his robe all over the house."

Bea nodded. "It makes a woman feel safe."

And you don't feel safe here with me?" he asked gently.

"It's this house. Would you mind if we sold it and never came here again?"

"You just furnished the goddam place!"

"I know," she said contritely. "Your godfather thinks it's real pretty and hinted that he could use it for the overflow of guests to the house on Epsom Downs. And after they move out officially, it would be a pied-à-terre for him and his wife when they visit England. He would take it off our hands at once."

"Emma hasn't seen it since it's been painted."

Bea shook her head. "She won't come here and I know how she feels. Even I feel a bit haunted." He wandered off to the kitchen, carrying the new coffee machine, and Bea closed her mouth. She had been about to tell him how Emma and she had never been able to drink champagne with any enjoyment after the Bristol bombings, but that was in her past, not his, and she slowly realised that he had his own fraught memories and needed none of hers to burden him. Perhaps when we are old and memories no longer have a sharp edge, she thought with a wry smile.

Coffee? She shook away the sleep. Dwight was making

coffee, but this was different. She looked up into Emma's face and saw the steaming mug in her hand.

"I must have dropped off," she said, raising herself on to an elbow.

"You've been out like a light for over two hours and Aunt Emily said I'd better wake you or you won't sleep tonight."

"I feel better," Bea admitted. "I had no idea I was so tired."

"Drink up and come for a walk before we eat. Aunt Emily needs half an hour to finish her booking and we can get out of her hair."

"If this was The Princess Beatrice and I had to be on duty soon, I would have carried on and not noticed that I needed a nap, but here I feel so relaxed that I shall probably sleep all the time."

"You'll be lucky! I have plans for you, and now that I have the car, we can see some of the places that I've always loved. If you don't like them you can go back to the mainland," her friend added heartlessly.

"Are all you Islanders so territorial and pugnacious?"

"Of course." Emma laughed. "We have a local weekly paper that is full of very parochial features, usually ignoring momentous happenings away from the Island. One magistrate was reported as saying to a man from Portsmouth who was up before the bench for felony, "Go away, back to the mainland, and don't come back again, or I will send you to prison. We don't want your sort over here." In the local mind, this was more deadly than sending him to prison for six months!"

"I'll have to mind my step. Do you think I should wear black and no make-up?"

"Idiot! Get dressed. It's warm and dry and we can walk up to the shrubbery at Carisbrooke. As we haven't a lot of time to spare and the casserole is bubbling happily, maybe I'll drive part of the way."

"Is she all right?" asked Emily, peering over her spectacles and eyeing Emma with interest while Bea was getting ready. "Good face with a lot of character that could be for good or the other way, but she's chosen the good, I think."

"She's fine, and falling for Dwight was the best thing in her life so far," Emma said. "It's a miracle, as most of her family have a loose streak. I met her cousin and he was really evil, but as they need ruthless men in wartime he died a hero."

"Off you go," Emily said as Bea came into the room, looking as fresh as new paint and smart in a shirtwaister dress of blue Shantung silk. "You didn't get that on coupons," Emily said.

"No," admitted Bea. She cast her gaze upwards. "And I thought I was dressing down to blend with the scenery."

"Better go through the corn, then," Emily said dryly. "There are plenty of cornflowers this year with the poppies."

Bea kissed Emily on the cheek. "You say the nicest things," she said.

Emily backed away. "You can stop all that nonsense. Emma will tell you we have never been a kissy family with women."

"Nor men?" Bea looked sideways at Emma. "That accounts for a lot."

"Come on, Bea. Aunt Emily isn't used to your warped sense of humour. I put the potatoes to roast and I made a bread and butter pudding," Emma said. "Nothing to spoil, so we can eat when you have finished the paperwork," she told Emily. "See you in an hour."

"I could have done with her years ago," Bea said, enviously. "You don't know how lucky you are."

The car started at once and they drove up through Shide towards Carisbrooke Castle, past the lane to Mount Joy.

"We'll walk up there one day," Emma said. "I believe it's where some of Cromwell's troops camped and roasted the sheep they stole from the Royalists, way back."

"Is this going to be a history lesson, or do we talk about us?" Bea asked crisply.

"What is there to say? I have lost Guy and have a choice of a few jobs, none of which fill me with any sort of enthusiasm, and you will be leaving with Dwight for the States."

"Buck up, ducky," Bea said bracingly, forgetting that she had felt just as despondent yesterday.

"Your sleep seems to have done you good," Emma said, with a scathing glance.

"It has. Dwight will not be finished here for a while as he is ferrying planes from Europe to the States for the Pacific war, which is still pretty hot, believe it or not."

"You'll see him next week?"

"Not for another week or so after that as a few planes such as the B-17s and the newer enormous B-29s have to be flown further over to airstrips closer to the Marianas, from whence they can carry enough fuel to take them to Japan from a carrier. It may be a month before he comes back."

"You sound calm?"

"I am. He will not be sent on a bombing mission. In fact he grumbles that he might as well be a civilian, but I glory in the fact that he's safe. I told him to take time to call in to see his family if possible, as they haven't seen him for months."

"Can you stay here until he returns?" Emma's face brightened. "Here we are. We can walk up to the castle and round the moat."

"I shall stay for a week if I may and if I promise

34

not to kiss Aunt Emily, then we must both go back to London."

"Both of us?"

"Yes," Bea said firmly. "You are far too attached to this island and you need a prod to get you started again."

"What's wrong with that? I may take the job in Casualty."

"You know who goes with that package?"

"No!" Emma's face was stony. "Paul is a friend and nothing more. In any case he'll be away for a long time and may not come back if he gets involved with neurology."

"Come back with me, Emma. I'm feeling as you are, in a kind of limbo, and I want to think a few plans through, but I need you."

"You'll have to do without me soon and I shall not have you here," Emma said unhappily.

"All the more reason for doing a few things together now."

"I can't come and stay at the cottage," Emma said bluntly.

"I know. Dwight and I stayed there and it looks very good but it is impossible. Too many ghosts sidled in and not only from Heath Cross. I recalled far too much there about the early days. We are selling it to Dwight's godfather."

"I'm glad." Emma took a long deep breath and gazed out across the deep basin of the valley that was now full of waving corn. The breeze ruffled it until it seemed as if it was a rippling lake of cool, greeny-gold water. Behind them, the gaunt grey walls of Carisbrooke were followed by the deep, grassy moats, where three children were ecstatically rolling down the slopes and then breathlessly running back up again to roll again.

"I like this place and Dwight would go mad about it as

35

it's really old." Bea laughed. "There's hope for me when I'm ninety-two. He loves everything ancient. I must bring him here before we leave for Texas. Do you think Aunt Emily will adopt him too?"

"She'll love him if he eats all she puts before him and smiles in that nice boyish way."

"So he gets to kiss her but I don't?" She bubbled with laughter. "You are a crazy lot."

"Takes one to know one," Emma retorted. "If I come to London with you, where do I stay? I haven't accepted the surgical theatre job at Beatties yet, and I can't just arrive there expecting to be given bed and board, even though we are officially still on the staff but on leave for another week or so."

"We stay in St James's. Pa is away, doing diplomatic visits to Amsterdam and several charities that have sprung up to relieve the suffering of Holland and Belgium. It's fashionable to be charitable just now," Bea added dryly, "But the poor man can't do it all from behind a comfortable desk, so he has to be seen to be involved and that means sharing the meagre rations of a starving continent. Not his style at all! I told him he was lucky not to have seen a death camp. Some of the politicians went over and were shattered by the experience. Sorry, I forget," she said, contritely.

"It's all right. I can talk about it now. I told Aunt Emily and it seemed to get it out into the open as if I was talking about a dear friend who went away. To be honest, I had seen very little of Guy for months before he died, as I had to concentrate on my exams and he didn't really agree with not finding me wait-ing for him at all times. I sometimes wonder if we would have got married, even though we were in love, and he is becoming an aching dream. Everyone knows about Belsen, Auschwitz and Buchenwald now. Be fair!

Your father did a lot for refugees in the Free French forces."

"Fed them on wonderful Swiss food and wines, you mean? Sorry, Emma, I know my father. He wants a seat in the Cabinet, so he treats a period of what to him is real hardship as an investment, or he wouldn't be seen dead over there." She gave a short laugh. "He'll be out on his ear if the general election goes the other way. They say that the people in the Forces are sick of war and hardship and think that a Labour Government will bring them prosperity."

"Surely they can't turn Churchill out now that he's been such a tower of strength and bolstered up the morale of the nation for so long? On VE night the crowds were shouting for him and loving every word he said."

"He's been a fine leader in wartime, but many think he might be a pain in the neck as a peacetime politician, so who knows? We may have Clement Atlee for PM.

"Who is Atlee?"

Bea gave a tired smile. "She doesn't even know the name of the leader of the Labour party."

"I don't need to know. A grateful nation will never turn on Churchill now. Are you sure it will be all right to stay at the apartment?" Emma asked nervously. "Remember the time when we went there and a couple of Australian officers arrived in the middle of the night saying that your father had invited them?"

Bea laughed. "Our antipodean friends are like that. If someone suggests that they visit if they are in the district, they take it as a firm invitation to arrive at any time and stay for a week! Even Pa was a bit miffed. He wasn't concerned about our virtue, alone in a flat with two good-looking and very masculine men, but he had invited a liaison officer with the Free French for lunch the day after and found he had to pay for all of them."

She looked at Emma. "It will be fine. I did check with him and he hasn't given a key to anyone but me. Now that I am married to a man of some importance in his eyes, I am welcome and he treats me with a certain reluctant respect."

"It could be fun," Emma said slowly. "I do have to make up my mind soon. I have to earn my living and begin to live a little."

"We've walked round twice and you've shown me where King Charles I was incarcerated. Now can we go back? I'm starving."

"The car's over there. The trouble with you is that you have no sense of history," Emma said sternly.

"That's the last thing I'll need in the States," Bea said, and slammed the car door briskly. "Drive on! I can almost smell that casserole. Did you make masses of mashed potato without lumps?"

"Of course, and some roasties," Emma said.

"Good! Remind me to offer you a job as housekeeper at the ranch."

"It's just ready, and so am I," Emily said when they got home and beamed. "The fresh air has done you both good. Come and have some sherry. Dr Sutton gave me a bottle and I seldom drink it, but I will today."

Bea fetched a large bottle of red wine from her room and a packet of coffee beans. "Dwight insisted," she said when Emily said, "You shouldn't."

"We can all get squiffy and Aunt Emily can tell me what really goes on with her and that nice Dr Sutton."

"I'm waiting to hear what your plans are," Emily said, later when the plates were empty and the last of the wine was being drunk. "Emma is drifting about without a paddle and you might be able to steer her in the way she should go."

"Take no notice of her," Emma said. "When Aunt Emily compares me to a boat, I know she's tipsy!"

"In vino veritas," Bea said owlishly, after two large glasses of sherry and a lot of wine. "I have a plan! Do you remember Nurse Day from The Middlesex, who we met at Heath Cross? She met me and said she wanted to investigate private nursing. It pays well and she wants to save for her wedding."

"I don't think it would suit us, do you?" Emma asked.

"Admin. at Beatties try to make it sound awful, but that's because they want us to stay with them after training. I hear that it can be very nice. It would mean we could take a case or so and then have an unpaid rest, as it wouldn't be a salaried post, just fees for that one job. We could work as hard as we liked or have a break until we needed to work again. I could meet Dwight when he is over here and you could have a social life with us in between jobs. How about joining her? She wants to go to an agency and be vetted by the woman who owns it. It's all very posh. She takes only nurses from the very top hospitals in London, which means us."

"It makes sense," Emily said. "I have to work tomorrow, so I'll say goodnight."

"What? No tea?" Emma asked.

"After all that wine?" Emily went to her room.

"Surely tea would sober her up if she feels she has drunk too much," said Bea.

"Not the way she drinks it, laced with whisky," Emma said.

"Let's sleep on it and talk about it tomorrow. At least it would be different. No ghosts," said Bea. "And we'd be based in London. I could do with a few theatre visits and a few night spots."

Chapter 4

"There she is!" Bea waved wildly and called, "Day! Over here. Day!"

"I suppose she has a first name?" Emma asked.

"I think she's called Lucille, but you know how it is in hospital. Lucille Day," she compromised and the girl looked towards them, smiled and came over.

"Is this Emma?" she asked. "I got here early and we have time for coffee before our interview. I found the place and it's only a minute or so away from the National Gallery."

"Handy," Bea said and led the way to the steps of the picture gallery next to the bombed out museum. "Did you come to London this morning?" she asked.

"I live in Sussex, but my boyfriend has an uncle who lives in Acton so I can give that address as well as my parents' phone number if the agency is trying to contact me."

"We stayed overnight, too," Bea said and Emma knew that she didn't want her father's address to be common knowledge in case the agency was what he would consider infra dig.

Workmen in long canvas aprons were carrying shrouded pictures into the gallery from the underground stores and Emma noted with a kind of relief that the harrowing wartime paintings were not now in the lower gallery.

Faint sounds of music issued from another room and

she recalled that there might still be lunch-time concerts, possibly now being rehearsed.

"I remember a concert here," she said. "Myra Hess, Thibaud and Cortot all in one concert. Can you believe it?"

"You came here with Guy?" Bea asked gently.

"No, someone else." It was a shock to recall that it had been her childhood sweetheart, Philip, with her that day. Yet it now seemed to her that it must have been Guy, as if the occasion was more memorable than the people concerned.

"What do you know about this agency?" Bea asked. She peeled off her gloves and placed them in the suede handbag that matched her coffee-coloured suit. Her halo hat finished a picture of expensive understatement and Emma was glad that she had followed her example and dressed smartly, wearing a pale green silk dress from Switzerland which was a birthday present from Bea's father, a plain straw boater, white court shoes and carrying white gloves.

"It's a bit intimidating," Lucille said. "My cousin went to it and she didn't get a job, as she was told that her hospital training didn't rank high enough as it was LCC and not a voluntary hospital."

"I think they'll have to change their ideas as more and more old hospitals are being upgraded and many are very good, as we found at Heath Cross," Emma said.

"It's snobbery." Lucille said with a contemptuous sniff. "I shall be all right as The Middlesex is considered good," she added confidently, then eyed the other two girls with a touch of consternation. "Do you think I should have worn a hat and gloves?"

Bea shrugged. "I have no idea how this woman's mind will work, so I wore a hat," she said simply.

"I did bring this," Lucille said reluctantly. "I wore

41

it to a wedding and it's the only one I have." She produced a tired half hat made of pink feathers. Emma dared not glance at Bea, but knew that they remembered an auxilliary nurse at Heath Cross who proudly displayed a similar hat to them before her wedding, complete with a huge, silver paper horseshoe to carry for luck.

"You have such pretty hair. Why hide it?" Bea said with a pleasant smile.

Lucille bundled it back into her bag. "I know it looks common," she said. "My mother said it was, and seeing you two today, I know she was right."

"I feel as if Sister Cary from the Home on the Downs in Bristol will inspect me," Bea said when Lucille was in the ladies' room. "At least we can cope with practically any situation after being regularly humiliated by that woman. I often wondered if she was related to Himmler."

"There now, she said we'd thank her one day," Emma said, and laughed.

They walked slowly, so that they would arrive at the imposing mansion in Mayfair looking cool and calm, and Emma wondered if she'd ever lose her apprehension about meeting a fresh situation, but she took courage from Bea's obvious enjoyment of the experience.

"That house over there," said Bea, pointing to a tall, narrow establishment, with very white net curtains at the windows that must have come from a secret supply as they were too fresh to have come from a factory turned over to war work.

"What about it?"

"My Pa said it is a notorious bordello. What fun if that is the house we're looking for and we'll end up making stacks of money from immoral earnings."

"I'd tell Dwight," Emma threatened.

"I think it's over there," Lucille said in a hollow voice. "I'm scared."

"No need to be." Bea pressed the bell and they heard it reverberate through the house. "She'll either take us on or she won't, so why worry?" she said airily.

"Yes?" The maid who answered the door looked solemn and very old.

Bea told her that they had an appointment with Mrs Davies and she led them into a dark-panelled room with huge ceramic vases on the broad mantelpiece and heavy pictures of stags and grubby looking sheep on the walls. The maid disappeared and Bea looked out of the window, while Lucille seemed fascinated by the sonorous beat of the grandfather clock by the empty fire-grate. Emma inspected the mahogany desk; a dust-free edifice with a large leather-bound blotter covered with unused, dark purple blotting paper. It matched the gothic lettering on the stationery stacked in the well-polished pigeon-holes of the desk. I wonder what they'd say if I dripped ink onto that blotter? It's obviously never used, she thought. Would an alarm go off? The twin inkwells were dry and the desk had no sign of work in progress.

"Is this really the place?" whispered Lucille. "It looks like a funeral parlour!" She backed away from the clock and bumped into a chair.

"Mind the coffin," Bea said and giggled at Lucille's stifled cry.

"Don't do that!" Lucille blushed. "I'm so nervous."

"At least you have more colour now," Bea said. "Remember, they need us! We are well-trained and can get work anywhere we like, so if she looks down her nose at three wonderful nurses . . . sorry, we must call ourselves Sister now, then she's mad."

"Mrs Davies will see you now, all together," the maid said.

Bea took a quick glance at the others and led the way as if she was in charge.

The next room was lighter and had floral prints on the walls. An elderly woman sat in a large captain's chair that seemed to engulf her and she rested very white hands on the table before her. Her first sharp, examining glance took in the clothes and demeanour of her visitors and she seemed to accept what she saw, but her gaze lingered on the bare head of the third applicant as if disapproving.

Bea removed her gloves in a casual manner, as if expecting to be served tea and dainty cakes. Emma sat straight and wondered why the face seemed familiar. As if to make the comparison even more pronounced, the woman looked towards the window, showing her profile. Emma wanted to laugh. It was the profile of a younger person, a man, a star of the stage, famous all over the country and beyond, but it was ridiculous. There couldn't be a connection with this place.

One by one they gave details of names, addresses, and training schools. Mrs Davies checked them against a paper and seemed satisfied.

"That will be all from me, ladies," she said and rose to her feet. "I meet applicants to make sure that they are the right type for our agency, and then Miss Merchant takes over to tell you a little more about the work." She put a hand to the neck-frill on her pin-tucked blouse, consulted the old-fashioned pendant watch, and turned away.

They waited for five minutes. "Good thing to know we're the right type," Bea said dryly.

Miss Merchant was quite different. Her neat blue tailored suit was well cut, if not new, and her hair seemed lacquered to her head, and caught up in a bun at the nape of her neck.

"I'll run through a few basic facts first," she said in a pleasant, low voice, in contrast to her slightly forbidding appearance. "If you go out into private nursing, in many houses there will be less facilities than you are used to having at your fingers' ends in hospital." They nodded. "Patients are diagnosed and assessed before you are called in, which means that we know exactly what to expect in most cases unless there is a sudden crisis, and dressings and medicaments will be there under your care as soon as you take over. You will have at least one cupboard that you can lock for this purpose." She looked from one face to another. "Remember that you will be the only one in the household who has the skills required and you have a great responsibility as you are in charge and are accountable only to the doctor in charge of the case."

"Do they always let the sister have a locked cupboard?" Bea asked.

"I will give each of you a copy of the agreement the relatives must sign before they have one of our sisters," Miss Merchant said. "Any violation of these rules must be referred to this office immediately and I may withdraw our care and suggest the names of suitable nursing homes that might be willing to take the patient."

"That's a bit hard, isn't it?" asked Lucille. "We are well trained and have met most conditions."

Miss Merchant regarded her with assessing eyes. "If you were alone with a physically strong man who wanted to take illegal drugs, and who would, when desperate, take anything, from linctus containing morphine to strong pain killers, and who 'forgot' to tell the agency of his addiction, would you want that key in his hands? Or in the hands of the relatives who 'forgot' to tell us the worst?"

She smiled coldly. "We have all met people who fake symptoms to get attention. In private practice this happens a lot and some patients think that, as they are paying a large fee, they can expect that attention twenty-four hours a day, ad nauseam."

"Would we be on call for that long?" asked Emma.

"No. If night care is required, we supply another sister, but usually a relative will find someone to sit with the patient and call the sister only in a dire emergency."

She handed out the stiff cards of rules and told them to study them later. "We take no alcoholics on revulsion therapy, or, if we are asked for that, we have special nurses who are very highly paid for such work as it is very unpleasant. We take no active tuberculosis cases. We refer them to a sanatorium if this is diagnosed, and we put a time limit on your work. No sister works with a case for more than one month, and you report back to us as soon as you finish a case, for your remuneration and details of the next case, if you want one at once. But we recommend a break of at least four days between them."

"Do we supply uniform?" asked Lucille.

"Yes. So long as it is neat and tidy we leave the colour and style to you. Many girls now wear American-style white coats." Miss Merchant coughed gently. "We impress on our clients that you are professional women of considerable standing, from good backgrounds. You must have good accommodation and food and never be classed as servants. In some stately homes, there may be butlers and housekeepers who rule a tiny empire of their own and resent anyone else with authority. You must never become too familiar with the people below stairs. We had an incident where a sister took sherry with the butler in his pantry." She looked shocked. "That must never happen."

"What about food? If we don't mix with the staff, do we eat alone?" asked Bea.

"In some houses, you may be invited to eat with the family and many sisters do this, but, if not, a tray in your room does give you a little leisure away from them."

"So we might need something to wear for evenings?"

"It is quite likely," Miss Merchant said. "Sometimes a wheelchair patient or one chronically sick in some way is lonely and needs to think of you as a friend. Never become over familiar or emotionally involved. I know that you are taught this in hospital, but when you find yourselves in a different environment, in a lovely house, with every comfort around you and the sense that you are important to the well-being of the family, it is easy to read more into a sister-patient relationship than is wise."

"Would we have to travel far?" asked Emma.

"Occasionally, but most of our clients live in London or the Home Counties. We have two sisters working in a stately home in Buckinghamshire."

"I hope we are told a little about the cases before we arrive there," Bea said. "I would want to know the names of the families, as I might know them socially and not wish to mix duty with pleasure. Sister Dewar moves in the same circles as I do, so the same would apply to her."

"I quite understand," Miss Merchant said more warmly.

Full marks for putting her in her place, Emma thought. I can see that our rating has soared in the last minute. She checked a smile when Miss Merchant hesitated, then put the list she had on the desk to one side and opened the drawer to bring out another list on pale pink paper.

"If you are willing to start work almost immediately, I think we can arrange something," Miss Merchant said.

"I can," Lucille said eagerly.

"Could you report to the private patient wing of Guy's tomorrow to look after a twin room with two iron lung patients?" Emma noticed that this case was from the first list. Lucille nodded without enthusiasm. "Good. Will you go through to the secretary who will brief you and tell you the length of the case, as Guy's will want to use their own staff once their holiday rota is finished."

Lucille hesitated, then cast a regretful glance at the others and left the room.

"Now," said Miss Merchant, as if she had disposed of a tiresome fly. "I need a sister who has good experience of diabetes. The lady is an actress who has been rather naughty about her insulin and needs a few weeks on a strict diet and well-administered drugs to stabilise her. She hopes to be back in a play in the West End in two weeks. She collapsed in near coma during a matinée and this time is really frightened." She named the actress and Bea's eyes widened.

"You know her?"

"Not personally, but a member of my family has met her," Bea said quietly. "I think it could be interesting. I enjoyed the diabetic clinic."

"And the other suggestion is an officer who had shrapnel embedded in many places. He has had extensive surgery and is almost ready for the next operation, the last of five, we think. He needs surgical dressings daily and encouragement to move about more." Miss Merchant looked at Emma. "It's only fair to tell you that the last sister left yesterday, complaining that he was difficult to get on with. Can you cope with that, Sister Dewar?"

"How many sisters has he driven away?" she asked dryly.

The woman's glance seemed to flicker over the desk, but not at Emma. "Four," she said.

"Good, I like a challenge," Emma said. "Where is he?"

Bea grinned. "Shades of Heath Cross," she said. "The best of luck, Dewar!"

"He lives in Scarvel Manor in Kent. His name is Sir Arthur Jumeaux and he was wounded at Dunkirk."

48

Emma nodded. "I can but try," she said and mentally decided that what she needed most at the present time was a bloody-minded officer with smelly wounds, just to make her feel at home.

"You must be mad!" Bea said when they were out of the building. "He's a long-term patient who knows all the answers and has a chip the size of a brick. That, together with at least a half-French background, if his name means anything, makes for temperament, and he'll be naughty."

"You can talk! Hasn't she a history of drink as well as diabetes? But she's a superb actress." Emma looked across the table in Lyons' Corner House in Coventry Street off Leicester Square and picked up the menu. "I think you *do* know her, Bea. What mischief are you planning?"

"If she plays up, a bit of blackmail!"

"What!"

"Not the money kind, stupid. If I'm not mistaken, she was one of Pa's floozies way back when he took them to the apartment, before she became a serious actress. He really liked her, and for a time they could have got serious, but that was before the divorce and he couldn't afford to get tangled up too far as Ma was searching for convenient correspondents."

"She married a Frenchman, didn't she?"

"He was killed in Normandy and she is now a much sought after widow."

"You won't make mischief, Bea?" Emma pleaded.

"Much as I have despised my father, I'd hate to make two people unhappy, now that I have Dwight and know what real love means, but I shall watch and wonder, and maybe they could meet again. Who knows?" Her eyes were dreamy.

"Forget your power complex and remember to pick up the insulin before you report on duty in Chelsea."

"Squashed again by my Puritan friend," Bea said, and examined the menu. "I'm starving."

"We ought to buy uniform," Emma said. "White coats seem easiest and not too expensive. They have some in that shop in Regent Street."

"It will have to be eggs, bacon and beans," Bea said and sighed. "I can't face restaurant steak and kidney pie after the one we ate at Aunt Emily's."

"You know that you can take Dwight there when he comes back?"

"Yes. Aunt Emily said as much and now that the cottage is to be sold, we need to have friends or good hotels, if we aren't to stay at the Airbase every time he has leave."

"I wonder if we can use the telephone where we're going?" Emma asked.

"There must be a public phone in the local post office where you are going. Even a village like that has one at least, and in Chelsea there are masses I can use. I think I'll feel more at ease using a public phone at first," Bea said. "I can tell you how lousy she is and what a miserable time I'm having without anyone overhearing what I say."

"But we'll exchange numbers of the telephones in the places where we work in case of emergencies," Emma said anxiously. "Why do I feel like a first year nurse who has to report back every five minutes?"

Bea wore her most Siamese kitten expression. "Once you get inside that manor house, who knows if we'll ever see you again."

"Don't! I think I'm having second thoughts."

"It can't be worse than nursing surly German prisoners," Bea said. "At least he'll have nice manners and know how to hold his fork."

"He must have been very ill," Emma speculated. "Dunkirk was ages ago and he still has at least one operation to endure. No wonder he's difficult."

"I'd offer to exchange cases but I want to see what La Belle Miranda is really like."

"You'd be treated as well or as badly as I shall be," Emma said and shook her head.

"Not true." Bea narrowed her eyes. "I can be objective about any man now, but you are vulnerable."

"Don't be silly. I'm off men and the memory of Guy will be with me for years."

"If you are there for a month, you'll get to know him well and you can be too caring under that detached facade. It will be a one-to-one relationship, all day and every day, with both of you in a raw state as far as needing warmth is concerned, so be careful and run away to Auntie Bea if the heat gets bad."

Emma laughed. "If he's driven away four nurses, he must be ghastly. I can ring the agency for a replacement if I can't handle him. At least I know that Miss Merchant wouldn't be surprised if I did that."

"Uniform!" Bea asked for the bill and they strolled out along the battered streets, past bombed out buildings and holes in the road, until they came to the unscathed shop specialising in nurses' uniforms and medical jackets. Miss Merchant had given them forms that entitled them to buy dresses and aprons without giving up their clothing coupons, but they had no need to buy aprons as they still possessed the aprons they'd had to buy at the beginning of their training, to wear during the three months' trial period when the hospital didn't supply them free. Emma had regretted buying them. They never wore them after that first trial period as the hospital issue was different and exclusive to Beatties, but now it was a relief to know that she had only a limited expense for what might be a short time.

As if thinking along the same lines, Bea said, "We may not like the work and if I go away I'm unlikely to need them again, and any hospital that you work in will supply uniform, but we must look smart."

They each chose four identical tailored dresses of white cotton with pockets for scissors and watches and any small items they might want to carry with them on duty, white court shoes with silent rubber heels, and frilled caps, not only because they couldn't rid themselves of the discipline of wearing them, but also because they knew that they gave a certain dignity and authority.

"I have enough clothes for a week or so," Emma said.

"Take it for granted that someone will do your personal laundry as well as uniform," Bea advised. "If they are difficult, insist on two days off to fetch more from the Island. That should make them think again. You must not mess around trying to do it yourself," she added firmly. "People accept you on your own valuation in good houses with staff to do everything, so never let them take advantage in any way."

"You make me feel as if I'm going to prison," Emma said soberly.

"Oh, they'll have to let you off the leash for a few hours in the afternoons," Bea said airily. "That card of rules might be handy. It lays down conditions and makes it easier for us if they get mean."

"You will be in touch soon?"

"I'll write first and then we'll arrange a time to telephone when we are off duty. If they object to an incoming call, we'll use the call-boxes at given times," Bea said.

"How cloak and dagger! If we hang about call-boxes we'll be suspected of being bookies' runners," Emma said.

"What fun. I might take it up as a career," Bea said.

"Let's go back to the apartment and sort out our things and then go to see *Brief Encounter*. Celia Johnson wears abysmal hats, but Trevor Howard is a gem."

Chapter 5

"What happened?" Bea sounded anxious.

"Nothing terrible, but a bit annoying. I was told that I could use the phone whenever I liked, and I didn't like to do so at first, but when your letter came with the number of the call-box and the time you could be there, I thought I'd try that."

"Did the phone pack up? One minute I heard your voice and then sudden silence before we'd even said hello. I was all right as the call-box is in the local post office and there is a chair where I can wait for ten minutes or so, but in future, ring me at Miranda's apartment, as she hates using the phone and hardly ever answers it. Her maid gives her messages and I can be quite private when you ring. You haven't explained the cut off."

"Someone listened in on the other phone," Emma said. "I distinctly heard the other receiver being gently taken up and someone breathing."

"How low! Who was it?"

"I think it was Sir Arthur. He has a phone by his bed, and I suppose he's so bored, he just listens to any conversation he can overhear."

"Well, you can use a call-box and call here any time," Bea said. "What's he like, this sneaky man? Does he look as mean as he sounds?"

"No. As yet I haven't formed a firm opinion, but he

reminds me of so many men who came back wounded and lost hope." Emma sighed. "He worries me a bit as he doesn't smile, and yet I have the impression that once, he was a very interesting person. You'd approve of his mouth!"

"Well that's a start. He can't be all bad. Good-looking?"

"Quite, in a dark, rugged way. It's rather pathetic. He *was* like that, but he has lost it all and his hands are thin and his body emaciated."

"TB?"

"No. I did check his notes and X-rays and he's been tested and is clear, but his blood sedimentation rate is up, showing something toxic."

"How does he treat you?"

"With reserve and icy politeness. I almost wish he'd say something outrageous and find fault, but he sits waiting for his dressing to be done, puts out a hand to have his pulse taken, etc, and says very little."

"No wonder he wanted to hear the conversation over the phone. I expect his other nurses had a lot to say about him when they rang friends. Perhaps that's why they left or were dismissed!"

"I'm trying to get him interested in books and the wireless, but as yet he just says 'thank you' when I ask if I should turn it on, then he switches it off as soon as I leave the room."

"Rather you than me," Bea said with feeling. "I'm enjoying my stint here. Miranda is a peach; a very frightened peach, but nice. I've made out her diet sheet just as we learned at Beatties and I give the insulin in parts of her anatomy that she can't reach, to rest her poor arms and thighs from the twice-daily needles. I dress in uniform for my part as efficient Sister, to make sure she remembers why I'm here, but I do call her Miranda and we have meals together. I see an improvement and she could be back on the stage next week, with me in the wings to make sure she doesn't have a hypo. I feel as if I'm nursing a horse. I carry sugar lumps everywhere we go, and make sure she eats up all her carbohydrates."

"You go out with her?" Emma asked enviously. "I have three hours off each afternoon, but the village is small and there's really nothing to do there. The grounds are pretty and I sit by the lake sometimes but I think I'm almost as lonely as Sir Arthur."

"Is he in bed all the time?"

"No, he sits in a chair and walks to the bathroom and I think he could do more. Oh, damn! There go the pips and I have no more change. I'll ring again soon."

She walked along the village street and bought some chocolate with her sweet ration and a quarter-pound of black-and-white striped mints, more to have a lot of small change for her next phone call than because she wanted sweets. The letter she had written to Aunt Emily was duly posted and Emma wondered when she could telephone her as her aunt was not at home during the day and Emma was not off duty in the evenings.

Just as well, she thought. I really don't want to answer a lot of questions just now. A letter can tell her that I'm fine and the work is interesting, but she can't tell me about the Island and make me homesick."

The ten-minute walk back to the manor took longer today as Emma lingered to enjoy the sight of dragonflies darting over the lake as she walked through the park. A girl dressed in brown cord breeches was cutting the long grass by a clump of trees and she reminded Emma of a girl who had wanted to leave nursing to go into the Land Army. Would all those girls give up the land when the men returned to the farms?

She looked up at the tall turret at one side of the manor

and smiled. A perfect Rapunzel tower, she thought, but no pretty heroine awaiting her love. It was warm and sunlit in the garden and she sat on a stone bench with her face lifted to the rays, until she glanced at her watch and knew that she must go in and change into uniform.

An ancient Rolls-Royce was parked by the entrance. It was the first time in five days that there had been any sign of a visitor and Emma hurried inside the house, pleased to think that someone had made the invalid's day brighter.

"Who are you?" The autocratic voice was brisk, the searching glance taking in Emma's spotless, blue summer dress, plain sandals and her neat hair coiled into a French pleat.

"I'm Sister Dewar."

"One of the Scottish Dewars?" The tone was warmer.

"No, nor the Berkshire ones," Emma replied, her lips twitching with amusement, as she recalled Bea's horrific cousin asking her just that question and Bea replying that Emma was a one-off, unique, and he could stop being an insufferable snob.

"Oh? I thought that nursing sisters wore uniform," the lady said.

"So they do, on duty," Emma said. "If you'll excuse me, I have to do that now. I shall be on duty in fifteen minutes."

She walked away, leaving the lady looking after her and pulling on her gloves with some force. "Sister?"

Emma turned and smiled, with an enquiring lift to her chin. "Did you want me?"

"You *do* know who I am?" Emma shook her head. "I am Arthur's mother, Lady Jumeaux. Are you going to stay?"

"I have been here five days and my contract is for one month, Lady Jumeaux," Emma said.

57

"That tells me nothing. My son is sick and needs constant companionship."

"I'm sure that you visit as often as you can, Lady Jumeaux," Emma said tactfully.

"That isn't enough. Frankly, we don't really have much to say to each other since I moved out to the dower house a mile down through the park." The proud facade crumbled. "Do what you can. I think he likes you," she said. "He wasn't always like this."

She was gone and Emma saw the Rolls move away, driven by another woman who had down-trodden companion written in every line on her face.

Sir Arthur was flushed and when Emma took his temperature it was slightly raised. "What is it?" he asked.

Emma shook the mercury down in the thermometer. "It's fine," she said calmly. "Would you like dinner later today? I see that you had tea with your mother so you may not be hungry for a while."

"Yes, later," he said. "So you met the Grand Dame of Kent?"

"Lady Jumeaux introduced herself," she replied mildly. "I'll tell Martha that you would like dinner at eight?"

He nodded. "Do you object to having dinner with me?"

"That would be nice. It's lonely in my room," she said with a warm smile, and she left the room to give the message.

"What's that?" he asked suspiciously as Emma returned with a covered surgical tray. I have only one dressing a day, and all the scars are nearly dry."

"While I make your bed, I might as well take a look at that patch I found this morning when I washed your back. I'm sure there is a piece of metal just under the skin and if I can reach it now, you will be far more comfortable in bed, as it must be giving you discomfort when you turn over."

58

"I hope you know what you are doing," he said, morosely. "None of the others did this."

"Maybe it hadn't worked to the surface," she said, mildly. "And I do know what I'm doing. This is nothing new. You can rest for an hour afterwards and be ready for dinner."

A glimmer of a smile made her pause to watch his face. "The others made me rest after my mother visited as she sends my temperature up."

"Look on me as a counter-irritant."

"What's that?"

Emma laughed. "We apply one irritant to inflame the skin to relieve a deeper one, as in inflammation of the lungs," she said.

For the first time she heard him laugh and it was a good sound. "Come on then, irritate me," he said and pulled off his pyjama jacket to expose his back.

Earlier that day when Emma had dressed the four almost-healed patches where shrapnel had been removed, she had noticed that the skin and thin muscle was stretched over a small lump and a patch that fluctuated under her fingers, as if there was fluid there. She carefully sprayed the patch with a freezing local anaesthetic, cut a small cross with a scalpel, then gently probed. The unhealthy skin parted and a gush of offensive discharge flowed into the dish she held ready. She pressed the area firmly and drained off more and the metal eased out, leaving a gap that allowed free drainage.

"Christ, what is that?" he asked, nearly overcome by the foul smell.

"You'll feel a lot better without this lot," Emma said briefly, trying not to inhale the smell and blessing the fact that she was wearing a mask.

He twisted his head to see the dish and gagged at the smell again. Emma handed him a towel to put over his nose and then rapidly washed the cavity with weak hydrogen peroxide to fizz out the residue. She packed the gap with plugging gauze saturated with Balsalm of Peru and petroleum jelly to keep it open until all infected matter had drained away, and applied a dressing strapped firmly in place.

"Sit in the wheelchair and I'll take you to the small sitting-room," she said. "You can't stay here until the smell has gone."

She returned to clear away and put the dish, with its contents well-sealed, ready for the doctor to inspect the next day. The tiny room where she could sterilse the instruments, contained dressing-packs and there was a large sink and scrubbing-brushes for the exclusive use of the sickroom.

She opened all the windows and put two air fresheners by the bed and one under it and left the bed open to air. The smell of Airwick caught at her throat even more than the smell of discharge and she had a sudden vision of the ward at Heath Cross when the German prisoners of war were admitted with stinking wounds.

"How do you feel?" she asked when she went back to him. She checked his pulse and found it more vital than it had been after his mother's visit and his colour was good.

"How do *you* feel?" he asked. "How the hell can a pretty girl face such things?"

"I've seen and done worse," she said quickly.

"Girls that I knew before the war would have fainted," he said.

"I think you might find that those same girls are now doing jobs that take a lot of fortitude," Emma said. "The war rubbed a lot of rough edges away and made others more resilient. A great leveller," she added and smiled. "I dislike foul smells as much as you do, so shall we

60

blow away a few cobwebs and I'll push your chair round the terrace?" She glanced at him, wondering how far she could go as he had not had a meal outside his bedroom for weeks since his last operation. "I think we'd better have dinner here in the sitting-room, rather than in your bedroom. I want it to air out a lot more before you sleep there."

He looked startled, as if she was dragging him away from a safe cave, but she ignored his expression and rang for the maid. Sir Arthur recovered his usual noncommittal expression and gave the order to the surprised girl, and Emma wrapped him warmly in a thick bedjacket and rug and pushed the chair out into the early evening sunshine.

They stopped by the low wall of the terrace and a large stone griffin eyed them with scorn. "Why do they look like that?" she asked.

"Are you an authority on the King's Beasts?" he asked with a smile similar to the griffin's.

"I have seen some, mostly on the roof of a huge place in Bristol where there were gargoyles on the leads, which looked down at the mortal world with an expression, if anything, much much more evil than these, and there are a lot on the terrace of Osborne House on the Isle of Wight."

"You seem to like old houses."

"I love space," she said. "When I look at a view like this, and there is no sound but the birds, the war fades away and there is such peace that I am tempted to stay for longer than is good for me. I find it like that at home when I can walk on the Downs and watch the sea," she added.

"You like it here?"

"Very much, but for me, it could not be perfect unless I knew that the sea was just over there beyond that range of trees."

"I've never been to the Isle of Wight," he said. "I've been to Rome, Brussels, South America and New Zealand and, of course, France with my father, but not the Isle of Wight."

"You are laughing at me," Emma said.

"No, I think I envy you. When you talk about it, your eyes shine and I sense that it is your favourite place."

"You could go there. After the last operation, why not stay at Osborne for a while in the convalescent home for officers? It's a beautiful place and you could explore the Island once you are stronger."

He stared at her. "Impossible," he said. "I think it's getting cool, and it's nearly eight, so join me for sherry before dinner."

He leaned forward as if to propel the wheelchair by the force of his thoughts and Emma took him inside the building, left him by the toilet and peeped into the bedroom. The air was now pure, so she half-closed the windows, made up the bed, put fresh water in the carafe and a bowl of fruit on the bed table, then washed her hands and combed her hair.

Two beautiful cut-glass sherry schooners sat on a silver salver, with decanters of amontillado and fino sherry, and Sir Arthur was already seated close by the window where a small table had been laid for two people.

The housekeeper, Martha, met Emma as she arrived at the door. "That's the first time he's had a meal out here for weeks," she said. Her tone was not encouraging, as if she almost resented the man gaining increased independence from a stranger.

"It's good isn't it? Today, a piece of metal forced its way out and he should feel better without that poison inside him," Emma said, as if none of the credit was due to her efforts.

The woman smiled. "Lucky that it came out," she said

and called to the maid to bring in the first course in ten minutes.

"My G.P. rang and I told him what happened today. He's coming tomorrow about ten to have a look," Sir Arthur said.

"Good. I want him to see the metal and possibly take a swab of the discharge, in case it would react to penicillin. As a serving army officer, you would qualify for some," Emma said.

Sir Arthur finished his soup and rang for the next course of chicken and mashed potatoes. He ate with more enthusiasm than Emma had noticed so far and finished his food without pushing it around the plate and leaving most of it. Maybe it was the glass of wine that he drank, but his eyes took on a brighter gleam and he began to talk of the manor as it had been before the war. Emma listened and formed the impression that he was a man who had never been ill. He rode and hunted, played rugby and and worked hard, and could not come to terms with his current feebleness.

"You are recovering now," she said gently. "Another week and you will look back on all this with disbelief and be able to pick up the threads."

"Never," he said.

"Have coffee in bed," she suggested when he grew tired, and tucked him in, with a pile of pillows supporting him.

"You see, I'm as weak as a kitten," he said resentfully. "And you forget I have another op to endure."

"Let me show you something," Emma said. "I wasn't going to say anything until the doctor came, but I think you may sleep better if you agree with my opinion that you may not need any more surgery."

She brought in a glass pot with a screw top, filled with clear disinfectant in which the shrapnel was securely

63

imprisoned. "Look at the X-rays," she said and held one up to the light. "The pictures are only two-dimensional so we can't see at what depth the metal was. Obviously it has worked its way along the muscle sheath and surfaced where I found it, but it was not as deep as they suspected. Now look at the piece we took out today. It's exactly the same shape and I think this is all that was left. Now all you have to do is to eat well, exercise and drink pints of water and soft drinks."

"Good God, you're right! It fits. It fits!"

"As snugly as Cinderella's slipper," she said, laughing. "Now go to sleep and have breakfast in bed before the doctor visits. I'll tidy you but leave the dressing until he comes."

Emma walked out on to the terrace and the scent of nicotiana. The old buildings were softly grey in the dusk and the griffins were blurred images. She thought of the neglected stables and over-grown tennis court and sighed. It was a lovely place and so much happiness could be generated here.

"But not by me," she told the honeysuckle.

She peeped into Sir Arthur's room at ten and he was asleep, breathing easily and lying comfortably on his side. In the morning when she checked on him, he was still asleep, as if he had abandoned his tensions and accepted with relief what she had told him.

When the doctor arrived Emma went to meet him. He raised his eyebrows as he listened to music coming from the sickroom. "Yes, he asked for his gramophone," she said.

"That's a miracle," he said dryly. "He keeps the place like a morgue. Let me see what you found before we go in," he asked.

"The X-rays are here, with the specimen," she said, and watched his face as he compared them.

"You say you removed over six ounces of thick, green discharge?" She nodded. "Then you've saved him a lot of trouble. I was afraid that he'd succumb to toxic absorption, but now that the source of infection has gone, I have a course of penicillin which should deal with the residue and he'll be fine. Have you used penicillin?"

"Yes, and I dealt with a lot of shrapnel from mortar fire, so this was familiar. He does seem better this morning," Emma said.

"Too proud for his own good. Hated being ill and refused to see his friends. His mother took fright, as she hates illness, and fled to the dower house, so he's been very much alone, poor devil."

"I guessed as much," Emma said.

"How long can you stay?" the doctor asked suddenly.

"Another three weeks unless I'm needed, but he will be fine by then and need no dressings."

"Stay on, if you can. You've saved his life – or at least his sanity – once, and who knows? you may do more for him," he said with a humorous glance that took in her face and figure.

"No," she said, quietly. "My fiancé died and I am not ready for another man."

"My apologies," he said gruffly. "Let's see what you've done to my patient," he added in a loud voice as they went into Sir Arthur's room.

Emma turned off a frantic rendering of Latin American music and fetched the dressing tray.

"Don't you like Edmundo Ross?" Sir Arthur called.

"When you can dance to that, I can take a holiday," the doctor said. "You look much better, Arthur." He helped him off with the pyjama jacket and Emma did the dressing. The packing was moist, but there was little discharge so she irrigated the cavity again and put on a dry dressing with no plugging. The doctor grunted approval.

"Now for my trick," he said and produced a bottle with a rubber film across the top. It contained an amber-coloured fluid. Emma fetched a sterile glass syringe and injected the first dose of penicillin into Sir Arthur's right buttock.

"Couldn't it go in my arm the next time?" he said.

"Tell him, Sister. You're the one who seems to know all the answers."

"Shut up, Hugh! You don't speak to Sister Dewar like that."

"He was joking," Emma said quietly and smiled. "But it's a well-known fact that nurses give better injections than doctors. Penicillin is so new that they haven't yet purified it enough to make sure it doesn't cause an abscess if it is not given into deep muscle. It can be painful if not given in that way."

"I'm afraid you must have an injection four times a day for four days," Hugh said.

"Hell!" But Sir Arthur smiled. "I have to get moving more now. What do you suggest?"

"I have an invalid tricycle that would make you stretch that leg and generally tone up your muscles more than a wheelchair could do. I'll send it over in the Post van. You could have physiotherapy, but all the pretty girls have gone to massage soldiers," Hugh said.

Emma had tidied the bed and waited by the door. "Tell him that he can dress in proper clothes if he wants to feel normal," she said in a whisper.

"When I come next time, I shall expect to see you in a pair of trousers and a sweater, if not a suit, with a glass of malt ready for an overworked doctor," he called back into the room. "See you in three days time."

"You are a genius," he said as Emma walked with

him to his car. "It isn't just the dressing. What do they call you?"

"Emma," she said.

"And I'm Hugh. Do what you can for him," he pleaded. "He does like you, very much."

"I'll see you in three days time, Hugh," was all that she would say.

The tricycle arrived and caused a lot of interest as the maids and Martha, the housekeeper, peeped out of the windows to watch Sir Arthur, who was dressed in trousers firmly belted to stop them falling off his thin body and a huge Fair Isle sweater that had a little moth in it. He rode slowly and painfully at first and Emma restricted him to ten minutes at a time, but gradually he rode with ease and confidence and the next week slipped by with progress made every day.

The bedroom was stripped of anything that would remind him of a sickroom and reverted to being a small reception room where visitors could wait. His main suite upstairs was in use again and seemed to make a lot of difference to his morale. In the afternoons he rested on a chaise longue in the loggia and Emma took her time off duty. Once, she met Bea in the next town for tea and heard all about Miranda, but Emma said little about her work as she was vaguely aware that Arthur now looked at her differently. They used first names and had an easy relationship. Arthur re-discovered light music and talked of buying more records when he could get into town.

One morning when Emma was looking for clean socks in the chest of drawers in his dressing-room, she saw a metal box and picked it up to look under it.

"Bring that here," he said. He was sitting on the edge of the bed waiting for his socks and Emma left the box with him while she selected a pair that matched his suit.

The open box was on the table beside him and she

stared. Among gold cuff-links and tie-pins was a cap badge. "You were a marine commando?"

"Was your fiancé in our mob? I thought he was a medic."

"No, but I knew a man who died after a raid and he left me his badge," she said softly. "Major Eddie Ripley."

"I knew him." Arthur's face was tight with emotion. "Damn good soldier, but absolutely no conscience," he said. "Gave us all the creeps."

"Me, too," Emma replied and backed away from the box.

"Emma, do you have to go away?"

"Yes, Arthur. I have other people to nurse and you don't need me." Please God he doesn't ask me to marry him, she thought, then the housekeeper brought in the mail.

"One re-directed several times, posted two months ago," she said. "It looks like a service letter."

"I'll get some coffee," Emma said and escaped.

"Might be from Miss Priscilla," Martha confided as they walked down the stairs together.

"Is she nice? He can do with a little feminine company," Emma said.

"They grew up next door to each other. Her family have Coot's farm about a mile south of here. She joined the ATS and has been in France and now Germany, but I heard in the village that she's coming home on leave this week before she gets her de-mob."

"Does she know about Sir Arthur?"

"She will by now. I met her mother and told her that he needs company."

"The sooner the better," Emma said fervently.

"It's like that, is it? You must get a lot like that."

"He's been hurt so much that I hate to depress him further and I must leave next week."

"I'll suggest to her mother that Prissy comes casually and stays to lunch."

"And when she does come I'll say that I promised to meet a friend for lunch," Emma said. "I'll be back later that afternoon. It'll be a good excuse to stay away for a few hours." They exchanged conspiratorial smiles.

Chapter 6

"So, she didn't turn up after all your scheming?" Bea seemed very amused.

"Backed out at the last minute. Martha was livid as she'd prepared a very good lunch for them and the silly woman had told Arthur that Priscilla was visiting him, so he even put on a necktie."

Bea looked at her watch. "Miranda said they'd pick me up at four. It was lucky that she wanted to visit friends in Kent and I could meet you, but I'll have to make sure she's done nothing silly, like eating with her friends, unless she's stuck to what she's allowed. I wake up dreaming of cutting bread to the size of those awful measures, and as for jam, which she adores, I have to be very strict."

"It sounds as if she is better."

"They had a dress rehearsal yesterday and she was fine. Can you get time off to see her? She wants to meet you as she was a great fan of your Uncle Sidney. She adores the early movies and thought him very handsome."

"I can take a day off and sleep in London. Officially, I am leaving soon, so I can do as I like, more or less. Arthur is up and uses his tricycle to get about the estate and has given orders for a lot of work to be done. When do you leave Miranda?"

"I've arranged with the agency that I am to stay for another two weeks after the month is up. She depends on me now and needs to ease herself into a normal situation again. It's coming right, but two more weeks will be fine for both of us as Dwight is still in America, and even when I leave, I shall keep tabs on her health for a while."

Bea eyed her friend with interest. "Miss Merchant said that Sir Arthur had arranged for you to stay on, too. I thought you wanted to get away from him?"

Emma looked shocked. "That's news to me! I am ready to leave next week and he knows that. I am going back to Aunt Emily for a week or so, before coming up to stay in St James's with you."

"Watch out, Emma, he has his eyes on you as the future Lady Jumeaux."

"I know." She sounded troubled. "He showed me the family heirlooms the other day, which include some exquisite jewels from Marie Antoinette's court, handed down through his family, and he asks what I think about the alterations they are doing to the stable block as if I shall be there when it's finished." She sighed. "He's really very sweet and I am quite fond of him. I hate to hurt him after all he's suffered, but the whole set-up would stifle me."

"Here's your bus. I'll wait by the Market Cross for Miranda. Let me know what happens in the next thrilling instalment of Emma Dewar's love life," she said as Emma climbed on to the bus and gave her a dirty look.

Emma walked from the bus to the gates of the manor and stopped. "Hello," she said.

"I thought I'd meet you," Arthur said and swung the tricycle round to ride back by her side. "You look wonderful. I've seen you in mufti only twice and I like it better than uniform. Why not dress like that all the time?"

"I can't," she lied. "The conditions of the agency are strict and it would give a false impression of my position here."

"Let it. If, as I hope, you decide to stay here, you can't wear uniform all the time." He glanced at her, his face set and anxious. "You do know that I love you, Emma, and I want to marry you?"

"You mustn't say that, Arthur. A month ago, you didn't know that I existed. I'm the only reasonably pretty female you've seen for months and we have become close because of what I do. But when you are really better, you will meet other girls and find that they have more in common with your life here than I could ever have."

"Remember what I've said, but don't give me a definite 'No' just yet." He stopped by the terrace and swung round to the ramp leading to the hall door. "Every day I am stronger and feel that life might be good again. You have given me my health, my pride and my manhood. I feel it stirring again and I want you very much."

Emma pushed the tricycle to help it up the ramp. "I'll stay dressed like this for dinner," she said. "I think I can offer you a great deal as a friend, but I'll dress in uniform again tomorrow so that there is no misunderstanding about my position here. We can be very good friends, once you have recovered from the patient-nurse fixation which is nearly inevitable in situations like ours."

"I suppose lots of men have fallen for you when you touch them with those gentle hands?"

"Hundreds," she admitted cheerfully. "All sorts, shapes, sizes and nationalities." She smiled at him with real affection and held his hand for a second. "But none quite as nice as you, Arthur."

"Do you mean that?" His hungry expression made her wish that she'd not said it. "You will stay for another two weeks? The agency told me that it would be all right."

"So I heard," she said wryly. "Sorry, but I have made

plans and I have to be away on the date that I agreed with the agency when I was appointed here."

"But you will come back?" he asked eagerly, and she knew how much it cost him to lose face over her decision.

"We have a few more days and I shall make you work hard so that you will not need a nurse again," she said.

"That's not what I mean and you know it." He swung back towards the park. "Come on, we'll go round to the stables and back by the lake." She began to protest that she had things to do in her room but he smiled grimly. "If you insist on being my nurse, then be that now and walk me out for fresh air," he said.

Emma relaxed. It was warm and the sun made dappled light through the trees of the drive. Some of the weeds had been torn up from the gravel and an air of good husbandry was creeping back into the neglected borders. Arthur knew the name of every rose and every shrub and he seemed contented until they reached the lake. Moodily he gazed out at the water lilies and then turned to her. "Marry me, Emma," he said softly. "I promise you that I'll make you happy enough to forget Guy and to make a new life for both of us."

"I can't forget Guy, so it wouldn't be fair to you," she said. "Besides I wouldn't fit in here."

She looked past him towards the spinney on the edge of the estate and saw a horse and female rider approaching, picking a way between the untrimmed saplings. The girl eased the mare into a canter as they reached level ground and her face was pink with concentration and something more like embarrassment.

"Prissy! What are you doing here? It's good to see you."

Priscilla stayed in the saddle and Emma knew that this was a deliberate ploy to keep above them in all respects,

73

looking down and having the advantage. She did look well in the saddle, her scarlet shirt flowing gently over full breasts down to the trim waist of her breeches.

"Hello, Arthur." She looked at Emma with guarded interest.

"This is Emma, or as she would rather be called, Sister Dewar," Arthur said with an edge to his voice.

Prissy laughed and seemed to relax. "Difficult patient?" she said and Emma smiled. "Always was a bit bolshie," she added cheerfully. "Needs a firm hand like this one," she said and stroked the mare's neck. "Christ, Arthur! She nearly threw me in that copse. It's a disgrace! Creeper everywhere and seedlings old enough to do a lot of damage if the hunt comes through."

"Come back to the house and have a drink," Arthur said. "What happened to you yesterday? Thought we were having lunch together."

"Sorry about that. Had to take the other mare to the farrier." Prissy turned the mare and cantered off. "I'll put her in the paddock and meet you on the terrace," she said. "I'll want to hear from you just how bloody-minded he's been," she told Emma, leaving her in no doubt that her presence was required over drinks. No tête-à-tête after a long parting of friends? Was there an undercurrent of shyness at the thought of being alone with Arthur?

Emma went to find Martha to warn her that there might be three for dinner. Martha shrugged. "We can manage that but did she say why she didn't come here yesterday when we expected her? It put us all out. I made a special pudding."

"She said she had to take a horse for a new shoe, as she'd thrown it."

Martha stared and then laughed. "I might have known the ATS wouldn't have changed her," she said, and looked more cheerful. "I've known that one since she was so high and when she was made to face something she didn't like, such as boring relatives, she'd make an excuse about a sick animal or a horse going lame."

"I think she's feeling shy," Emma said.

Martha eyed her with curiosity. "I thought before you turned up here that they'd make a go of it when they realised that they suited each other and weren't still children together."

"They are right for each other," Emma said firmly. "I shall be gone in a few days time. I've done what I came to do and I've grown fond of him, but that's all. You do know that my fiancé died in the war?"

Martha nodded and sighed. "Happened to me in the first lot and I never did get over it completely," she said, as if Emma was about to go into a nunnery. "Tell her I'm laying up for three and expect her to stay."

Emma carried the drinks tray out on to the terrace, feeling guilty. It was so easy to make Guy the excuse for evading all difficult male contact. If I'm honest, she thought, I now have only good, but misty memories of him, as I'd have for any dear friend, but he makes the perfect excuse for avoiding being hurt and giving pain.

Prissy arrived and went to the cloakroom to wash her hands and comb her hair, as the low branches of the copse had tangled it. She emerged with the well-scrubbed air of perfect healt and her vitality seemed to fill the space around them, but Arthur didn't even give her a brotherly kiss of greeting. Martha made the excuse to see her by bringing some cheese straws to nibble with the sherry and Prissy said that she couldn't stay to dinner.

"I can't leave the mare in that paddock until you've grubbed up that yellow weed. It's lethal," she said accusingly. "I hitched her up in the stable and even there I had my doubts, and hauled away some musty hay that could give her colic."

"I have plans for the stable," Arthur said defensively. "Now that the war is over, at least for us in Europe, I can make plans."

Emma felt the other girl's gaze exploring her face and knew that Prissy was unsure of her status with Arthur. "I admire anyone who rides well," Emma said. "I can stay on a horse if I must, but it isn't my favourite pastime," she added deliberately and watched Arthur look at Prissy with interest for the first time.

"Prissy can ride anything on four legs," he said. "Won all the cups in the gymkhanas and is out front at every meet of hounds, aren't you, old girl?"

Prissy blushed and put down her empty glass. "Must dash," she said. "I'll be over next week to look at the stables with you and I know someone with a hunter for sale."

"Then I'll say goodbye," Emma said. "I am leaving for good in a few days time."

"Are you?" The relief was almost palpable.

"When I'm gone, make sure he gets enough exercise and eats well to build up some muscle," Emma said.

"Goodbye, then. Nice to have met you," Prissy said with obvious insincerity, and fled.

Dinner was a quiet time and Emma sensed that Arthur was tired and often lost in his own thoughts. After breakfast the next day, he suggested that Emma should take him in his wheelchair to the village as it was rather too far to manage on his tricycle.

"Dress in mufti," he insisted. "We can go to the bank and then have lunch at the pub. It's time I did normal things and it will be good to see a few familar faces again. I'll take a walking stick and leave the chair in the pub until I get tired."

Emma regarded him with suspicion. He had made no further reference to his proposal, but she decided that he was determined to be seen with her as if they were friends or more, in a place where the locals would soon pick up the notion that they were far closer than was true. She dressed neatly, but in a blouse that looked as if she'd kept it from the sixth form at school and a plain navy skirt.

"I said no uniform," Arthur remarked, then grinned as if accepting her reproof. "It isn't important. At least you aren't wearing a cap, and you are beautiful in whatever you wear."

People came to speak to him, showing every sign of being very pleased to welcome him back to health, and with the aid of the stick, he gave a good impression of complete recovery.

Bread and cheese and pickles seemed the dish of the day that looked edible and he ordered cider. "This is good," he said. "A few weeks ago I knew that I would never come here again and I'd leave the manor in a box, but you came along and worked miracles." She shook her head, but he went on, "It's true. My doctor was afraid that I'd die of toxic absorption before I could have the next op, but you did that operation and saved me."

"The shrapnel was asking to be let out," she said. "Anyone would have done the same. It wasn't an operation."

"Using a scalpel to cut the skin and then easing out the metal?"

"The skin and muscle was very thin and needed little help to open," Emma said, defensively. "Quite a common condition where I worked."

"But even though you had done it before and knew it was possible, you used your own judgement and initiative." She nodded. "And you wonder why I owe you so much and want to spend the rest of my life saying thank you?"

"The penicillin helped," she pointed out. "Once the gubbins had gone and there was no risk of an inert abscess that hadn't drained, it cleared up the residue."

"Marry me?" he said as if he was asking her if she wanted more cider.

"No."

"Give me two good reasons that I shall not find ridiculous," he said and set his jaw in a determined manner.

Emma laughed. "I can give you several," she stated firmly, and ticked them off on her fingers as she told him. "One, I don't love you and haven't recovered from Guy." There I go again hiding behind his memory, she thought. "Two, I wouldn't ever fit in here without having the sea close by."

"That all?"

"No." She took a deep breath. "I'm not good with horses and and I am against hunting. I'd be bored if I lived here with no work to do and I think you should marry Prissy."

She glanced up and found him frowning. "You met her for hardly more than five minutes," he said. "Why Prissy and not you?"

"When she's overcome her shyness at meeting you again and realising that she's in love with you, she'll be a great support for everything you want to do here. Also she will get on well with your mother. Prissy is perfect for you."

"That's no reason for marrying anyone. My mother doesn't come into this at all."

"It does in a community like this, with you being the leading citizen and with a family history going back over the centuries." Emma gave a wicked chuckle. "Prissy will enjoy going with you to Buckingham Palace when you collect the Military Cross, and she will be a wonderful hostess at hunt balls."

78

"I love *you* and you are so beautiful," he said. "I daren't touch you without wanting you."

"That's another thing. I'm not fond of babies and you'll want an heir. The manor should be full of lovely, healthy children and Prissy has the right kind of child-bearing hips," she added and laughed. "Look at her really well and you'll find a lot of beauty and passion there, Arthur. One more thing. Prissy will love it when you call her 'old girl', but I'd run a mile from any man who called me that!"

"You may be right," he conceded. "If you refuse to marry me, I might as well take Prissy, but I shall never forget you, Emma. A part of me will be sad and lonely without you and that's for ever, but I can't fight a dead man, and I know now that Guy will never let you go."

She wanted to cry, Guy has nothing to do with this, but held back. It was kinder to let him think what he liked. A rival among his living contemporaries would be an enemy to be confronted, but swathed in the mystery of a valiant death Guy was invincible.

"I know I'm right," she said gently. "Be nice to her and make it soon. She'll adore looking after you."

"Let's get back. I want to telephone the chandler."

"And Prissy."

"Not until you have gone. Get packed and I'll arrange a car to take you to the station when the time comes, but before that, just enjoy my home and perhaps love it and have second thoughts?"

"See you later," she said when they reached the manor. "Be happy," she whispered, and kissed his cheek.

It would be so easy to stay, she thought when she walked round the lake two days later. The weather was cruelly fine, the flowers heavy with honey-bees and the water lilies sat pale and cool on the green water. When it was time to depart she felt a twinge of sorrow that was more acute than she'd expected. The car was coming at eleven, Arthur said, and Emma had her cases ready in the hall. She rifled through the morning mail, and found two letters for herself and a poster reminding everyone to vote in the general election.

"That settles it, I have to be back in London, to vote," she remembered.

"Churchill will get back in," Martha said comfortably. "I don't think I need to vote. The local MP has had this constituency for years and his father before him, and we know who we like."

"I should vote. There are a lot of ex-service men and women who have had enough of war and want the country to give them something better. They might not feel the same as you do, Martha."

"That's not true," Martha said. "People will never forget that they are grateful to Churchill. Everyone fought for his country. Sir Arthur gave a lot for his country and he will vote Tory, as ever."

"You may be right," Emma said mildly, but recalled seeing the faces of some of her patients, left with an arm missing, or so badly wounded that they'd never work again. Arthur had a wonderful home and plenty of money, but what of the others?

She looked up. The crunch of gravel under car wheels told her that either the car to collect her was early or there was a visitor. The ancient Rolls stood by the porch and Lady Jumeaux climbed out and walked briskly into the hall.

"Good morning," Emma said.

With one sweeping glance, Lady Jumeaux observed the slim figure dressed in the immaculate cotton suit that had been Emma's main personal extravagance during her American visit with Bea, and the bright, well-ordered hair and soft make-up. The sight gave her no pleasure and she set her mouth into a hard line. "Good morning," she said and saw the suitcases. "Going away for a break? I thought you were here for good, if the village gossips have it right."

"A car's coming to collect me at eleven," Emma said.

"And when you come back, I suppose you'll continue to wind my son round your little finger? His doctor tells me that he depends on you for everything now."

"Did he say that? How strange," Emma said, determined to keep her temper and not to give Lady Jumeaux any excuse to accuse her of rudeness.

"Prissy came to see me this morning and said she'd met you," Lady Jumeaux continued, obviously upset by the lack of response she had from this elegant and lovely girl.

"I hear that she is leaving the ATS and coming home. That must please her family and friends," Emma said. "It's good to think the war is over and we can get back to normality."

"Men like my son will never do that."

"You haven't seen him for several days and I think you'll find him very much better. In fact he will no longer need a nurse, as he exercises on the tricycle, walks with a stick and the wounds have healed well."

Lady Jumeaux gave a bitter laugh. "You say he doesn't need a nurse now? I suppose you mean he does need a wife?"

"Of course. Arthur is much too fine a man not to fulfil his obligations here and he will be able to live a full life very soon." Emma smiled. "You must be very proud of your son. I do hope you see more of each other now. Illness makes many people edgy with their dearest friends and family, but now he is so much more cheerful and confident of the future, that I'm sure you will become close again."

"How dare you dictate to me about my own son! I suppose you think that once installed here, I shall have to kowtow to you as mistress of this house?"

"I don't know what you mean." Emma looked the picture of injured innocence. "I am leaving today and I have no intention of coming back here. I'm afraid I'd find Arthur's relatives and friends a bit boring."

"What?" Lady Jumeaux was lost for words and, behind her, Arthur waited for her to recover. He was smartly dressed and walked without his stick. His colour had improved and the few pounds he'd put on in weight over the past two weeks showed off a potentially fine figure and deportment.

"Yes, Emma is leaving me," he said. "I asked her to stay but she has to go away. Not my choice but hers," he added to make what he said, certain.

"She admits that you no longer need a nurse," she said defensively.

"And she says that any other relationship is out of the question."

"So I should think!"

"I don't know why you say that, Mother. I asked her to marry me but she turned me down. I asked her several times because I know that she is the love of my life, but she tells me she doesn't want me and that I should marry Prissy and have lots of children." He smiled, with an ironic lift of his eyebrows. "Can you believe it? She refused all that I can offer."

"Then you are a fool," Lady Jumeaux told Emma.

Emma laughed. "Don't tell me that you want me to change my mind? Or is it too much for you to take in, that anyone might prefer a life away from here? Did you think I should be so honoured to be asked, that I could not, in my right mind, refuse? I have become very fond of Arthur and I shall never forget him, but I know that marriage between us is out of the question."

"I had no chance. I can't fight a dead man," Arthur said simply, and Emma felt very small.

"Is the car out there?" she asked.

"Ready for you, Madame," Arthur said. "I've been practising when you've been in the village and I find I can drive now. I shall take you to the station, if you don't mind riding in a rather out of date model?"

"Take the Rolls," Lady Jumeaux said.

"No, thank you, Mother. I have my own . . . everything, and have no need for patronage."

"Don't be too hard on her," Emma said when they were halfway to the station.

"Why not? She was hard on me when I was a child, and she left me when I came back very ill and needed help."

"Some people can't face sickness."

"Some people have no heart," he said and smiled sadly. "Others have heart but won't give it away."

He parked the car and they waited outside the country railway station until they heard the train coming in the distance. "You must let me know how you get on," he said urgently.

"No, my dear. No letters, no contact, at least not for many years. I refuse to come between you and your future wife and I know that you must forget me."

On the station platform he held her close and she raised her face to his kiss. He smelled of good soap, his shaven face was smooth, and there was no trace of weakness in his kiss or embrace. Almost unwillingly, she held him and felt a surge of longing that she had lost since Guy's death.

Emma picked up her cases and boarded the train. She wound down the window and he put up a hand to touch hers. As the train moved away in a flurry of steam, they were both crying.

Chapter 7

"Miss Merchant wasn't exactly pleased when I told her that I was leaving after my month with Sir Arthur but I told her, ever so demurely as if the very idea shocked me, that I had to leave as he wanted to marry me and it was out of the question."

Bea chuckled. "Did she tell you that you were mad?"

"Not in so many words, but I'll bet if I get another case she'll suggest a woman, or a man so decrepit that he will be past it."

"Difficult! The poor woman might think you are a lesbian who hates men, so what is she to do? Will you be safer with a woman or another man?"

Emma giggled. "I've missed your mad brain," she said. "Are you sure I can stay here? With the election, your father might have guests who want to use the apartment, but I do have to stay in London to vote."

"My Pa is staying with friends at the Carlton, where they are having lots of meetings. With no staff to cook for him, he's better off there. I don't know what he's up to, but he has his ear to the ground over what's happening in politics and I think he's very uneasy about the election. True he has a safe seat, but if the others get in with a clear majority after being a coalition, bang goes his chance of a seat in the Cabinet. In a National Government, he could have a chance and if not, he might make something big on the opposition benches, but he'd hate it."

"He's not going to lose his seat, so why should you worry, unless you feel strongly about the Party? I didn't think you were interested." Emma said. "Personally, I can't get worked up over it and whoever gets in has a terrible job to do in the near future."

"I shall stay with you here and just see Miranda each morning and after the theatre. I give one injection and she gives the other now and we're gradually making her take responsibility for her diet. She had such a scare that she'll behave and cope well now that she's stabilised, and her maid has got the hang of what goes into the food, with the help of Dr Lawrence's excellent book on diabetes. I shall be out of a job until Dwight comes back in two weeks time."

"You're a lot happier about him now. In time, you might even be calm and sane, but he'll hate that," Emma said, teasing her.

"Everything he mentions seems somewhere so far away that it could never touch us. He writes good letters and tells me a few things that the general public haven't heard."

"Isn't that censored?

"Most of the letters come through the diplomatic bag in the care of my father, who puts them in fresh covers and sends them on. Since Dwight went to the White House and met the President, he has been promoted again and is told a lot of military secrets, probably of a low grade, but impressive. I suppose I am considered OK as Dwight's godfather approves of me and my Pa is important."

"Does he like President Truman? Some say he is brash and not quite the same class as Roosevelt, but as he was Vice President when Roosevelt died they had no choice but to appoint him."

"He's a very shrewd man and, when he's accused of being rash, he tells them that he will take the blame if anything goes wrong. Dwight says he has a plaque on his desk with the words, 'The Buck Stops Here,' which is a reminder to him and everyone else that he is in charge."

"But Roosevelt had a lot of influence and Truman is not well-known outside the States."

"The President was a very sick man and some people were almost relieved when he died. They thought that he might not make such a good job of the peace as he'd done in war. Rather like Churchill now. Two old, tired warhorses with millions loving and admiring them, but now maybe unable to do the job for lasting peace. The Americans are hotting up the war in the Pacific and we have got the Japs on the run in Burma at last after that terrible war there, so let's hope that, as Vera sings, there'll be bluebirds over the white cliffs of Dover, and the boys who are left will come home."

"I was appalled when Arthur told me about the Burma campaign, where many of his friends died or were taken prisoner in the jungle. He said that the Japanese have a completely different idea of life and death and they swear to fight for their emperor to the death, as they think he is God and if they die for him they will be blessed in the afterlife. They despise anyone who surrenders."

"Kamikaze pilots have done a lot of damage to shipping in the Pacific islands, and, when fighting on land, they never give in, but fight to the last man and would rather die than be taken prisoner," Bea said.

Emma shuddered. "Arthur said that after the way they treat our men, taking a delight in humiliation and forcing them to make the Burma Road and railway, so that many dropped dead from hunger, disease, torture and fatigue, the Allied forces now have no mercy either. When confronted by a yelling mob advancing towards them, they mow them down like lines of rats as they come on and on, until they are all dead or taken prisoner, but surrender is rare."

"They sound inhuman. Most Americans secretly dread being taken prisoner by them as they face torture and humiliation and hard labour under starving conditions." Bea looked serious. "Dwight said that they had a point about survival. He wouldn't want to go on living if he was captured, but, thank God, he will never have to face that now. He will not go on any more bombing raids, but feels that he is useful ferrying the planes over the Atlantic and then down to the islands and the airbases."

"Does he listen to Tokyo Rose?"

"They all do, even though the powers-that-be discourage it. She has a nerve! She is an Amercian-born daughter of Japanese parents, who happened to be in Tokyo when war was declared and stayed on to do their propaganda over the wireless."

"Do they believe her?"

"They try to ignore her, but last year, when the losses in the Islands were so bad, she was jubilant and every American man with red blood in his veins wanted to strangle her!" Bea sounded pensive. "She's still out there, boasting about Jap supremacy, but says much less about specific targets, as the US spy network gets better and better and the White House has the sense to keep quiet about some things that the general public need not know, like the balloons."

"Barrage balloons? What's secret about them? We have them all over the place," Emma said.

"Not that. These were huge balloons, thirty-three feet across, with cages under them carrying fragmentation explosives and fire-bombs. The Japs sent them up to thirty thousand feet to drift across the American coastline, hoping they'd come down or be shot down and do a lot of damage, or at least be a scary tactic."

"I've never heard of them."

"They kept it quiet as they were afraid that, if the Japanese thought they were successful, they might have loaded the balloons with germ warfare. When nothing appeared on the news about them, the Japs believed that they had been very ineffective and stopped making them. Some did come down and kill a few people and made forest fires in Alaska. Others were shot down, and some pilots, seeing them come silently out of the clouds, thought they were unidentified flying objects from outer space. That's all we need! Little green men with large heads, saying 'Take me to your leader!' and invading the planet."

"Idiot," Emma said and only half-believed all that Bea told her, although she knew that the tales of atrocities were true. Arthur had told her that after the natives of one island had suffered greatly from the Japanese, when the tide of war turned and they had the chance to retaliate, they reverted to their ancient culture of head-hunting and cannibalism and took a horrendous satisfaction in every prisoner they caught.

"The election here has taken the headlines away from the Pacific war, but there's a big sea-battle going on with both sides eager for confrontation. Dwight says the enemy has sent over so many planes piloted by inexperienced and very young men, that the US Air Force shot them down easily, and they're calling it a turkey shoot."

"The Yanks are so laconic about serious things, it's weird," Emma said.

Bea laughed. "He said they hoped to make an end run and finish it soon."

"A what?"

"You really will have to learn the jargon for American football if you come over with us. It's an outflanking tactic, or so I'm told."

"Foreigners!" Emma said scathingly. "You'll have to teach them cricket. We have sensible names for the players' positions, like silly mid-on."

"We'd better get to the polling station," Bea said. "Pa wanted me to wear a blue rosette, but I'm not even sure I want to vote Tory again. He'd kill me if he knew, but I feel like a change."

"Clement Atlee isn't exactly glamorous," Emma said. "He never seems to smile."

"He has a lot of very keen intellectuals in his team," Bea said. "Now we are cosy with the Russians, they are willing to forget the sharp left communist element that Dwight scathingly calls 'pinkos' and speak only of our valiant Russian allies who fought at Stalingrad. This crowd are not your actual cloth-cap image, but lecturers and scientists and many able administrators like Sir Stafford Cripps. Shinwell would encourage the miners, and even if they have to have a coalition, they'd all have to pull their socks up and work for the nation."

"You seem to know a lot for someone who hates politics," Emma reminded her.

"I absorb it through my pores, when Pa gets going" Bea said. "Two to watch later might be Aneurin Bevan, who has a nice Welsh voice and can put on a cloth cap and muffler and convince the workers in the Valleys that he is one of them, having left his Rolls outside the valley! I've met his wife Jennie, and she has the most exquisite hands of which she is very vain. The other is Ernest Bevin, who worked alongside Churchill in the National Government and sent the new conscripts down to work in the mines as Bevin Boys when coal was scarce. He's different from the usual politician, but again one of the people, a plain, tweedy man who calls a spade a spade. Dangerous," Bea added.

"You should be in politics," Emma suggested.

"That's what Pa says," Bea said calmly. "I might join something when I go to the States. I think I'd go down well and maybe do some good."

"I doubt it. Remember how the women looked at you when we went to the General's parties?"

Bea made an impatient gesture. "They were just self-indulgent softies who had never seen anything of importance and had no idea of what we had gone through."

"They'd be the ones you'd have to influence, as they have money and status on their side and some of them did care a lot," Emma reminded her.

"Well, let's do our civic duty." Bea looked up at the scarred paint and grimy windows of the church hall. "Why do all polling booths look like something very drab from Russia?"

"Don't you know there's a war on?" Emma quoted. "Soon we shall have to find other excuses for everything." They showed their polling cards in the church hall, and walked across the bare floorboards to the individual booths which had been hastily erected from plywood and untreated deal shelving. Bea looked heavenwards as if asking for inspiration and made her cross on the voting paper.

"Did you have the courage to vote Labour?" Emma asked as they walked out into the sunlight.

"No. I had a sudden vision of Churchill on the balcony of the Foreign office on VE night, and I couldn't reject him." Bea sighed. "Like it or not, I suppose that blood was thicker than water when it came to the decision. I know my Pa would be impossible to know if he thought I'd done otherwise."

"Me, too," Emma said. "If they lose this time, at least we shall know that it wasn't due to us."

"Our two votes?" Bea laughed.

"What now? London seems very busy, but we'll manage to get some food in one of the big stores or the American place in Leicester Square."

"The Quality Inn?" Bea smiled sadly. "I don't think I've been there for years, ever since the day we met my cousin Eddie there, or rather, he tried to muscle in on our meal and take over afterwards."

Emma gulped. "Please! I thought I'd forgotten him."

"Well, he won't be there now," Bea said firmly. "And be honest, does any girl forget a man who tries to rape her?" She looked at Emma. "Sometimes it's good to remember such things, to give you a sense of proportion when a really good man comes along and wants to marry you."

"I should count my blessings and marry Arthur?"

"Not Arthur. He's not the only man who wants you."

Emma looked annoyed. "If you mean Paul, then forget it. He's in Southampton testing reflexes and I haven't heard a word from him since I came away. There was never anything between us," she added. "He was just a friend."

"Funny!" Bea looked slightly malicious. "I thought I saw him last week."

"In London?"

"Actually, I didn't see him. He telephoned the apartment."

"And?" Emma asked, feeling that Bea was at her most exasperating.

"Nothing." Bea shrugged. "I wasn't there. Pa told me that he had rung and would be at St Thomas's for a while."

"What else?"

"As I said, nothing. My Pa isn't the type to have endless conversations with my male friends, and as it was me he wanted to contact, he assumed I'd ring back when I got the message." Bea laughed. "After all the affairs my father has had, it's strange to see how he gets annoyed if I even mention a man other than Dwight."

"And have you rung back?"

"No, I've been busy," Bea said. She regarded Emma with a shrewd expression. "If he wants to contact you, he can do so, but I'm not going to be piggy in the middle and do his work for him."

Emma bit her lip. "It's not important," she said. "As he didn't ask about me, forget it."

They found an empty table and picked up the glossy menus. Girls and one or two men too young to be called up hurried about with platters of attractively arranged food, a concept still unfamilar in England as most cafes served small portions of meat and two veg or fried fish and chips.

Seeing Bea's incredulous expression, Emma said waspishly, as she felt slighted that Paul hadn't mentioned her name, "You'll be living on stuff like this soon, so you'd better get used it."

"Whale steaks? I tried whale meat last week and it tasted fishy," Bea said. "And for heaven's sake what is snoek? It is listed under fish, so I suppose it must be something unmentionable from the sea. The salad might be good as the Americans do like crisp lettuce and use imaginative dressings. Do you know, I rather like Spam fritters and hash browns. That with salad might be quite nice."

The food arrived fresh and hot and Emma looked across at the other tables. "It hasn't changed."

"At least one thing has. We don't have to run away from Eddie this time."

Emma cut a slice of Spam into small squares and added a piece of fried potato to a piece. "Arthur knew Eddie," she said. "They were in the same marine commando unit." She smiled. "Arthur was too polite to ask if I knew him well, but he didn't care for Eddie except as a fine soldier."

"Did you tell him?"

"I couldn't say, 'by the way he tried to rape me in a dance-hall in the West End of London and I found him a bit rough! It would have seemed odd to tell him that, after he knew that Eddie left me his cap badge. Arthur has one like it and when I saw it, it made me feel cold as if Eddie might appear."

"Ice–cream that doesn't look like lumpy custard?" Ben interrupted. "I see some over there and they've even got wafer biscuits. Do you think that awfully-pink one does taste of strawberries? I'm tired of synthetic vanilla."

"Just coffee for me," Emma said. "What shall we do this evening?"

"I have tickets for Miranda's play and an invitation to meet the cast in her dressing-room after the show."

"You are looking like an Egyptian cat again! What are you scheming now?" Emma asked.

"Miranda acts under a pseudonym as her early career had dubious overtones. My father doesn't know that the bright star is his former girlfriend, so I think he might like to meet her again."

"You are a cat! A real one!"

"I think not," Bea said with dignity. "Pa is lonely and a mite uncertain of his political future. I suggested that he should like to show his confidence in the election results, which will not come in until tomorrow and the next day, by being seen enjoying the company of his dutiful daughter and her friends, meeting the cast of a very prestigious play."

Emma eyed her with suspicion. "You sound as if you've written it up for the gossip columns."

"Do I?" Bea said airily. "I may have mentioned it to a

reporter friend of mine who is sick of writing about the election and the war and says he wants to do his own column about famous people."

"You'll send Miranda into a coma!" Emma said. "She may not want her early life exposed."

"My father is a pro when it comes to people. He'll act as if he has never set eyes on her, and then be charming. Miranda knows he's coming to see her and she seems pleased, so she will act as he does and enjoy the meeting."

"And you will purr with satisfaction," Emma said. "Do you really fancy Miranda as a stepmother?"

"Could do worse. She is a very nice woman and Pa needs someone away from the political scene. She told me how they met and a little of what came after, but she isn't all that forthcoming about him."

"Is he coming to the play?"

"No, he's with his constituents until polling ends and will meet me at the stage door. I've arranged supper for a small party at the Bagatelle; just us and my father and Miranda and her leading man and a couple more from the cast, to show that she isn't Pa's guest alone."

"And the Press?" Emma asked dryly.

"Just my friend and a photographer."

"Arthur would enjoy that."

"Meeting an actress and a politician?

"No. Edmundo Ross and his band play at the Bagatelle. Arthur loves Latin American music."

"Marry him! He gets better and better."

"He also likes horses and hunting and one or two sports that I'd hate and will want hordes of children."

"What you need is . . ."

"Shut up, Sister! I know what I need and it isn't a man."

Bea chuckled and finished her ice-cream. "How about

an affair with a handsome actor? Or a flyer? Dwight has loads of friends who are just dying to meet someone like you."

Emma shook her head. "Haven't you noticed? When Dwight takes us out and includes his friends to make up a party, I do have fun, but he watches them like a hawk in case they get fresh with me. He is like a fussy chaperone."

"Nothing like an old married man to be puritanical. He's very fond of you, Emma, and hopes you'll marry and live happily ever after, like us." Bea was serious. "Don't undervalue that. We are both concerned about your future."

"I know." Emma looked away. "I shall miss you both." She wrapped her untouched bread roll in a paper napkin and took another from Bea's plate. "Let's feed the ducks. Ducks never answer back."

"Perhaps I should have eaten my roll. They seem to think it delicious," Bea said. They stood on the bridge in St James's Park and looked down at the water. The sleek birds that knew no wartime rationing but whose numbers had been decreased by night prowlers fancying duck for dinner, fought over the bread, their green feathers shining like splashes of emerald satin. Sparrows, so tame that five at a time perched on Emma's hand, ate the tiny crumbs. Bea watched her with amusement. "I bet you carry sugar lumps for the donkeys on the beach," she said.

"No, I save my sugar ration for Aunt Emily. She likes everything sweet."

"How is she?"

Emma hesitated. "I've written twice, but had no reply. I'll have to ring her, although she hates talking on the phone. I didn't ring when I was with Arthur as I knew I'd feel homesick," she explained.

Bea looked sceptical. "You must get in touch today!

Who knows, she may be torturing herself over who she voted for, and will need moral suport."

Emma laughed "She will vote for the Liberals. We have a very good MP on the Island, who gets in every time. Aunt Emily knows him, so she makes sure he treads the party line!"

"We could do with her in Parliament."

"Maybe I should phone. If Stafford Cripps gets in, she'll need smelling-salts, as she is convinced, for no reason that I know, that he will ruin the country."

"Strange," Bea said slowly. "Pa thinks the same. He says that he might be the next Chancellor and will put very harsh taxes on the rich."

"Would that be bad for your father?"

"Not really. He has bank accounts in Switzerland and very few liquid assets in this country now. He also managed to get appointed to the War Graves Commission before everyone knew there were well-paid jobs going there. His contacts in Holland and Belgium will be a great help. Did you know the Dutch have had to eat flower bulbs and the mash left from sugar beet that they usually throw to the farm animals? Indigestible but life-saving, Pa said, and he has organised relief in a big way, so he's becoming highly respectable."

"He's a really good man at heart," Emma said.

"He's very cunning. If he had to shed his sleek haircut and dress in the drape-fronted suits that the spivs wear and speak with a cockney accent, he'd fit in well," Bea said dryly. "He's a barrow boy by instinct, in spite of Harrow and Cambridge, which makes him good in politics. Maybe I'll buy him a kipper tie for Christmas."

"Stop being cynical and let's go back and make coffee," Emma said.

Already the placards were screaming the opinions of

newspaper proprietors, prophesying the election results according to the political beliefs of the various editors, but Bea refused to buy any papers as she said they'd find out soon enough.

Aunt Emily was out and Emma felt relieved. "I'll try again tomorrow," she said, putting thoughts of her and the niggling annoyance that Paul caused her out of her mind, and feeling excited about seeing the play.

Miranda looked beautiful and, as Bea said, "Bone structure helps and she really does look good even off stage." Her recent illness had left a translucent fragility that was right for the part and charmed the audience. Many left the theatre with tears in their eyes.

"I wish Pa had been here to see her," Bea said. "Come on, I have to make sure she has her injection before she forgets and socialises."

Maisie, Miranda's maid, was in the dressing-room with the insulin ready and Bea let her carry on, knowing that Maisie had a fiercely protective side to her quiet nature and would care well for Miranda after Bea left.

"Now for it," Bea whispered as her father was ushered into the room set for the party. He carried two large bottles of very good champagne, and when he saw Miranda, he managed not to drop them, but advanced with every sign of meeting a lovely woman for the first time.

He kissed her hand. "I'm afraid I missed the play, but I shall come back," he assured her. "I really must see you."

Miranda gave a throaty chuckle. "I shall look forward to that," she said and looked at Bea. "Am I allowed champagne? I feel like celebrating."

"If you drink what my father brought, you can have two glasses. It will be very dry," she said.

Chapter 8

"You look like a mother sheep whose lamb has escaped." Emma said with malicious relish. "I never thought I'd see the day when you would go all protective over another woman."

"She's still in my care," Bea said defensively.

"And who pushed her into a situation that might have an element of danger? Cheer up Bea, you're tired and so am I. Your father took her home, so what? It means nothing more than a courteous act to an old friend. Times change and people do too. Neither of them would want a scandal and Maisie went ahead to get Miranda's room ready for her to slip into after a hard day. She knows how to test for sugar and acetone and will ring you here if she's concerned."

"As usual you are right," Bea admitted. "I did take Pa aside and warned him that she was a bit frail and he promised to look after her." She put a hand to her cheek. "Do you know, he even thanked me for asking him to the party and kissed me for the first time in years."

"You did a good thing," Emma said. "If the election goes the way it seems will happen, Miranda will be just the solace he needs. I think she's still in love with him."

"Gonna make a sentimental journey," Bea sang.

"Ouch! You are not Doris Day," Emma said.

"I'll buy him the record just to annoy him," Bea

said, more cheerfully. "What did you think of the cast?"

"They look better behind the greasepaint," Emma said. "Most of the time I understood about half of what they said. It was all stage jargon about people I'll never meet." She laughed. "I think the one with the profile wanted me to say he looked like Ivor Novello."

"He does a bit. Why are you looking like that?"

"I've just remembered. When we saw Mrs Davies at the agency I thought her profile was like his."

"Not surprising. She is his mother, Mrs Novello Davies." Bea was enjoying her amazement. "That's why so many stage people ask for help through her agency." Bea shrugged. "You don't have to believe me, but I swear it's true."

"I suppose it could be true. Many people have unexpected backgrounds, although men like Arthur have 'county' written all over them and couldn't come from any other background."

"Do we wait until tomorrow to hear the first results over the wireless or torture ourselves tonight?"

"I'm too tired for that but I have had so much wine that I am stimulated. Not a happy mix. Shall I make coffee? We can slip into bed when sleep catches up on us,' Emma said.

"Cocoa, not coffee," Bea said. "If only we had a fire to gaze into while we dream and drink cocoa."

"Too hot for that, although Aunt Emily has a fire winter and summer as her mother did. My mother believes that fires start on December 1 if the weather is freezing." She yawned and handed Bea a steaming mug. "Cocoa in bed I think. Here you are, Bea. Goodnight."

Emma slept and then heard a door slam as Bea ran to answer the phone in the hall. She found her watch and saw that it was almost ten o'clock. She wriggled her toes and stretched, feeling refreshed and warm and supple. The kettle was already nearly boiling and she called, "Tea or coffee?"

Bea came into the kitchen. "Tea," she said. "Pa retained his seat and had a good majority, but it looks as if there's been a landslide victory for Labour. Not all the votes are in yet from the outlying districts, but it's really all over bar the shouting and it will be a Labour government and not a coalition." She sank onto a chair. "He's a bit upset but said he had been expecting it for ages. His main concern is Winston, who he thinks will suffer a great deal over this and maybe leave politics."

Emma put bread to toast and brought out butter and marmalade. "I'll try to get Aunt Emily today. I know she'll be very upset. I ought to go down to the Island," she said, as if it wasn't what she wanted to do.

"Not keen? Paul is away, so you can relax."

"If I go there, I shall want to laze about and I must plan my future."

"Take another case through the agency or go back to Beatties. They still want us," Bea said.

"I'll think about it and maybe take another case, but isn't it good to have a little time off? A month with no days off was very long in such a cloistered sort of place, and I see the wisdom of most of the agency rules, that we work longer than that only by arrangement, if it suits us."

"That dratted phone again! If people ring asking for Pa, I shall go mad. They must get him at the House or at the Carlton. All the ones who matter know where he is. I've told him that I refuse to be his secretary when I'm here and he says, let it ring."

"It might be for you," Emma said uneasily. "I hate letting a phone ring unanswered in case it's important."

"Just this one, then we go out and let it ring all day if

that's what it wants to do," Bea said, giving the telephone a mind of its own. "Hello! Buckingham Palace here," she said.

Emma heard her chuckle. "Just rehearsing, as the country will soon be a Republic the way it's going, and I might get there yet as daughter of the President, if my father turns round in politics and does a Vicar of Bray act!' She listened. "Yes Emma is with me, and we do have some time off. That sounds good. We can exchange news and mutual sympathy, unless you voted Labour? Make it about twelve as I have to see my patient first." She gave him the address in Chelsea where Miranda lived.

Emma rescued blackening toast, scraped it over the sink and then put it on Bea's plate. "A little charcoal is good for you," she said. "Who was that? Someone I know, as I heard my name mentioned."

"You should have concentrated on important things like my toast and not listened in," Bea said sternly, then gave a sweet smile. "Knew you'd be thrilled. Paul is picking us up for lunch from Miranda's apartment."

"Paul?"

"Yes, ducky," Bea said with exaggerated patience. "Remember Paul? Nice, young, handsome doctor who is everything a girl could wish for, except Dwight of course, and you aren't having him."

"What did he say?"

"You never listen. He asked if you were here and wants us both to go to lunch with him."

"And if I wasn't here?"

"Then he and I would have lunch together. As he's a friend of yours, he's one man who Dwight trusts to be with his beautiful wife without pushing her into bed."

"Do I come to Miranda's flat with you?"

"Yes, she wants to talk to you without having to say 'hello, darling' to a crowd."

"Why do they do that?"

"Half the time they forget names, and it's safer to call someone 'darling' than to say the wrong thing. I used to do that when I was insecure, but now I am more exclusive and Dwight wouldn't like it. Actors are very sensitive and take offence easily, or the ones who haven't made a name yet, do," Bea said shrewdly. "It's quite meaningless, like kissing the air when they pretend to kiss on both cheeks, but I prefer my endearments to be sincere. I'm becoming old-fashioned."

"Have you finished in the bathroom?" Emma smelled the warm scent of expensive bath salts.

"Yes, I got up early to listen to the election results and then to write to my husband. He'll want to hear the political news first hand, as he's anxious about my father, would you believe it? Go and make yourself pretty and use my Coty Chypre bath salts."

The pale pink bathroom was steamy. Emma wiped a circle clear on the mirror and surprised a smile in her reflection. It would be good to see Paul again, as a friend. Knowing that Arthur had fallen in love with her was good for her morale even if she would never marry him, and she could face Paul with confidence, knowing that some men found her attractive; but she was puzzled. Why should she need to put up a defence?

Carefully, she avoided getting her hair wet and sponged her body with the scented soap that matched the bath salts. Almost angrily, she watched the water run from the bath and gurgle in the pipes. Why did she have to impress Paul or convince herself that she must do so? He was a good friend and had known Guy. That was enough for a relationship between them, just as she had bonds with many of the men she had met at Beatties.

103

Friendship and a real affection that was no threat to their girlfriends or wives, and it was no more with Paul, she told herself. Paul would find a girl at St Thomas's or . . . on the Island or in Southampton and they could still be friends.

Miranda wanted to know all about Emma's Uncle Sidney and was disappointed to learn that Emma had met him only briefly when he was dying of tuberculosis. "When I was touring in the States, I saw all his films and thought he was very romantic and a very good actor," Miranda said. "Even when the magazines hinted that he was queer, I didn't believe them. He was engaged to be married, wasn't he?"

"Yes, but she was killed in a road accident." Emma smiled and left Miranda with her illusions. Sidney had been handsome, generous and loving and had given pleasure to millions, so why muddy the waters of his memory?

Paul arrived on time and insisted that Miranda should join them for lunch before her matinée. Bea was pleased as she had been worried and wanted to see that she had the right food. Hatchetts was nearly empty and the food was appetising enough to satisfy Miranda and safe enough for her diet. She ordered a taxi and left the others to finish their meal while she went to the theatre to prepare for the afternoon.

"Matinées! All those dear old biddies with tea trays rattling in the sentimental parts," she moaned. "But they do like me."

Dwight thinks it's a barbaric habit," said Bea. "How can an actor concentrate when Aunt Fanny is pouring out second cups and eating crunchy pastry?"

Miranda blushed. "Your father is coming to a performance next week when he is less busy in his constituency. Thank you for inviting him last night, Bea."

"Really thank you?"

"Really," Miranda said, and, picking up her gloves, left.

"What have you been plotting, Bea?" Paul sounded amused.

"Nothing," she said nonchalantly. "I come from a long line of matchmakers."

"How much do you charge?"

"I do it for love. Now finish that piece of mousetrap cheese and follow me."

"Where?" the other two asked.

"You may not have noticed but we are in for a storm and summer storms can make a body very wet, and I am not going for a walk in a dripping park," she explained carefully. "I am going to the flicks. Come if you want, but even if you don't come with me, I shall wallow in *Casablanca*, which I have seen three times and can't wait to see again."

"What about *Henry V*? With Olivier?"

"Is that on?"

"At the Odeon, Leicester Square."

"Which is it to be, Emma?" Paul asked.

"*Henry V*," Emma said. "I haven't seen that one." She knew that *Casablanca* would reduce her to tears if she heard "As time goes by". It was a film to watch alone with a pile of handkerchiefs or if she happened to be in a party, but with no personal ties. She felt his level, grey gaze on her and opened her bag to find a lipstick. "Coming to the ladies?" she asked Bea and walked away from the table.

There was a queue for the film as if the general public needed to forget war and elections and lose themselves in something so extravagant that they could believe that the seamy side of life didn't exist.

"Good psychology," Paul said and bought a bag of peanuts.

"Nuts are good for the brain?" Bea asked flippantly. "Give me more."

"No, not the nuts. Good films are therapeutic," he said and grinned. "You can see that I am getting involved with psychiatry."

When they had their tickets, Bea peeped in and asked the usherette if the main film had begun. "Can we wait for five minutes? I don't want to see the Pathe news."

"I'll go in and bag your seats," Paul said as more people came into the cinema. I'll sit on the left, if possible, and stand up when I see you come in."

"That's what I like about Paul. He accepts what I say without making me feel silly by trying to persuade me that I want to do the opposite." Bea was pensive. "I hate the news. Once, I saw a plane load of American airmen coming back to base after a raid and they pointed out the shell holes that had nearly brought the plane down over France. There were no familiar faces, but I thought it could have been Dwight. I want no more shocks after all we've seen."

Emma nodded, suddenly pale. "Quite by accident, just when I was convincing myself that I was getting back to normal, I saw a newsreel about Belsen and I had to leave the cinema as I felt sick, knowing that Guy died there. In many ways it seems years ago and at other times, it's only yesterday."

"It's only three months," Bea said gently, then flicked back her hair as if determined to dispel all gloom. "I hear the end of the news. That stupid Cockerel they have crowing on it should be shot and roasted. There's our gallant escort," Bea said and led Emma over to Paul.

The wonderful voices and diction and the great spectacles of the battle scenes, that had so little to do with the battles seen on the news, brought a deep, artistic satisfaction, and the spontaneous cheer that filled the cinema when the English archers let fly the dramatic, zinging curve of arrows, was intensely moving. It was good to see a romantic British victory, even if it was centuries old.

When the news came round again, Bea got up and the others followed her from the dark cinema. "They filmed *Henry V* in Ireland," she said. "Makes one aware that they had far more than we did during the war. But if they turn out films like that with such marvellous props, they have my blessing."

"It was wonderful," Emma agreed.

"Bea looked embarrassed. "I have to leave you now, children," she said.

"Where are you going?" Emma felt panic rising and wanted to cling to Bea's strength.

"When my father phoned, he asked me to join him at the Ritz for tea at five and then go on to a reception for his faithful constituency workers. I'm the gloss that tells the world he is a good father and a safe bet for the future," she added dryly. "When I get really broke I may sell his life story to the horrid papers, but for the moment, I shall smile and then shake hands and let fat ministers without portfolio or charm, breathe all over me."

"So that's why you wore that suit! I thought it was to impress Paul!" Emma spoke lightly to hide her sudden apprehension.

"So, Emma will have to put up with Danish pastries or fruit cake in the Old Vienna cafe in Lyons' with me, while you have cream cakes and sandwiches in very elevated company," Paul said, smiling.

"See you rather late," Bea said. "I shall call in to Miranda's to check on her, after her evening performance, and be home about midnight."

"I'm dying for a decent cup of tea," Paul said.

Emma watched Bea's retreating back and wondered if

she need have been quite so obvious with the promise to be out of the way for hours, so that Paul could be alone with her.

"Aunt Emily sends her love," Paul said as they walked down to the park. "This is better. The sun's out and a brisk walk over to Green Park and back is what we need after hours sitting in that stuffy cinema."

"When did you see my aunt?"

"I popped down to talk to Dr Sutton and went to see her. She has received your letters and said that she'd write soon, but she's a bit on the busy side just now." He glanced at her. "But not too busy to make you stay away," he said.

"She's always busy and really should let up more. What is it this time? More work at the British Restaurant, training others to staff even more of them?"

"No, she has her sister staying with her."

"My mother?" Emma stopped walking and looked fraught.

"Not unless your mother is called Janey." Paul eyed her with almost professional interest.

"I'd almost forgotten her existence," Emma said with relief. "Aunt Emily is very fond of her and often said she hoped she'd come further south to live as they haven't seen each other for ages."

"Her son, George . . . remember George? is in the Navy and when his stepfather retired from the sea and set up a small marine accessory firm in Edinburgh, the family stayed in Scotland, as George was stationed there."

"So why did Aunt Janey go to the Island?"

"George is in Plymouth awaiting a re-fit to his ship and her daughter, Vikki, has got married to a man in Aberdeen, so your aunt thought it was time to get away from another hard winter up north and they've bought a property in Hampshire."

Emma's laughter had a hint of hysteria. "How is it that you know more about my family than I do?"

"I'm nosy," he said. "I get my information from Dr Sutton mostly. Your Aunt Janey married the son of a doctor colleague of his and he hears their news."

"Of course! I remember now. Janey was the one who lost her husband in the First World War and married his best friend, Alex Barnes. I saw very little of them as George was a few years older than me and Vikki was older still, so we didn't play together."

"Dr Sutton said that Vikki was adopted."

"It was still a family affair," Emma said. "Her father was my uncle. His wife went to America on the stage and my grandmother cared for Vikki until Janey adopted her. It was just as well as they wanted more children, but Alex and Janey didn't have any."

"So you do know a few things that I haven't found out." Paul smiled. "Better brush up your family history if you go down to see them."

"I feel like a hypocrite. I haven't thought of them for ages, but now that you have mentioned them, I'd like to see Aunt Janey again."

"That's natural. You haven't forgotten her, but you've had a lot to fill your life so far." He paused. "Too much," he added quietly. "You must feel overwhelmed by events, and in a kind of limbo now." He brushed some dead leaves from a seat and they sat down, watching the water and the swans.

"Perhaps after the war, we shall all slow down a little and have time to think," she said.

"There's a difference between thinking of past events with pleasure or pain and then putting them where they belong, into a memory slot, and going to the other extreme, dwelling on them in an obsessive way and refusing to look forward."

She looked at his profile. His face was calm and yet a pulse throbbed in his temple as if he was under stress.

"Guy has been dead for only months, weeks really," she said, quietly. "At times I feel that I heard the news only yesterday. You are right. I am in limbo. I have filled the time with work. When I forget him for a while I feel guilty. When I enjoy laughing with friends, I feel I'm betraying him. If I put on lipstick, I feel that he might be watching and believe I have forgotten him and I am trying to attract other men. I am confused. A part of me wants to be free. I even resent some memories. I have yet to look far ahead." The words came in small disjointed phrases as if being forced from her by an inner pain.

Hot sun made her close her eyes, or had she the need to shut out the painful beauty of the park, the grace of the swans and the warmth of the man at her side?

"Talk about Guy," Paul suggested.

"No, I'm still raw."

"Then talk about you."

She looked up, surprised. "What is there to say? I love my work and I can do whatever I like now that I am fully trained in most areas of nursing. Apart from the fact that I can't have Guy back again, there is a lot I can do."

"Take time off. Aunt Emily says that you are financially secure up to a point, so you can buy time."

"You *have* been nosy," she said with a faint smile that lacked resentment.

"She talked to me," he admitted.

Emma stood up and brushed her skirt free of wrinkles. "I must remember that you are into neurology and fast becoming a psychiatrist who will need conscripts to be grilled. I shall have to be careful. If you can get Aunt Emily to tell you all her dark secrets, you must be good."

"I'm interested in people," Paul said simply. "But it makes me hungry."

"Guy used to say that work that was completely absorbing drained him of a lot of energy."

"Better," Paul said approvingly, and took her by the hand as they strolled between the high, gilded wrought iron gates that had escaped the drive for the collection of metal in war time, to make Spitfires. They walked up Pall Mall and into Haymarket past the theatre and the exclusive Prunier's Restaurant. "Very expensive and I like my fish and chips out of newspaper," he said.

"I prefer mine on a plate in nice surroundings," Emma said.

"Well don't look at me. I don't take girls to such exclusive eating places," Paul said easily. "You have been spoiled. Fresh fish, straight from the sea and cooked by Aunt Emily with a kind of magic, would make you turn up your nose at that place and it would be money wasted," he said.

"Do I detect a mean streak?" she asked and laughed. "Prunier's is world famous. I had a patient who said that when he was out in Normandy, he longed for a special dish they prepare and the dream kept him going."

"I never got to Normandy," Paul said with regret. "I am on the reserve. They took me for training then left me to get on with what I do best, even after I requested to be sent on active service." He shrugged. "One pompous devil on the selection board told me, 'Gold is where you can make it, my boy. Hard though it may seem and we all feel it, some of us have to stay behind and man the shop." So anyone want to buy a nice uniform, hardly worn?'

"They may call you up now and send you to fill in forms in the wilds of Scotland," Emma said heartlessly.

"What is it? You seem pensive. Don't you think I could fill in forms? I can do joined up writing," he said.

"I have an idea. What if I go into the forces now? There are lots of naval and military hospitals that will need staff for years, and I rather fancy the nice tricorne hats they wear in the navy."

"Try to think of your most unfavourite ward sister, now promoted to admin and very powerful, and imagine being trapped with her for months and not being able to leave the service."

"Horrid thought. I think I'll stick to private nursing."

"Here you are. Situations vacant," Paul said when they were sitting in the ornate crimson and plush imitation of a pre-war cafe in Vienna, complete with racks of newspapers slung like pennants from a thick rail. He laughed. "I thought you wanted a job? Why look at the births, marriages and deaths? Expecting news of a friend or enemy? Or just morbid?"

"Well, she didn't waste much time!" Emma stared at the announcements then gave a short laugh that could have meant pain or pleasure.

"Anyone I know?" Paul ordered tea and cakes, then craned his neck to see the announcement.

"It's Arthur's engagement," Emma said with a suspiciously shaky voice. "I bet Lady Jumeaux put this in the paper before he could back out!"

Paul regarded her solemnly. "Would he want to back out? The newspaper requires the signatures of both parties concerned to prevent hoaxes or pushy parents who want the match or a shotgun wedding! Obviously you did a good job on him and he has a future." She was silent. "Just the tiniest bit jealous?" he suggested. "Even though you refused him, maybe you thought of him as your property."

"That's rotten!" Emma blushed. "I didn't mean that. I feel a bit sad, that's all. It's just that he's forgotten me so soon after he swore undying love for me."

Paul's eyes were bright and challenging. "Wise man! He took you at your word and cut his losses. Men who

112

have faced death know that life is precious and look forward. I still say you did a good job and he owes his happiness to you. Have you any regrets about him, Emma?"

She gave a reluctant smile. "No regrets. All those horses and dogs . . . sorry, hounds and what goes with the life there." She sighed. "I shall always have a very soft spot for him and if we meet again much, much later, I know we shall be pleased to see each other."

"Correction. He would not welcome it, as you will always mean a lot to him and you could upset his marriage."

"He does have a lot to look forward to in life," she admitted. "To be honest, I don't think he's had to choose second-best. I was only a fleeting passion in a nurse-patient situation."

"I doubt if you are a fleeting passion for anyone," he said and looked at the huge mahogany-framed clock that ticked loudly on the wall behind them. "But time flies and I have to leave you," he said. "Life and patients can't be ignored. 'The bird of time has but a little way to flutter, and the bird is on the wing.' Almost Omar in case you didn't know." He laughed.

"I did know," she said. "It makes me sad and vaguely panicky."

"Read it and see how short life can be and make the most of it and of people who are your friends."

She looked away. "Are you on call?"

"At six," he said. "I offered to sit in while the Professor examines two soldiers who are in bed, supposedly paralysed from the waist down."

"You think they are shamming?"

"Not consciously. Both of them went through hell and I think their minds are refusing to face any further action."

113

"I've heard of functional disorders like that, but we didn't deal with them as we were mainly surgical," Emma said.

"It's amazing what the human brain will do to avoid confrontation," Paul said. He grinned. "Ever been under hypnosis? I'm getting good at it."

"*No*! And I have no intention of having that sort of treatment. I am as sane as the next person."

"You don't have to be insane to be unsure, or disturbed," he pointed out. "Those men are really the sane ones. Who in their right mind would want to go back to noise, danger, pain and privation?"

Emma collected her jacket from the bentwood stand. "I'll get back to the apartment," she said almost formally. "I must ring Aunt Emily and start to pack. I think I'll go down to see her before I ask the agency for another case."

Paul left her by Admiralty Arch. He kissed her cheek and grinned. "That's not for you. Give it to my favourite lady on the Island."

"She doesn't like being kissed," Emma said.

"Then keep it for yourself," he said and walked away.

Chapter 9

The face looked familar and yet Emma knew that she had never seen the man before in her life, or if she had, it was so long ago that she had forgotten, and that made him a stranger. He was tall and moved with the ease of someone used to exercise and maybe hard work. He turned and looked at her, and he too seemed puzzled.

Emma turned away. Who do I know in the Navy? He might be an ex-patient. Emma recalled seeing men in hospital pyjamas and then afterwards, when they changed into their own uniforms or civilian clothes, and they appeared to be different people. The sea air was wonderful after the heat of London. She breathed deeply, looking ahead at the distant shore of the Isle of Wight. The open prow of the ferry was a mass of coiled ropes and pieces of greasy equipment and most of the passengers sat inside the covered lounge area, but she stood outside, preferring the fresh air and the anticipation that always filled her when she saw the land appear, closer and closer.

Aunt Emily had been so pleased when she heard that she was coming home, that it made Emma feel guilty that she had not telephoned more often over the past few weeks, but after Guy had died, she had withdrawn from the unspoken sympathy from her beloved aunt. At least Emily had company now. Aunt Janey must have been a very welcome guest.

The man in naval uniform, with one-and-a-half gold rings on his sleeve, was watching her and Emma smiled. Of course, he was like the man in the picture that Emily kept on the piano. Aunt Janey and her husband Clive on their wedding day. The man in the sepia photograph was grinning and his uniform cap was at the same rakish angle as the one she now saw. The grin was the same and he seemed to guess what she was thinking. "You must be George Barnes," she said.

"And you?" He hesitated, the rather wide mouth soft and smiling and his eyes filled with interest. "You remind me of someone and I think I've seen your picture."

"Emma Dewar," she said and laughed. "I think we may be long-lost cousins."

"Kissing cousins?" he asked hopefully.

Emma backed away. "No, not in my branch of the family, and I take after Aunt Emily. No kissing," she said firmly and nearly spoiled her dignity by stumbling over a coil of rope.

He grinned. "OK, but it was worth a try. You must be going to Aunt Emily too. I hope you are staying for a long time. I have leave and we have a lot of catching up to do."

"From the time that we were children," she agreed, but thought that he might need keeping in place. It was going to be too easy to slip into a familiarity that wouldn't happen if they were really strangers meeting for the first time. "I can't remember much about you. You were a rather fat, little boy and a bit spoiled, my mother said."

"That really isn't fair! You can't remember that. You were a baby when we left the Island and Mother married Alex who became my stepfather." He gave her a sideways look. "Cutting me down to size when I get out of line, like the good hospital sister that I hear you are?"

"Habit," she said briskly. "We're nearly there. Are you being met or do we share a taxi?"

"Mother will be there. She learned to drive years ago and she bought a car from a local garage here, mostly for me to use, I suspect."

"She sounds much more enterprising than my mother," Emma sighed

"She's wonderful," George said. "I've been lucky. Alex has been the only father I've ever known and he is super."

"Your real father died at sea, I seem to recall," she said slowly. "Did your mother mind you going into the Navy, too?"

"Of course she worried about me, but I would have had to join one branch of the Services and I wanted to be a sailor, so why not the sea? I could be shot down from a plane, mortally wounded in Normandy, so why not risk a few torpedoes?" He sounded relaxed but his eyes held a darkness that Emma had seen so often, when a man recalled friends dying.

The ferry lurched as it hit the jetty and they gathered up their luggage. "I hope she brought the car up the pier," he said. "We could take the train, but we'd have to get out at the Esplanade as this train doesn't serve Shide station."

Emma laughed. "I'd never have guessed that," she said.

"Sorry. You know this place better than I shall ever do," George said.

"You don't intend staying for very long?"

He frowned. "Who knows where we'll be in five years time? I go to sea, come back and have a break, with any luck find a nice girl and see a few shows, and then it starts again."

"You'll leave the Navy one day and may want to settle down." Emma smiled, a teasing glint in her eyes. He was very attractive but the thought of him settling down was amusing.

"She's over there by the Lincoln. Do they expect you on this ferry?" She shook her head. "When we go over, don't say anything. She'll think I've brought a girlfriend and she didn't approve of the Wren I brought up to Scotland. Couldn't you put on a lot more make-up and a tighter skirt? Unfortunately, you look as if she might approve of you!"

"Idiot. I pity Aunt Janey if she has to put up with you."

"She loves it," he said with a complacent grin.

"George! Over here."

The plump, but still shapely woman eyed her son with affection. "Hello, Mum," he said and hugged her.

Emma came closer and Janey Barnes regarded her with interest. "You came with George?" she said and laughed.

"Just for a night or so," George said carelessly. "We met on the boat. What did you say your name was, honey?"

"Stop it at once! You don't catch me with that one. It's Emma, isn't it? I knew she couldn't be one of your uninteresting little girls."

"How did you know?" Emma asked, when she emerged from an enveloping hug.

"It's good to see the real person. I've seen enough snaps of you over the past few days," Janey said dryly.

"I'll drive," George said.

"You will sit in the back with Emma," his mother said firmly. "I'd like my tyres to last for a bit longer. I hope you scrounged a few petrol coupons. It isn't fair to use Paul's."

"Is Paul here?" Emma asked.

"No, I did meet him briefly, but he had to leave suddenly. He seems a very busy man," Janey said, with a flickering glance towards Emma.

"Boyfriend?" George asked.

"No." Emma replied so quickly that he raised his eyebrows and changed the subject.

"How is Aunt Emily? Is there room for all of us? Very nice but surely a burden on the bathroom?"

"She had a shower put in the downstairs cloakroom. You can make as much mess there as you like, so long as you mop it up and keep out of the bathroom upstairs," Janey said.

"Anyone would think I'm untidy."

Emma listened, fascinated by the affectionate banter, and envied them. Fate was unfair. If Janey had been her mother, instead of the cold woman who seemed to hate life and everyone in it, would her own life have been happier?

"I hear that you have bought a house in Hampshire, near Calshot," Emma said.

"It needs a lot of repairs, but we can move in after they've done the plumbing and made the roof safe. Alex is busy setting up his marine-tool and boat-building business, so he's staying in a local boarding-house, and I can stay with my sister for the first time in years and have a wonderful time." Janey Barnes sighed. "I didn't know how much I loved the Island until I came back after all those years," she said.

"You could have bought a place here," Emma said.

"No. Some things belong to my childhood and my youth," Janey said quietly. "I've had to move on since then and I'm happy with Alex. However, we shall rent a small cottage here for summer holidays and for George to use if he wants to go sailing."

"Is Father OK?"

"Much better down in the south. When he was invalided out of the Navy, he was really wheezy, Emma, but he hasn't had an attack of asthma for months now." She shrugged. "Good food and rest and no real worries have worked wonders and he's a very healthy man. His new interests have filled his mind and he likes his workers, as they are by the sea and of the sea and understand a sailor."

"Is Aunt Emily home today?" asked Emma.

"No, and it's too early to fetch her from work, so we'll have some tea and then Emma can take her car and bring her home."

"Do you have a car here?" George asked. "I thought you worked in London."

"It isn't mine. A friend lent it to me, more to take Aunt Emily for drives when I'm here with her than for my own use," she explained and knew that it sounded unlikely.

"Paul with the petrol coupons?" His smile was mocking. "You are looking po-faced. Was that why he left in a hurry, because you looked at him like that?"

"Will you please mind your own business?" Emma said through gritted teeth. "You and I met only a few minutes ago and you know nothing about him or me or anything to do with me." She spoke softly so that Janey wouldn't hear.

Janey Barnes swung the car expertly into the narrow driveway and switched off the engine. "Take the bags in before I put the car away, George," she suggested. "I'll make sure the kettle's boiling."

Emma took her bags up to her small room. Emily had insisted that the room would be hers whoever came to stay at the house and she could use it at any time to store her things while she was away, so she unpacked and put her clothes on the bed until she would have time to sort them. Her aunt called her for tea. A small album of snaps lay on the dressing-table. She had intended showing them to Aunt Janey, but now she hesitated and put the album away in a drawer. Guy's picture was in the earlier ones and he was her own private memory. George was not going to see the pictures until she knew him better.

George was examining the framed photographs on the crochet-edged cloth covering the baby grand piano in the sitting-room. He looked up, smiling. "You look better in this one than that," he said. Emma saw that he held a picture of her in a short frock and crumpled socks, standing by the leaning tower of a sandcastle. Her hair, always unruly before she tamed it under a nurse's cap, stuck out, badly cut and overshadowing her eyes. The other picture was a studio one of her in uniform, with immaculate cap and glistening hair.

"Aunt Emily hoards snaps," she said. "There's one of you here, taken when you were a baby, naked on a bearskin rug and dribbling."

"Where?" He grinned. "Nearly fooled me. It can't be me. Anyone who really knows me would see that this baby has no sign of a birthmark on his bottom." He gave an exaggeratedly lecherous smile. "I can prove I have one, any time you like, cousin."

"The photographer painted over it, or did something to remove it," Janey said, laughing. "It is you, but he didn't want a proud mother to think her baby had any blemish."

"You are blushing," Emma said triumphantly, and felt happy.

"This one's not me!" George insisted, picking up a small snap of a boy with very tidy hair and an expressionless face.

"That's Lizzie's boy," Janey said and made a wry face. "I suppose I ought to see her now I'm on the

121

Island. I shall hate every minute, but she is my sister."

"Has she ever bothered with you? Even long ago when my father died?" George asked gently. "Aunt Emily described all her family to me when I came here when the ship first went into dock for repairs. Of all your family, Aunt Lizzie and her twin, Clare, sound very selfish people who care only about themselves." He looked embarrassed. "Sorry, Emma. I forgot that Clare is your mother."

"Most of the time I forget it too," Emma said. "We don't get on and I haven't seen her for ages." She gave a tight smile. "Aunt Emily keeps me informed about the family and I expect she's told you all about me."

"No," he said. "Strangely enough she hasn't said much about you. What dark secrets are you about to tell me?"

"Nothing," Janey said firmly. "Drink up your tea, Emma, and get over to the restaurant for Emily. I'll put the kettle on again, as she'll want her strong tea. I wonder it doesn't give her heartburn."

"It does," Emma said. "She takes soda mints several times a day in between cups."

"George, I think we need more wood in here. I know it's warm, but Emily likes to have a fire even if she has to have the windows open!"

George bent over her and kissed her cheek. "See this gold," he said, displaying his sleeve. "That means I *give* orders not take them, or at least not from my equals."

"Take it off, it's much too warm for today," Janey said sweetly. "I'm quite dazzled. Then get the wood."

They watched Emma leave in the car and Janey caught George by the shirtsleeve. "Don't ask questions that she isn't ready to answer," she said simply. "Emma has suffered a great deal. She lost her fiancé only a few

122

weeks ago, so keep that animal magnetism tamped down. She's your first cousin and she's not for you."

"Where?" he asked and his eyes were haunted.

"Not at sea, thank God, but probably as bad. He was with the first medical team into Belsen and died of typhus."

Janey went back into the house and cut bread-and-butter as if she would like to destroy the loaf. George waited on the garden wall until Emma returned with Aunt Emily and then he seemed to come back to life and made a great display of carrying in a basket of logs.

"I could do with you more often," Emily said without even saying hello. "You all spoil me. Are you cooking supper, Janey?" she asked hopefully.

"As you refuse to be taken out for a meal, yes, I'm cooking," Janey said. "It will be ready in half an hour, so have a cup of tea and listen to the news. George has turned on the set and is trying to get rid of that awful hum. I thought you needed a new high-tension battery, so I bought one and he's putting it in now.

"I have the accumulator charged up regularly," Emily protested.

George wiped his hands on a piece of rag. "Mucky contacts and verdigris on the terminals, a slack battery and a loose knob," he announced. "All done and you'll be able to hear *ITMA* a treat."

"Fancy that," Emily said, as if he had waved a magic wand over the mahogany case of the huge wireless set and produced a miracle.

He sat by the set and listened. Janey watched him without seeming to do so, but Emma sensed her concern.

Bracing facts about the mopping-up operations in Europe and Burma and the planning of the reprisals and curbs to be imposed on defeated Germany made comforting news, but as soon as the war in the Pacific

123

was mentioned, George tensed and leaned forward as if to glean more than the bland announcer told him.

Self-styled experts told them about the detonation of the first atomic bomb in Alamogordo in the desert of New Mexico, and George grunted in disgust. "That isn't fresh news. It happened a short time ago," he said. "I suppose they are telling us that now to frighten the Japs as they wouldn't admit we had the Bomb."

"What do you know about it?" asked Emma. "I know it happened, but I had my information from an American."

"Mata Hari now, are you?" he replied. "That was classified information."

"My best friend is married to an American flyer who has been ferrying aircraft out for the war in the Pacific," she said. "I am her safety-valve, I suppose. She is allowed to tell me things that must go no further until it is made public, as Dwight knows me well and his godfather, who is an American General, approves of me," she said simply. "Nursing, we receive a lot of personal confidences and it becomes a habit to be discreet."

"So you know that the American cruiser *Indianapolis* was torpedoed?"

"Dwight said it should not have gone unescorted, when it was made to join the fleet at Leyte for the new assault on Japan, but they had tried to play down its role. It had just carried very sensitive material to do with explosives to Tinian, he said, and a convoy would have told the Japanese that it was important enough to be pursued. Why are you interested? Have you friends in the British Pacific Fleet?" Emma asked.

"I've been there and I'm waiting to hear if I'll be sent back," George said. "It's no secret that the Americans have lost a lot of tonnage in warships, but now that they have the superfortresses, the B-29s that can strafe Japan from the Marianas and give cover to the fleet, we are on the way back."

His eyes had the haunted look again. "Slowly, we are hearing of Japanese atrocities and the soulless kamikaze mentality that makes them give their lives for the Emperor who is their God. I have friends, who we think are in Jap. prison camps, and now that we hear news of the terrible, inhuman things that happened in Burma, I wonder what in hell has happened to them."

Emma shuddered. "Don't," she said softly and Janey gave her son a stern look that silenced him.

Christ, I'm a fool, he thought. I'm piling on her agony.

"I'm hungry," Emily said, as if that had precedence over the war and all its horrors.

"Come and help me carry in the dishes," Janey said to George, as if she wanted him under her control in case he said something even more tactless to Emma.

"Some day, everyone will know about the torture and hellish conditions in those camps," he said defensively. "But I'm sorry. I forgot that Emma might have seen something of the results of the German camps. Losing her fiancé . . . Oh, hell!"

"Exactly," was Janey's comment. "Now stop looking like a dying duck in a thunderstorm, as my mother used to say, and take in this dish. It's hot and heavy, so don't drop it."

"We could do with you on board," George said cheekily. "I'd love to see you call my captain a dying duck in a thunderstorm when things get a bit grim."

"Are you going away?"

"Ouch! You're right. This is hot." George swept up the dish and hurried into the dining-room. Janey picked up a vegetable dish and followed, her eyes misty. How like his father he was; sweet and impulsive and volatile.

Passionate, too, she thought. He would be as passionate in love as his father had been and he was already looking at his pretty cousin with more than a family interest.

"Pork with apples and a herby crust?" Emily sniffed her approval. "It's amazing what gets left on my doctor's doorstep. I suspect that this pig was killed, quite by accident, of course, outside the farmer's quota, but I have got past worrying about the Ministry of Food, after what they impose on our restaurant."

"I made some pork pies, too," Janey said. "I thought I could take one over to your doctor as he has lost his wife. I suspect a man alone doesn't get much variety of food."

"He does very well," Emma said and regarded Aunt Emily's innocent expression with amusement. "I'm sure he will enjoy your pies, Aunt Janey, but he does have a lot of friends, and one in particular," she added.

"More gravy?" Emily said hastily.

"More everything," George said. "What's for afters?"

"Fresh raspberries and cream," Emily said.

"Real cream or that stuff they make from margarine and milk?"

"Real cream. I do have Carnation in a tin, but I never touch it. I like the real thick cream from Wootton."

"I never thought of you as a black market spiv," George said, his eyes mischievous.

"Just for that you can clear away *and* do the washing up," Emily said, and later he found that she was serious.

"I'll help," Emma said. "Let them talk about the old days and then I'll make some coffee."

"What are your plans, Emma?" he asked.

"I don't know what to do," she admitted. "I had one private nursing case which was good in parts. I rushed into it and maybe it was a mistake to work again so soon

. . . after my training," she added hurriedly. "I haven't signed on for another." She shrugged. "I need a breathing space and I have a few alternatives that need studying." She sighed. "Suddenly I have all the time in the world and it's strange and empty." She wiped the same plate for the third time and George took it from her and gave her another. "Why am I boring you with all this? I hardly know you."

"You do know me. You know more about me because of our family than many of my friends who have been mates for years will ever know. We can relax with each other, Emma. I have an older, adopted sister and we get on well. I always wanted a real sister or a younger brother, but none came. Are you an only child?" He grinned. "That shows how out of touch we have been, but now, meeting you here, it's as if you came back from another room having been gone for half an hour."

She stacked the clean plates and folded her tea towel. "Thank you, George," she said and he knew that she wasn't thanking him for doing the washing up.

"What are *your* plans?" she asked.

"I hoped you could tell me that! You seem well briefed about the war."

"I haven't heard from my contacts for ages," she said airily.

"Something wrong?"

"I just remembered that I really haven't heard from Bea, the wife of the Amercan pilot I mentioned. She said she might come down here but I don't think there'd be room now." She told him about Bea helping her father with his constituency chores and a little more about Dwight being unable to fly on active service beyond ferrying planes to the war zone in the Pacific.

"Lucky chap," George said. "He's done his stint in Europe and now deserves a break from active service, but it's hairy out there and he could get involved. They've lost a lot of planes and they say that everyone is waiting on tiptoes for something really big. Don't say anything to Mother, but I think I might have to leave soon to join the British Pacific Fleet. My ship is in dock but they need good officers and they'll fly me out to the Marianas."

"Maybe the war with Japan will end soon," Emma said hopefully. It will be good for Bea when it's all over, but it means that she will go to the States with Dwight and I shall miss her."

"I think we have a way to go yet," he said slowly. "Write to me, if you have the time," he said, then hesitated. "When I come back, we must meet."

"So you really are going away?" He nodded. "Does your mother know?"

"Tomorrow, I shall take her out to the West Wight, which she loves to visit although she has said that she prefers this side of the Island for everyday living. I have a week here, then London and a plane to the States to join the British Fleet."

"You must spend as much time with her as possible," Emma said.

"Make the coffee and I'll see that there's enough wood for tomorrow. Fires in July? She's mad."

Emma heard laughter as soon as George joined the others. She made fresh coffee and opened the tin of biscuits that Bea had insisted were Emily's staple diet. She carried the tray into the sitting-room where the French windows were wide open to the evening air. Already moths flew in and the distant sound of cattle and the smell of wood smoke made her feel peaceful.

George was laughing and Emma watched him, growing familiar with his face, his voice and the warmth in his eyes. It would be so easy to be, what did he call it, "kissing cousins"? But a part of her was glad he would be away soon. Warning bells said firmly that she wasn't ready to have another man to worry about, just yet.

"We're going to Yarmouth tomorrow," Janey said. "We'll take a picnic in the Lincoln as it has more room than your car, Emma."

"It looks as if it will be a fine day," Emma said. "Enjoy it. I envy you, but I have to stay here in case Bea phones, and if I don't hear from her I must try to contact her."

George gave a solemn wink of approval, but protested mildly that she ought to join them as he wanted to see how she'd manage the walk over Tennyson Down.

"Not very well as they have it all covered with barbed wire to keep people away from the radar station above the Needles," she replied. "I suppose that some day they'll give the land back to the Islanders, but they haven't cleared away all traces of the First World War yet!"

"I'd like to meet Bea," Janey said. "Emily talks about her a lot."

"That's because she brings me these nice biscuits," Emily said. "But I must say she is a very nice girl."

"Praise indeed," Janey said.

"If she comes down, I think it will be a bit cramped here, especially as she promised to bring her husband sometime."

"Dwight is in the States," Emma pointed out.

"He'll be back," Emily said cryptically. "I spoke to old Bert Cooper and asked if he has a nice cottage to rent out. He makes a habit of buying up cheap houses, especially ones with a bit of bomb damage, doing them up and using them as holiday lettings. He leaves it all to his son now, but still keeps a finger in the pie."

"Bert? I thought he must be dead!" Janey was amazed.

"Very old, but as tough as old leather," Emily said. "Never goes far, but has all his marbles and still strikes a hard bargain. He has a soft spot for us and I can get what I want. You and Bea could stay there as far as sleeping goes, and I might know someone who will want to buy a place here. We'll see what Bert offers." She smiled. "When Dwight comes here, they'll need a bit of privacy and they can stay there while you come back here to sleep."

George chuckled. "You think of everything. What colour cushions will you put in there?"

"You seem confident that Dwight will be back soon?" Emma said quietly.

Her aunt's dark brown eyes were pensive and fey. "Soon after the big bang," she said and she looked into the now intent faces round her. "They'll all come back and we shall not lose any more of our men. At least not to war."

Janey kissed her sister's cheek and, for once, Emily didn't object to the contact. "Thank you dear", Janey said. "That's a weight off my mind."

George held the door open while Emma carried the coffee tray into the kitchen. "Mother really believed her," he said.

"She isn't often like that, but when she is, I've never known her to be wrong. But what big bang, George?" She shrugged. "One of her curious figures of speech, I suppose."

"I wonder," he said and was suddenly withdrawn and silent.

Chapter 10

"Emma!" There was desperation in the ecstatic greeting and Bea's hug was a cry for help.

"Put me down and tell me what's wrong." Emma demanded. "Better still, get in the car and tell me while I drive."

"It's just relief at seeing you. Dwight's godfather was in touch and said a radio messsage had come from Dwight. He can't come back here yet and from the General's tone of voice, there's something very nasty happening out there."

"Dwight isn't on active service," Emma reminded her.

"That's true, but the General said something about being an observer when a new explosive is ignited. Personally, I think it's like the atom bomb that Oppenheimer invented. They tried it out once on an atoll in the Pacific and again recently in the desert and I think they may do so again, but why now? They will not be able to use it, as nearly all our enemies have surrendered except the Japanese, and each news bulletin tells of more of our victories especially in the Pacific Islands."

Emma avoided a cock pheasant in the road and wondered how safe such birds would be once the shooting seasons started again after the war. Would mankind ever be satisfied with shooting birds and not men?

"George is going to the Marianas, too," she said.

"Who is George? I really think, Dewar, that if I am away from you for more than a day, you could refrain from picking up stray men."

"That's better," Emma said. "Aunt Emily will be glad that you haven't changed."

"Well, who is he?"

"Very good-looking and great fun, and staying with Aunt Emily."

"Where does he sleep? I knew I shouldn't have come. Your other aunt is there too, you said on the phone."

"Calm down. George is my long-lost cousin, Janey's son. He is in the Navy and has to report to London soon and fly out to the BPF."

"I don't have to share with him, do I, nurse? My husband wouldn't like it," Bea said in her best south of the Thames whine. "Roses!" she said and pointed as if she had never seen such flowers before now.

"Yes, roses and lavender and old-fashioned gardens," Emma said dryly. "What brought that on? Don't tell me you like gardening?"

"The war will be really over soon and Dwight will leave the Air Force and take me into the desert," she said sombrely. "I'll need roses and old-fashioned pinks smelling of cloves. Do you think they'll grow in Texas?"

Emma laughed. "I bet they have wonderful gardens. Dwight's people are rich and can afford the best, but I doubt if they have pinks. Carnations, yes, and roses and lots of flowers with exotic names like hibiscus and climbing plants that cascade over rooftops."

"How do you know?"

"I've seen them on the films. You remember the apple blossom in *Maytime*? And they say that the deep south has magnolias. When we went to parties that the General gave in Epsom, they had sheaves of American Beauty

132

roses, so they do care about flowers. I could hardly bear it. They were so elegant against the pale velvet drapes." She sighed. "Everything was new. None of the women had blouses made of parachute silk or coats made from blankets, and the soft leather shoes made my wooden-soled stacks look clumsy."

"That blouse you embroidered was the envy of all of them. It was unique and it did wonderful things for my figure," Bea said complacently.

"That's one reason I swopped it for the suit you said was too short for you. It clung to every curve and I hate men trying to imagine what's underneath."

"That's fun," Bea said cheerfully, "Even my jealous husband can't be mad when men look at me in that way, as he knows they never get past first base." She chuckled. "I think he enjoys seeing them burn and shift on their seats as their pants get tight."

"Nearly there," Emma remarked and turned off from the main road.

"Am I tidy?" Bea opened a silver powder-compact and eyed her reflection. "Must look good for George," she said. "By the way, American Beauty roses have no scent and no thorns. What good is that in a rose or a woman?"

"Which is why Dwight married you," Emma said. "You have both. What is it?" She sniffed, as Bea sprayed herself with perfume.

"*Je Reviens*," Bea said, and looked woeful. "And I shall come back," she said as if promising it to herself. "I can't go away for ever."

"You are still here," Emma said with deliberate lack of sympathy. "Enjoy the present." She looked ahead and her eyes pricked with unshed tears. "Remember? 'We look before and after; we sigh for what is not. Our sincerest laughter with some pain is fraught; Our sweetest songs

133

are those that tell of saddest thought . . . for love of love or for heart's loneliness.' I believe that it's foolish to be haunted, Bea. Please don't be miserable or you'll set me going."

"Sorry, ducky. You appear to be so damned normal that I forget." She stared out at the field on the left. "I may not be an accepted native, but this isn't the way to Aunt Emily."

"She suggested that we might like to share a cottage," Emma said. "An old friend has some that he is keeping for the boom in the holiday trade after the war and this one is free." She giggled. "In your new sentimental mood, I think you'll like it."

"Roses round the door?" Bea gazed in wonder as they stood by the car in the driveway. "And honeysuckle!" She leaned on the car, helpless with laughter. "Wasted on two lone women. It's a honeymoon cottage or something from a fairy tale. Is it made of gingerbread?"

"I'll have to tell Uncle Bert what you said. He'll put that in the advertisements."

"Don't mention it to him yet. I want to stay here."

"Aunt Emily has rented it for three months," Emma said.

"That means you have decided to stay on the Island and be a casualty sister?"

"No." Emma looked serious. "I haven't made up my mind," she admitted. "Aunt Emily has been a bit fey, or she had too much whisky in her tea, but she said it would be useful when Dwight comes back very soon, for just you and him, if that's what you want."

"And you?"

Emma shrugged. "I don't know. She did say that none of us would lose any more of our relatives and that the war would end with a big bang. Aunt Janey was relieved. She knows when her sister is really certain and she sings now, believing that George will not drown at sea, as his father did."

Bea shook her head. "I have no idea when Dwight will be back in England and I'm worried. He's so high-ranking now that he might be drawn into things that he can't refuse to do."

"Like what? Surely he's only ferrying, and that's his own decision as he hates being idle and hates desk work."

"If he goes somewhere as an observer, he'll be right in the battle zone again," Bea said.

"I know he'll be safe and home soon. Aunt Emily wouldn't have bothered with the cottage if that wasn't so. We could just about manage in her house now, but not if Dwight comes home and wants you to himself."

"You said that George is going to the Pacific?" Emma nodded and Bea regarded her with uneasy speculation. "I hope he isn't in submarines."

"That's the one promise that Aunt Janey insisted he made when he joined up in the Navy, as her husband was a sub-mariner."

"That's a relief. I hate the sight of those dull, grey slugs just waiting to be sunk," Bea said.

"There's something more?"

"The General mentioned it to give me a hint as to what is happening, but it was also on the news on the day after he told me. British miniature submarines have attacked Singapore with some success."

"They aren't like the Japanese kamikaze subs, are they?"

"No, with any luck they come back to the mother ship having loosed their torpedoes and left a few limpet mines."

"Well, you and I can't win the war alone, Bea, but if we get more casualties sent over, we can at least help patch them up. I think I'd go back to Beatties if that happened."

"It's too far away now. The most we have over here is what David told me." She saw that Emma was curious. "He stayed at the apartment for a couple of nights and sends his love to you. He's very bitter about the way that Guy's family ignored your existence when they were informed of his death." Bea sighed. "It takes very little to make David bitter now after all he's seen. He's changed, Emma. Remember the lighthearted boy he was at Heath Cross, flirting with everyone and having an affair with Lindy?"

"He was Guy's best friend," Emma said. "What did he tell you?" She busied herself in the kitchen with coffee mugs and bread and cheese.

"They brought some released prisoners of war back to UK from camps in Europe."

"Belsen?" asked Emma. Her mouth was dry.

"Not to Beatties. They had men from Buchenwald, where they had been used as slave labour and came back like walking skeletons with swollen ankles from malnutrition, and such great psychiatric problems that David said he wished them dead. They were still suffering mentally as well as physically. They shouted in their sleep in German, begging not to be beaten again and they couldn't digest anything but fluids." Bea clenched her hands. "Pray God that Dwight comes back soon," she whispered. "They say the Japs are even worse, with torture and sheer mindless brutality, as they despise anyone who surrenders."

"I wish you hadn't seen David," Emma said. "Not just now."

Bea seemed not to have heard her. "He said they stank of decay and fear. Fear has a smell of its own and they were nearly dead from that alone."

"Coffee! You need it and so do I. Your room is at the top of the staircase and it's a double room fit for a returning war hero," she added lightly. "We'll have supper with the others tonight, but first we can settle in here."

"I'm glad I came. I thought I never liked chintz, but these chairs are charming. Quite old, I'd say, and the rugs are good. Was all this included?"

"Bert Cooper has a son who goes to sales and picks up good bargains. There have been a few just lately, with more sellers than buyers, from houses that had bomb damage or where the owners have moved away."

Bea carried the tray out into the garden and set it on a rather rusty wrought iron table. She waved away a wasp and told it politely to go away. "What if he doesn't?" Emma teased.

"Rude wasps get swatted," Bea said and did just that with a rolled up newspaper, then sat low in her canvas chair and closed her eyes. "I could purr," she said.

"When you purr, it means you are plotting," Emma said.

"What happened to Paul?" Bea asked. "Pour me some more coffee, there's a duck."

"If you talk about Paul, you can get your own coffee," Emma said severely. "I haven't seen him for ages and no, he hasn't tried to get in touch with me, and yes, I have no plans that include him. Right?"

"You use his car," Bea said with an Egyptian cat smile.

"Only as a taxi," Emma said. "I couldn't refuse it as Aunt Emily does enjoy a drive sometimes, and after all he was a friend of Guy's."

"Was he? I thought he was your friend." Bea topped up the mugs and ate her second piece of sponge cake. "Aunt Emily's?"

"No, Aunt Janey made that. She's a super cook and while she's here, she says she'll take over the cooking when Aunt Emily works at the restaurant. I think she enjoys spoiling people and she's delighted to be here with George."

"I can't wait to meet her and George. Is he good-looking?"

"You saw the photographs on the piano?" Bea nodded. "There's one of Janey with Clive, her first husband, George's father, taken on their wedding day. George is like him."

"A real heart-breaker?"

"If he's your type," Emma said carelessly. "He's quite good fun."

"Careful! He sounds very attractive and you are in a bad state just now. Arthur was easy to keep at arm's length, but George might be different."

"Quite," said Emma dryly. "But you forget. He's my first cousin and, traditionally, cousins don't fancy each other. It may even be illegal!"

"This I must see." Bea took the tray back and washed up the mugs and jug. She hesitated then closed the cake tin firmly. "If Aunt Janey cooks like that, I must not spoil my tiny appetite. I'll wait for supper."

"We can walk over there. It's only half a mile by road and if we take the short cut by the derelict water mill, it's even nearer."

The bees in the honeysuckle and the butterflies on the clumps of wild buddleia enchanted Bea and she sat on the bank of the brook and dangled her hand in the water. A dragonfly dive-bombed a leaf on the stream and flashed turquoise and gold as it skimmed the water. "Can we get into the mill?" she asked, eyeing the ancient wheel with interest.

"No, it's boarded up to stop children playing inside.

They say that the floorboards are so riddled with dry rot that if you trod on one you'd disappear into space."

"I wish that Dwight was here and we could stay here for ever," Bea said.

"Not really," Emma said. "You were made for the wide open spaces of America and the high-powered social life, Bea. I hope Dwight comes here and loves the Island, but who knows where we'll be this time next year?"

Bea shook the moisture from her hand. "If I have my way, you'll be with us in the States."

"Come and meet Aunt Janey," Emma said and reached a hand down to pull Bea from the bank.

"Is Paul away permanently?" Bea asked. "I thought he was taking over half of a GP practice here."

"Later, I think, but he still has a part of his course to take in Southampton and he attends seminars at St Thomas's, so he comes and goes."

"When did you see him last?"

"When we both went out with him and Miranda."

"I had lunch with him a few days later and he hinted that he might make neurology and psychiatry his subject, which would mean giving up the Isle of Wight job."

"He can't do that!" Emma's eyes were hot and dry.

"Why not? He'd be a consultant and have a very good life," Bea said. "He'd make a fortune in the States, with all those guilt complexes and sexual hang-ups among those who did nothing for the war effort." She regarded her friend with interest. "Why can't he do something that really suits him?"

"He'd make a wonderful family doctor."

"He's a very good doctor and a very nice man," Bea said seriously. "He's also in love with you and might be just what you need."

"Please don't. Paul understands that I loved Guy, and, for me, he was the love of my life. In any case," she added with a touch of pique, "Paul doesn't seem very anxious to impress me, as I have heard nothing from him since that day in London."

"Can you blame him? If you won't have him, then he might as well forget you and concentrate on unscrambling other people's minds," Bea said bluntly.

Emma stripped the leaves from a sprig of beech that had been torn from the hedge. "Do you think he would go to the States? I remember he said that he was interested in Red Indian folk medicine and wanted to study it some day." She peeled the bark and twisted the length of white wood into a tortured shape.

"I know he wants to do that and Dwight and I will help him in any way we can, if he comes out to us."

"He can't do everything," Emma said acidly. "People who do that end up doing nothing worth while."

"Well, ducky, if you don't want him, I'm sure he'll find an enterprising woman who will follow him to the ends of the earth," Bea said lightly. "Here we are. The gate's been painted. Is it still wet?"

"Just avoid the gateposts. I think George went mad with a paint brush and he's painted the water-butt too. We'll go in the back way and you can see even more roses."

"Is that him?" Bea asked in a hoarse whisper.

George was splitting logs and making a neat pile of firewood from the trimmings. His faded, red sailing trousers were covered with dust and his equally faded, blue shirt clung to his body in the heat. Emma called and he turned, resting on the long handle of the axe. He wiped his hands on his shirt and grinned. "You must be Bea. Meet the hired help, ma'am."

"Is Aunt Janey at home?" Emma asked,

"In the conservatory, shelling peas. I said I'd rather do this."

"There's enough wood there to last Aunt Emily for weeks," Emma said.

"Good. I hope she finds another slave after that, as I shall not be here."

"When do you go?" Emma asked in a small voice.

"Tomorrow, quite early, so I'd like a lift to the ferry at Cowes, if that's all right with you. I don't want Mother to come with me. She may be upset and her driving might suffer on the way back."

"You're joining the British Pacific Fleet, I suppose."

Emma saw his surprised expression when Bea spoke, and she said, "Bea probably knows as much as you do, and maybe more. Her husband is out there and he has friends in high places who keep her informed."

George grinned. "I'm glad I haven't got to turn you in as a beautiful spy," he said, and he stared at Bea with the expression that Emma had seen on so many men suddenly confronted by Bea's lovely face. Irrationally, she felt left out.

"Come and meet Aunt Janey," she said, and Bea followed her into the house.

"George is really quite spectacular," Bea said. "Are you sure it's illegal to marry first cousins?"

"Quite sure," Emma said firmly. "Or I think so. In any case George has, as Aunt Emily would say, a cabbage heart, a leaf for every one!"

"You could have an affair with him," Bea said.

"When for instance? Between supper tonight and the ferry early tomorrow morning?"

"Don't tell me you find him repulsive?"

"Of course not. He's exciting," Emma admitted. "It's nice that I know him now. It's good to find such a pleasant relative and that we can even flirt safely without it being serious, as we know that we could never fall in love, being cousins."

"Has he kissed you?"

"Of course not!"

"He will," Bea said cheerfully.

The peas from the taut pods fell like bullets into the colander as Janey sat with tensed shoulders over the vegetables. As soon as she heard the others come into the conservatory she stretched and smiled, a smile practised over the years when she had suffered or had to console others who suffered, and which made her eyes dry-bright.

"Hello, Aunt Janey," Bea said. "Forgive me, but I adopt all Emma's relatives as she has such nice ones." She bent to kiss her cheek.

"Hello, Bea. Have you met my impossible son? I warned him that you were expected, but he refused to put on something respectable."

"He's making himself useful," Emma said. "And we haven't come to waste your time. What can we do to help?"

"Nothing, thank you. I've finished these and the pies are in the oven. Why not take Bea for a drive in my car and then pick up Emily?"

"I'd like that," Bea said before Emma could protest that there must be something useful to be done before supper. She tugged at Emma's sleeve. "Have we time and petrol enough to get as far as Carisbrooke?"

"You seem in a hurry," Emma said as they walked to Janey's car.

"She wants to have him to herself for a while. He may not come back for months," Bea said. "Look. She has come out as if to wave to us, but it's an excuse to stay and talk to him and make use of every minute she has left of him."

"You should be a psychiatrist."

"Nice car," Bea said with approval. "Where did she buy it?"

"She liked it at first, but now she hates to ride in it."

"Why? Did she have an accident?"

"It seemed a real bargain when the garage man showed it to her, but she heard later that the owner had been killed in action and his wife needed the money desperately. It was too late to adjust the price up higher and she hates to think of it belonging to a dead soldier's widow who still waits for her pension to come through."

"Selling it now wouldn't help," Bea said. "I hope George makes her see the sense of that. If Janey hadn't bought it, the lady might have had to wait for ages to find a buyer at any price." She looked at Emma's profile as she drove carefully past the lane to Mount Joy, and the remains of the small chalk pit on the way to Carisbrooke. "George has a good mouth," she said. "He is a man who would care about his mother and about the lucky woman he marries."

"He has lots of girl friends," Emma retorted. "Janey says that she's lost count of every girl who comes with him on leave."

"We all have to do our research before we settle for THE one," Bea replied calmly. "All except you, of course."

"I had boy friends before I met Guy," Emma said as if annoyed.

"You had Phillip the faithful, who acted as a buffer between you and other men. You felt safe with him as you never did love him, and you felt safe with Guy, too."

"That isn't fair! I loved Guy."

"It's time you took a look at yourself, Emma." Bea's voice was the one that had quelled recalcitrant soldiers in her orthopaedic ward when they were bored and, apart from their broken bones, healthy in every sense of the word. It brooked no argument. "You are doing it again. I know that you loved Guy and that you intended marrying him, but only when it suited you. No, don't interrupt! Now you are hiding behind his memory to protect you from other men and other loves. It's not fair to you to keep buttoned up and it isn't fair to the men who want you."

"Don't be daft! You agreed that I wouldn't be happy with Arthur and I know he would get bored with me when I couldn't ride to hounds."

"We aren't talking about patient-nurse crushes, but about flesh and blood men in the real world."

"Oh, and where is the queue of men, lining up, panting for my attention?" Emma said scathingly.

"Paul and now George, if I read my antennae right," Bea said calmly. She touched Emma gently on her bare arm. "Give them a chance and give yourself a chance too. There have always been men hankering after you even when you failed to see them, and there always will be." She laughed. "We may be different in many ways, but we are really two of a kind. Let's face it, without undue modesty; we are both very seductive women, ducky. It's nice." Bea gave a chuckle. "I'm safe now, but you may need a few men passing through before you settle for someone, and I repeat, stop hiding behind Guy's memory."

"I wonder why I bother with you! You come here and eat my aunt's food and insult me!" Emma gave a shaky laugh. "When I think about it later, I shall be angry with you and then admit that, as usual, you are partly right." She parked the car by the entrance to the castle and they walked round the top of the moat.

"Is that the window?" Bea asked when they came to the far side and looked up at the steep grassy bank that led up to the window from whence King Charles I attempted to escape. "Poor man, he must have had hope that day, but later, utter despair, just as our men must have felt when they were discovered trying to tunnel out of the stalags in Germany."

"Dwight will never be a prisoner," Emma said gently. "The war is nearly over and he'll be home again."

"I know that, but I have this feeling of dread. Strangely, it isn't fear for Dwight directly, but for a lot of people he knows and I shall not be happy until he is in my arms again, as I'll need to comfort him."

Chapter 11

"I asked Aunt Janey to show me how to make really light cakes," Bea said, with a false innocence that didn't fool Emma for a moment. Breakfast was over and Aunt Emily had been taken to work by George while Janey sponged and brushed his uniform.

"Not now, surely?" Emma asked in a low voice.

"It's the best I can offer," Bea said. "She hates parting and he might as well have the thrill of you seeing him off."

"I wanted you to come, too."

"Coward." Bea laughed. "You are funny! You have this gorgeous man drooling after you and you're backing away as if he is after you with a gun."

"He isn't drooling," Emma said.

"Wake up, girl. When a man has that expression in his eyes, he's smitten, and it isn't what he feels for his usual bits of fluff."

"Thanks," Emma said dryly. "I'm glad I'm not a bit of fluff. By the way, I thought you knew all about sponge cakes."

"Today, I don't. I shall do everything wrong and have to be shown and Aunt Janey will want to tear her hair at my stupidity."

"She'll know," Emma warned her. "She'll see that you can't help doing it the right way."

"By that time, George will be across on the ferry and

you will be back again and we can laugh about it. I think I'll pick some roses. What bliss to go out into a garden and help myself to those old-fashioned roses that really do smell of heaven."

"You are becoming a country girl," Emma said laughing. "I can't see it lasting once you get back to London and the bright lights of Mayfair, but at least you're getting into the fresh air and relaxing here." She noticed that Bea's tension had slackened since she arrived. A good sleep and the warm, unpolluted air made her even more vibrant than usual. They walked in the garden, picking far more flowers than they'd intended, but lulled by the early bees and the soft background of lazy pigeons. Bea went into the house to arrange the roses in a highly-polished, brass urn that Emily kept on the window sill and Emma waited for George.

"Emma?" George appeared in full uniform, his cheeks clean-shaven and his eyes bright. He heaved his duffle bag into the back of the car and dangled the keys. "Mind if I drive?"

"Of course not. I like being chauffeured," Emma said.

Janey and Bea watched from the doorway and George gave a careless wave. "I said my goodbyes and I hate this bit," he admitted as he drove away from the house. "I'll hate saying goodbye to you, too, Emma. I've just discovered that I have a beautiful and wonderful cousin and the gods tear me away before I can do anything about it."

"I'm glad we met," Emma said. "When you come back, I'll visit Aunt Janey and you."

"Promise?"

"Promise. I had no idea I had such lovely relatives and now that your base will be in Hampshire, it will make visiting easy."

"You make it sound as if you are visiting an aged uncle," he grumbled. "There's more to us, Emma."

"No, George. You do know about Guy?"

"I'll give you time."

"That isn't the point. I was engaged to him and we were about to be married. We were in love. You and I are cousins and I can't see any future for us in any other relationship, however we might think we feel about each other when we are together."

"You could love me," he insisted. "I know it."

"I feel a deep family affection for you."

"Ouch!"

"It's good and I hope we keep it," Emma said. "I haven't decided what to do about my future, but a love affair or marriage doesn't come into it."

"May I write to you?"

"I'll answer any letters you send," she replied. "If I don't hear from you, I'll know that you are fully occupied. I've been like that many times and felt guilty when I realised that I haven't been in touch with friends I value a lot. The person going away finds a lot to do and time flies, so if we don't exchange regular letters we'll meet when you come back."

He laughed. "Ever the practical and reasonable nursing sister. I bet your patients loved you."

"Where you are going? I thought we were going to Cowes for the ferry."

"Mother thinks that, but I have to report to Portsmouth first so it's the Ryde ferry today. Tomorrow I shall be gone to the American Airbase to fly out and join a frigate on patrol, or so I was told. But there are bigger things than convoys to be covered. If I send you a grass skirt, you'll know I'm in the Pacific, somewhere like Hawaii." Under the humour, she sensed a kind of wariness, as if he couldn't make out what lay ahead and it worried him.

He parked the car and they walked towards the ferry

terminal. "Give me the car keys," Emma said as he absent-mindedly put them in his pocket.

"Thought you might come with me," he said and grinned.

"The ferry is about to dock, so you'd better get over there." Emma smiled. "I too hate goodbyes, so I'll not wave you off."

"Even cousins kiss goodbye," he said and took her firmly by the shoulders. His mouth was cool and lingering as if it felt right on her lips and he smelled of cologne. The strength of a man's arms was what she had missed. He was young and healthy and so close that she could feel the lines of his body against hers and she closed her eyes for a moment, remembering other embraces. She clung to him and the pain of parting was real.

Passengers hurried to catch the ferry and Emma drew away from the man she knew she would miss more than she would admit.

"Goodbye," she said, simply, but her eyes were wet.

"Some day," he said and picked up his duffle bag. "Love you until hell freezes," he said with a rueful smile. "Remember me."

Emma stalled the engine twice and then sat until her hands stopped trembling. She saw the ferry swing from the pier and turn towards the mainland and she knew that George stood watching the shore. I'm far too vulnerable, she decided. I must come to a few practical decisions that don't include men.

Now the engine fired and she drove slowly along the Esplanade and on to the Newport road. She stopped to buy newspapers and used up her sweet ration to give to Aunt Emily as she had a passion for mint humbugs, and having dentures, had no need to worry about damage to her teeth.

She thought of Aunt Janey and wondered if Bea was

working her magic on her, and, when she arrived at the house, she smelled good coffee.

"Pa sent me a supply from Ireland," Bea explained. "He seems to get about a lot more now that he is on the Opposition back benches and hasn't a chance in the Cabinet. His job on the War Graves Commission brings him many valuable contacts."

"Why Ireland?"

"He heard that families over there had no news of their dead sons and husbands, so he took over information and photographs of Service graveyards and the assurance that, after they've sorted out red tape, they will be able to go over to Europe, just as the English, Welsh, Scottish and the Northern Irish can do. Southern Ireland was neutral, but there were masses of men who fought with the British and suffered as much," Bea explained.

"Your father sounds like a very nice man," Janey said.

"He's improving," Bea said. "A very good friend died and it gave him a jolt as he faced his own possible mortality, and he's rediscovered an early love."

"George left a shirt in the linen basket," Janey said. "It's an old one, but if I throw it away, it will be the first thing he asks for when he comes home, so I'd better keep it."

"Don't wash it if it smells of him. You'll treasure it," Bea said. "Dwight keeps some of my underwear with him and a lot of boys away from home carry some keepsake."

Janey turned up her nose. "How earthy! I can think of better souvenirs. He wore it when he was chopping wood and it was a very hot morning," she said, but she carefully folded the shirt and put it in her room.

"Well, did he?" Bea asked when Janey was out of the sitting-room.

"Did he what?"

150

"Kiss you, you idiot!"

"We are now kissing cousins," Emma said demurely. "We may write and we may not."

"And his mother has spent the past hour telling me that she wishes you could marry him. Be flattered, because she adores her one and only son and wouldn't want just anyone for a daughter in-law."

"I couldn't marry a cousin."

"I wonder if it is still illegal? The law makes it sound like incest. It makes sense in some cases, but you wouldn't have idiot children," Bea said bluntly. "Two healthy people whose families had not been inbreeding for centuries, would have normal children."

"Thanks, I'm not a brood mare," Emma said indignantly.

"I've something to show you," Bea said as Janey came back into the room. "Another advantage of having a roving father is the fact that he brings me good clothes and his taste is perfect." She sighed. "The trouble is that I'd need a whole new wardrobe to go with this, and everything we wear now will be old-fashioned in six months, once the fashion catches on."

"I've always loved clothes," Janey said. "The war has made us all make-do-and-mend as the pamphlets urge us to do, and the only fashions have such a military touch about them that I'm fed up with dresses that look like army issue, and skirts that have one back half-pleat and no lining. Anything from abroad that doesn't carry the Utility label, and clothes that women make from old pre-war patterns and good material, stand out and people notice the difference."

"That has its disadvantages," Bea said. "However well they are made, the styles are still pre-war fashion, so keep any good material you can get until the new patterns come into the shops."

"Where did your father buy your clothes?" Janey asked.

"Have you heard of a Frenchman, called Christian Dior? He's a man to watch. Not yet, but next year, they say he'll do something very adventurous and the magazine editors are all agog." Bea saw their puzzled expressions and laughed. "I am about to educate you, my dears. I'll have to go back to the cottage for it. I'll be only a minute if I take your car," she said.

She fetched a cardboard box while Janey cleared away the coffee cups and made a space on the dining-room table after putting on the dark green, chenille table-cover that Emily insisted was not of just sentimental value, as it had belonged to her mother, but also practical, as it kept the table-top from being scratched. Emma saw that Janey was intrigued and guessed that Bea had kept this more frivolous interlude to take her mind off George.

"I have a copy of *Vogue* magazine, and in it, a British designer, Hardy Amies, was interviewed about fashion trends now that the war is nearly over. He and James Laver, the fashion historian and writer, say that clothes will be softer and more feminine, with less shoulder-padding and neater waistlines. They argued a bit about it, as I'm sure that nobody really knows what will happen. Amies was for a much more feminine shape now, with more material to show that austerity is over, but Laver, who is an authority on past fashions, announced that after wars or revolutions women tended to cut their hair short, wear skimpy, short clothes and have no real waistlines.

"I can't imagine wearing that," Emma said.

"It happened after the First World War, in the Twenties. The women had achieved greater independence in the war, when they had to work in factories and join the forces, so they wanted to show off a little and flaunt their new status. They wore short skirts and cloche hats over bobbed hair, and Laver thinks it could happen again."

"I remember it," Janey said and laughed. "I was slim and pretty and enjoyed the short skirts, but my mother thought them very immodest until the doctor's wife wore them and gave a kind of respectability to the fashion. Just now, I think I prefer the idea of no waist. I can fit in with that more easily!"

"They can't do a lot," Emma retorted. "We are still short of material and money and manufacturers aren't allowed to do as they want to do. I think the designers will have to be cautious as there isn't a lot of money for new outfits in this country."

"The designers have a ready market abroad in countries untroubled by rationing," Bea said. "Designers have been sending ideas to the States and to other countries like South Africa where they have no clothes rationing and still have lots of people to work in the factories that are not making munitions. There are huge numbers of rich people who have avoided the war and live in Switzerland and the colonies, all hungry for pretty clothes."

"Just as we are, after all the dullness of war, but with less chance of getting them except when presents are brought in from other countries. You are one of the lucky ones," Janey said. "I've given George strong hints that any dress material he can buy abroad will be very welcome."

"Let's see it!" Emma and Janey bent over the pieces of tissue paper as they were taken from the box and Janey carefully folded each piece as if it was precious.

Bea held up a suit of light woollen fabric, the pale grey lining making a contrast to the deep charcoal grey of the jacket, which was faced with the same pale grey silk. "Put it on," Emma commanded, and Bea slipped her arms into the sleeves and buttoned up the front.

It was a normal suit but with a difference. The waist was cinched in and the shoulders were narrower than the padded, more military ones that they were used to wearing. Emma held up the narrow skirt with its slightly flared hem. "It's longer than we wear. Will you take it up?" she asked. "It could be tricky with that shaped hem."

"No, it's just right as it is. The skirt balances the jacket, and with the plain grey blouse that's under that tissue paper it does look right."

"It couldn't be made here, with our restrictions," Janey said. "The longer skirt, cut like that, would take too much fabric." She eyed the skirt with interest. "I do like longer clothes. I could lengthen mine, if I put a false hem or inserted a band of contrasting material a few inches from the bottom." She smiled. "Emily will be in fashion. She has never worn skirts that ended at the knee."

"The hats are pretty," Bea said. "Knitted hoods and beany hats will look very odd now and the new ones are more like the halo hat I wore when we went to be interviewed at the nursing agency. I expect the changes will be gradual, but at the Paris shows which have started again, they show dresses that make the fashion writers gasp, and yet they will filter down in milder forms before the year is up, or so Miranda says."

"How is it that the French, who were occupied, can do all this while we are still floundering among the ruins?" Emma wanted to know.

"I asked the same question when Pa gave me these," Bea said. "He muttered about big business and the fact that many of the leading fashion bods, Jews in the rag trade, fled to America and have a head start on us now. Some have returned to Europe."

"It will be nice when we can buy what we like," Emma said wistfully.

"Miranda is wearing a wonderful bit of nonsense in her latest play," Bea said. "I think my Pa had something to do with it. The audience have eyes on stalks when they see her in it, and someone said that people come not to see the play but to see Miranda wearing the dress. She has a wonderful figure and superb legs, in silk stockings with sparkly patterns on the sides. The dress is short and straight and shimmering with thousands of beads and sparkling stones on a wicked black silk chiffon background. It is nearly transparent in places and the men go mad trying to see what bits of her are visible."

"Like the tango dress that a relative of ours, Vikki's mother, wore on stage," Janey said dreamily. "Before you were born, Emma, but the idea was the same. That was after the other war."

"And did she have short hair?" asked Bea, smoothing back the sleek blonde swathe that she had caught up in a pale snood, almost the colour of her hair.

"Everyone was horrified when she had it bobbed, but it suited her and soon the rest of us did the same, until hairdressing and permanent waves became too expensive, good cutters went into the forces, and we grew hair longer again."

"Time I helped get supper," Bea said firmly. "I'll leave these here to show Aunt Emily and Emma can fetch her from work while we toil over a hot stove."

"Would you have short hair?" Janey said.

"I think Dwight would divorce me if I had my hair cut," Bea replied complacently. "He says he agrees with the guy who wrote 'Gentlemen Prefer Blondes', and he likes long, blonde hair."

"Doesn't he know that a woman wrote that?"

"Who cares, so long as he believes it?"

"Thank you, Bea," Janey said quietly.

"For what?"

Emma smiled. Janey had not looked unhappy for one minute since Bea took over, and George had gone, with no tears shed, as if he had left for a short break and would be back soon. Mentally, she added her own thanks, and remembered that parting kiss and the magnetism of his young and vital body with pleasure. She felt no hint of pain from her own bereavement. Guy was dead and was becoming a warm, if sad, memory that no longer hurt acutely each time she thought of him . . . a gentle "pulling down of blinds".

"Well, fancy!" Emily said later. Her dark eyes snapped with humour, "I said that longer skirts would come in again and I was right."

"You said that twenty years ago, Emily!" Janey said indulgently.

"All things come to those who wait," Emily said cryptically.

"So you'll also wear the short cocktail dresses?" Bea teased. "Can you shimmy? That was your generation wasn't it?"

"Some did it. Almost as disgusting as that rock and roll the Yanks brought over here. I mean to say! All that tossing a girl over a man's shoulder and showing everything she's got on, what there is of it!" She sniffed.

"Dwight taught me, but he can't do it now after his fractures and he gets all possessive if anyone asks me to dance like that."

"So I should think," Emily said sternly. "George went off all right?"

"Emma saw him onto the ferry," Janey said. "It's a pity that they didn't have time to get to know each other."

"Just as well," Emily murmured. "I need a cup of tea before I have anything to eat." She felt the pot and Bea told her it was freshly made, so she poured the dark brown tea into a large cup and added sugar and milk.

"I can smell the mackerel. It's as well you are here, as it's a twenty-four hour fish and must be eaten on the day it's caught. Young Michael Attrill left more than I could ever eat on my own on his way home from fishing this morning, and they should be good. At least fish ekes out the meat ration."

"I baked them with a couple of apples and made a gooseberry sauce and mashed potatoes," Janey said and laughed. "There's sponge pudding to follow. Bea made it, as well as a couple of sponge cakes that I've put in a tin."

Emily glanced at Bea and nodded approval as if she guessed that she had filled Janey's time and mind while George left. "Are you making that nice chocolate sauce you did the last time you were here?" she asked.

"Pints of it," Bea assured her. "I brought a lot of choc- olate with me and some dried milk, and then Dr Sutton called and left a can of cream, so we can be really piggy."

"I hope the cottage is comfortable," Emily said. "I didn't have time to do more than look round and leave the linen before you came, but it seemed dry and sound."

"It's wonderful, and when Dwight comes back, I know he'll fall for it in a big way. Will it be available for more than three months?"

"He'll be back soon," Emily said firmly. "Bert has had an offer for it, but he'll stay his hand until I tell him I don't want it." Emily glanced at Emma. "If you want to buy it, you'd have first choice. I thought at one time you might work on the Island, but you seem to have doubts now."

Emma moved restlessly. "I can't make up my mind. I feel as if something will happen to convince me what I must do, but I do need this break first."

"George hopes to see a lot of you," Janey ven- tured, when Emma helped her dish up the meal, while

157

Bea laid the table and Emily sat enjoying her second cup of tea.

"Meeting you and George has done a lot for me," Emma admitted. "I feel as if I do have a family."

"I'll be honest. I wish that you and George were not cousins, but it may be possible for cousins to marry now. I think they talked of changing the law and it would be my dearest wish to see you with him."

"There's no question of that," Emma said sadly. "It's too soon to think of loving another man."

"If not my son, then there must be someone for you, Emma. You may say it is too soon to look ahead and I may sound as if my first marriage was soon forgotten, but what I say is true. If you drift and convince yourself that there will never be another man in your life, then you could make that true, as Emily did. I know she refused more than one man after her boy died. I loved Clive with all the passion in the world. George wrings my heart when he laughs and he's the image of his father. Clive was wonderful and when he died at sea, I was heartbroken and wanted to die too. But Alex comforted me, calmly and without putting any pressure on me to go to him, and gradually the two men merged into one in my mind. I found I needed physical love again and I married Alex."

"I've not met him, but his photograph makes him look very like Clive," Emma said. "George told me that Alex was the only father he's known and he obviously thinks a lot of him."

"He is a very understanding man and we have a love that will last, even if I have never felt the breathtaking passion and the pain of life with Clive. We are good together and we have a real love, not just a second-best. It's different. Not better, nor worse, but satisfying on all levels and lovemaking still gives us pleasure."

"I wish I'd known you years ago," Emma said. "You would have made life easier."

"How your mother and my sister, Lizzie, came to be born into our family, I'll never know! You take after your grandmother, not your parents. They were cold even when young. Clare was good–looking but vain, and thought that every man who looked at her wanted her. Not that she gave much back even if they were interested and she imagined most of it. She even thought that Clive preferred her to me and hardly spoke to me after we got married."

"I often wondered why she bothered to marry my father," Emma said. "She considered sex dirty, but they must have done it to produce me!"

"What are you giggling about?" asked Bea from the doorway. "We are hungry and want our grub and you stand there sniggering and letting the mackerel get cold."

"Here. Take this dish in and be careful. Use a cloth. It's hot," said Janey.

"If I lived here, I'd have a dog and a cat and some chickens," Bea said after they'd scraped the last vestige of chocolate sauce from the lustre jug.

"If you left as few scraps of food for them as you have now, the dog and cat would have to eat your chickens," Emily said dryly. "To look at you, I'd never believe that you could eat so much."

"Emma and I have lived a life of feast and famine," Bea replied. "We have to store up when we can, or we did when we were in training as the food was often revolting." She smoothed her flat stomach and grinned. "I can still fit very nicely into my husband's contours," she said.

"You can't shock me, you hussy," Emily said calmly. "Now, are you going to make the tea, or shall I?"

159

"I'll add the whisky and Emma can clear away," Bea said lazily.

"Just another half-hour and then I must get back to the cottage, if you have no bed for me here."

"Poor little girl, turned out into the snow," Emma said. "Come on, Bea, you wash and I'll dry."

Bea folded the tea towel and carried the tea tray into the sitting-room. "May I ring my father?" she asked with a glance at Emma that said "ask no questions". "He said he'd be there about now."

"Help yourself," Emily said. "I hate that contraption, but it has proved to be useful," she admitted.

Emma put a chair by the telephone in the hall and said softly, "I'll close the door and you can feel really private. Give him my love."

Conversation was sporadic as if the three women were expecting important news when they waited for Bea's return. They heard the soft sound of her voice, a faint ting as the receiver was put down and then silence.

Emma moved away to the window as if she found her chair uncomfortable. Bea was still alone in the quiet hall by the now silent phone and Emma's own tension built up to screaming point.

At last, she could bear it no longer and softly opened the door to the hall. "Bea?"

"Pa said not to worry," Bea said, but looked stricken. "He's sure it can't affect Dwight, but it all ties up now."

"What does?"

"There are masses of airplanes and ships in the Pacific, making terrible raids on Japan, but there's something more. Why do they want ships and planes to do nothing but observe. Observe what? Dwight is there, ready to be taken over Japan and the British Pacific Fleet is sending ships to the same area. It's all hush-hush as if the Allies are holding their breath and waiting for something big. My father knows what is happening and even he, cynical old bastard that he is, is appalled."

Chapter 12

News on the wireless was desultory, as if a blackout on anything important had been imposed and, in Emily Darwen's house, the women were restless. Bea and Emma had stayed up talking until midnight in the cottage, then slept badly even though the night was cool after the hot day. The distant sounds of cattle were comforting and shared no relationship with air raid sirens and war.

In early morning, Emma pushed aside her window curtains to see the dawn and leaned out to savour the rising scent of flowers. No blackout, she thought with pleasure. Things are getting better. Just a few more days or weeks and we can really look ahead again.

But when Bea came down to breakfast, looking pale and bleary-eyed, it was obvious that she had not slept for more than an hour or so. She refused to go back to bed. "I want to hear the news," she insisted. "Last night there was nothing fresh, but I feel that they are waiting for a big break of something awful. It has the same feeling that was everywhere just before D-Day and the invasion of Normandy started. Where can I buy a wireless set? If we stay here, I must be able to follow the news. Pa mentioned the Manhattan Project and then stopped as if he had said too much. When I hear a code name for anything to do with war, I feel chilled inside and know that there will be bad news for someone."

"I have a set at Aunt Emily's. It's bulky, but two of us can manage it if we take the car."

"I didn't know you had one here. How did you get it over to the Island, or did you buy it here?"

Emma looked evasive. "It isn't mine. It was lent to me."

"Paul?" Bea showed a glimmer of interest in something other than her darkest thoughts.

"Aunt Emily told him to use her cellar to store anything he didn't need in Southampton," Emma said with an effort to sound offhand. "He told her to let me use the wireless and his car as it would be doing him a favour. Cars and wireless sets get out of order if they aren't used."

Bea smiled her disbelief. "*Je crois,*" she said. "Let's get over to the house. I hope they are awake. It is a bit early even for Aunt Emily."

"I was going to make breakfast for them," Emma said. "I doubt if they'd bother today unless it's put before them. We can eat together. Bring those eggs and I've made soda bread ready for the oven as some milk went sour. It doesn't take long to cook and I know they both ate a lot of it while they were growing up. It might help as comfort food," she added with a shrug. "We can but try."

"You had of course forgotten that one of my passions is hot soda bread?" Bea asked wryly.

"I've made enough for all of us," Emma replied kindly, as if promising a treat to a child.

Bea burst into tears. "I'm frightened. Frightened as hell," she sobbed and Emma hugged her close. "For some, the war isn't over, and there's time, terrible time to have things go wrong."

"Janey must feel as you do and she hasn't Alex here to comfort her. She's lost one love of her life and she dreads the sea taking another. In one way, she must be glad to be with Emily, but the Island also has bad memories for her with the sea ever present out there waiting under all that lovely calm blue."

"And what about you? Don't you sense that something is wrong? You and George came together like magnetised iron filings and he is a wonderful man. Surely you worry about him?"

"I believe Aunt Emily. I have lost my lover and I know that I shall never suffer like that again. She's been slightly fey for years and now seems even more so. She knew when my father was dying and she tried to suppress uneasy feelings about Guy. Believe her, Bea. Dwight will be home soon," she said firmly. "Now this soda bread will go soggy if it isn't in the oven soon, so get moving!"

"I refuse to leave England without you," Bea asserted.

"And have me playing gooseberry with you and Dwight for the rest of my life? What a fate! Wash your face and I'll start up the car."

As usual, the front door was not locked and Emma and Bea entered the house quietly. The oven by the "Yorkist" stove was hot and the idling fire needed only a vigorous raking to make it even hotter, so that the bread cooked evenly and quickly.

"Umm," Bea said more cheerfully. "If they aren't awake now, the smell of that gorgeous bread will bring them down here soon."

Emma brought out the curl of fresh, golden butter that had seen no ration book and the homemade apricot jam. Bea scrambled eggs. By the time the tea was brewing on the hob, Janey and her sister peeped round the kitchen door to see what was happening. They both wore dressing-gowns of indeterminate vintage and Bea made a mental note to send them something more fashionable, if she could persuade her father to send them from Switzerland.

164

"Still wearing that terrible robe?" Emma asked in a teasing voice. "I gave her a very nice dressing-gown, but she keeps it for when she is ill, which is never. She soldiers on whatever happens."

Janey smiled. "Would you believe that mine is as old as George? I shall wear it until it drops to bits."

"Bang goes one bright idea to make you both look glamorous in the mornings," Bea said, and realised that Janey still treasured the gown her first husband had worn all those years ago.

Emma adjusted the volume control knob on the wireless set. The fretted mahogany front, backed with crimson silk, reminded her of the old piano, with the fretwork and velvet and candle holders, that Emily had sold when two notes ceased to function and she bought a more up-to-date baby grand.

The voice of the announcer made them pause before finishing breakfast, but the news had no sinister meaning and they ate with better appetites than they'd thought possible. The shipping news told them that the sea was calm all round the coast and it was to be a fine day with no hazards for boats in coastal waters.

"What shall we do?" Bea asked. "It's the weekend and the weather couldn't be better. I shall swim and sunbathe this morning once my breakfast has gone down, and then, do we have enough petrol to drive over to West Wight?"

"Shall we all go?" Emily asked.

"No work today?" Emma was surprised.

"It's Saturday and I'm taking the day off. I'm due for more than that and while Janey is here I want to make the most of it." She laughed. "I doubt if they can make a bad meal without me there today. It's salad and cold meat mostly, and sausages as an alternative."

"You gave us breakfast, so you can go on the beach

165

at Sandown while we get a picnic ready," Janey said eagerly. "It will do us all good to get away from the wireless and the telephone."

"Catch the train at Shide and we'll pick you up in Sandown by the pier at twelve. We can go on from there in the car," Emily suggested. "No, leave the washing up. It will give us something to do."

"I haven't been on a train for ages," Bea said while they sat on a bench on the quiet platform and waited for the steam train that would deliver them quickly to Sandown before going on to Shanklin, Ventnor and all stations as far as St Lawrence Halt on the far side of the Island.

"Dwight will be so excited by this!" Bea said. "He boasts about the huge, ugly trains in the States that go coast-to-coast, but wait until he has to ride on this!" she said giggling. "He'll want to stay on it all day." She climbed on board, regarded the lurid pictures of Isle of Wight views in the plush-seated carriage and lowered the window on its broad leather strap.

"You can buy a ticket to take you anywhere on the Island," Emma said. "It's a good idea for visitors, and as the train passes through some of the best countryside, it really does give a good impression of the Island."

"It won't break down, will it?" Bea asked as the train lurched over the points.

"It's been chuffing along since Queen Victoria lived here and there have been no real accidents," Emma said. "But if you sit there, you'll have smuts in your eyes."

"They watched the changing scene, the trees heavy with summer leaves and the sheep in the fields, dew ponds and patches of nettles that showed the sites of ancient dwellings. Emma closed her eyes and heard the steady clunket-clunk of the wheels that had sounded the same a hundred years ago.

The train whistle blew to give warning that it was approaching a station and the engine sighed to a halt in a cloud of steam.

"Bliss!" Bea said. "Where's the sea?"

"When we were children, we came to Sandown for our annual Sunday School treats and had to walk from here. It was always a hot day, or so I remember it, and we were ready to run into the water as soon as we saw the beach," Emma said. "The temperature of the water must have risen sharply with the immersion of about fifty hot little bodies! I hope it doesn't seem as far today. They have cleared a length of the shore where they had anti-enemy concrete piles and metal spikes, and we can swim there."

The sea was calm in the deeply sweeping bay under the white cliffs of Culver Down, and it seemed impossible that anything more aggressive than the greedy gulls could have menaced the shore or the ships that went by on the horizon. Warily, they walked with bare feet across the hot sand to the sea, leaving their towels stretched out ready for them after the swim, and Bea crested the breakers as if fighting an adversary. The surge and the undertow challenged them and after a while they were exhausted.

"Have you fought your dragons?" asked Emma when Bea lay on the sand with her eyes closed and her long, fair hair spread in a golden wave on her haversack. The warm air fanned their cool bodies and dried the bathing-costumes quickly. Bea's elaborate rubber bathing-hat, covered with enough bright rubber flowers to start a garden as Emma remarked, was already dry and hot in the sun. Emma's own cap was less ornate and less efficient and the ends of her hair were damp, but she combed her hair and enjoyed smelling of salt and the sea.

"Most of them," Bea murmured sleepily. "There was one dragon I couldn't reach, always on the top of the next crest and it escaped before I could kill it."

"Time to get dressed," Emma said quietly. The object of the day's outing was to make them all forget the war and danger and their individual dreads for a while.

"Gets everywhere," Bea said as she sat on the sea wall and tapped her shoes to sift out the large grains of dark sand. She wriggled into her French knickers and more sand was released from her now dry skin and cascaded down her legs. "I should have brought two towels; one to sit on and one to dry me."

"I love the feeling after a swim in the sea," Emma said. "I never want to shower away the salt. I'm sure it's good for me."

"Just as well we are having a picnic," Bea remarked. "If I sat in a restaurant now, I'd leave a circle of sand behind me."

The few other people sitting on the beach seemed set there for the day and one or two pale skins were turning lobster-red. Bea anointed her face with cream and applied bright lipstick. "Can't have a skinning nose for Dwight," she said and handed the cream jar to Emma. "You need some too," she said. "They will all come home, and we must look our best." Bea laughed shakily. "I do believe that now. First Aunt Emily, and now the sea has told me that Dwight will come home."

"It's five to twelve," Emma said. "Let's walk up to the road and wait under the shelter for the car."

Sandown Bay was fine and beautiful until they looked along the almost empty Promenade. The sea was the same as it had been when legendary gluts of mackerel had made the water almost black in pre-war days; the sand still had dark patches and golden areas and the cliffs towards Shanklin were covered in gorse and rough grass, with red valerian poised on the face of the sandstone rock;

but the remains of the sea defences under the breakers, were sombre reminders of the war.

The luxury sea-water swimming-pool that had fascinated Emma and her friends as children now lay empty and the huge rubber fishes and horses were long gone. Empty hotels, all needing fresh paint and repairs, were sightless eyes looking out to sea, and the remnants of cafes were boarded up.

"Just as well to bring a picnic," Janey said, as they walked along the sea front before returning to the car and driving on to the West Wight. "There's nothing here. Not a cafe open and no stalls." She took a deep breath of sea air. "I like Sandown. The only time I saw my mother take a holiday was here when she came for one day a year for her annual paddle in the sea and we all carried the food and bottles of cold tea."

Bea looked at her with a mixture of incredulity and envy. "I can't believe it," she said.

"They didn't have a lot of money with seven children to bring up, and in those days people like us had few holidays," Emily said. "I suppose your family have always gone to Nice or Cannes or somewhere smart for long holidays?" she added with a slightly malicious smile.

"Yes. I've been there and been bored stiff most of the time. When I have children I shall see that they have fun, and maybe I can do some of the crazy things that I longed to do, but couldn't do the first time round."

"So, you intend to have a family?" Janey asked with interest. She looked at the slim, lithe figure and the elegance that couldn't be hidden by a rumpled cotton dress and sandy shoes. "You'll have pretty babies. I wish I had been able to have more than one," she said with a note of regret. "I'm fortunate that Alex helped me with George and he grew up without being spoiled. He was a gorgeous baby."

"Not much wrong with him now," Bea said dryly. "Even I can see that, although I am a sober and godly matron."

Emma said nothing, but hoped that he was safe. In spite of the sun and the physical well-being of her body, soft and relaxed after the pounding salt-water, she felt empty. The war was over as far as it could touch her in England, and the need to work hard was less urgent. Would life become a routine of cases nursed in private houses, where she was unsure of her welcome or her status, or would she rise to administration posts in a hospital? Work behind a desk that wouldn't use her talents to the full?

"You shivered," Emily said. "Did you dry off as soon as you came out of the water or did you let your bathing-costume dry on you? That is a sure recipe for a chill!"

"I'm fine. Just a goose walking over my grave," Emma said lightly.

"Plenty of them about," Emily said and shrewdly left her alone.

The sweep of the military road to Freshwater was exhilarating and the last of the lingering depression left them. They ate lunch on the cliffs, cracking the shells of hard-boiled eggs on stones and dipping lettuce into home-made mayonnaise that Bea swore was better than she'd ever had in France. They watched the sea cream up to the Needles and the gulls hovering on the thermals above the Downs and they demolished a lardy cake and some of Bea's chocolate.

Bea laughed. "It happened in a house in Surrey when we began our hospital training and it's happening now. I feel happy for no real reason, even when there isn't that so-called essential element, a man, in sight!"

A small, blue butterfly settled on the rim of a cider glass and sipped. They watched until the small wings

170

flapped and the Chalk Blue made a zigzag flight to the top of a long grass to recover.

"Dwight would love that," Bea said and sighed. "He'll never believe I saw a butterfly with a hangover. I know he'll be back but what a bloody waste of time war is!" She looked at her watch. "This is lovely, but I think we ought to get back in time to hear the six o'clock news."

Janey was already packing up and Emma carried the picnic basket to the car. They drove into Freshwater village to buy fish so fresh that it smelled of the sea, with bright eyes and taut flesh. Bea argued that she wanted as much fish as possible to make up for the years she'd never been able to have it. She insisted that she liked a rasher of bacon with her fried flat-fish, while Emma said she preferred hers steamed with parsley sauce.

"You'll both have it fried," Emily said. "The parsley seems to have dried up in the garden and I haven't any cheese to spare to liven up a plain white sauce."

"With bacon?"

"There might be a few pieces of fat bacon fit for nothing else, but it will give it a flavour," Emily admitted grudgingly.

"You bought far too much," Janey said. "We'll all be growing gills after eating so much fish."

"We might have a visitor," Emily replied.

"Who is that? Your doctor beau?" Bea asked.

"A beau at my time of life?" Emily said scathingly. "Paul came over the telephone and said he would be staying with Dr Sutton for a day or so, and I asked him to supper."

"Would you like me to drive back?" Emma asked. She felt light-hearted and gave the swim and the picnic the credit for the change.

"It will be good to see Paul again," Bea said with sidelong glance at Emma. "I'm anxious to know his

171

plans, as Dwight and I would like him to come over with us and start up a clinic there."

"He couldn't afford that," Emma said hastily. "He said he has just about enough money to buy a partnership with Dr Sutton."

"He wouldn't have to buy a practice. Dwight says that anyone who is qualified can put up a shingle anywhere in the States and the clients come running if the practitioner is good. If he agreed to do some free work with the immigrant poor, then he'd be doubly welcome."

Emma gunned the engine and pretended to be absorbed by the road ahead, although they had passed only two cars all the way back to Newport. It wasn't fair! Bea had everything and now she wanted to take away the last of her friends, or rather Guy's friends. She drove in silence for a while, then sighed and her hands relaxed on the steering wheel. She knew that, as Bea had said, Paul was her friend and not Guy's. He had hardly known him.

Janey took over the car when Emma and Bea were left at the cottage. "I'll have a shower and run over in time for the news," Bea said. "Do you mind if I use the bathroom first?"

Emma shook her head. "Go ahead and I'll make coffee. All that cider made me thirsty." She could hear Bea singing in the bathroom. "Oh, not that again!" she called, laughing. "Even Vera Lynn knows more songs than 'White Cliffs of Dover' and you never quite manage the right pathos."

Bea gulped a cup of coffee on her way to find her still sandy shoes which she had left by the door. "Come over as soon as you can," she ordered, thrusting the empty cup into Emma's hand. "I'm hungry and they will be cooking that gorgeous fish."

Emma showered quickly and put on a clean, crisp cotton dress of tiny, red-and-white checks with a wide white collar. Her white court shoes were not suitable for walking over the field, if she took the short cut by the mill, and, reluctantly, she put on a pair of plain, flat leather sandals. I don't need to dress up, she thought, as if to convince herself that she had not made an effort to look good. Aunt Emily and Janey will never notice if I do and Bea has put on a very ordinary dress.

She went in by the kitchen door and found Aunt Emily preparing the fish. "No, you can't help," was her greeting. "Go and listen to the news and tell me afterwards what's happening, if anything."

Suddenly, Emma felt self-conscious. Her dress was so obviously new and very pretty and Emily had not missed the fact.

Bea stood by the wireless set as if willing it to tell her what she wanted to know and Janey sat by the window, gazing out over the garden. Paul got up from an armchair as Emma entered the room and took her hand briefly and formally.

"Hello," he said simply. "They've finished the weather forecast and you are in time for the news." He went back to his chair and sat deep into the cushions. He looked tired.

The bland, cultured voice of the announcer told the waiting world that the Potsdam Conference was winding up with a very efficient and satisfactory division of Europe as the Allies wanted it arranged, the mopping up operations in Burma were almost complete and the bombing of Japan had been so successful, using B-29s flying from China and the islands that, as an American spokesman said, they are running out of targets.

"That's good," Janey said, with a smile for Bea.

The voice over the air continued, "More British ships are now in the area with the British Pacific

Fleet, attacking Japanese positions and making Operation Starvation, the blockade of Japanese ports, very effective."

"Nothing new," Bea said and looked worried. "Did anyone else think he was just waffling?"

"Perhaps that really is all the news and everything will be back to normal soon," Janey said hopefully.

"Supper in ten minutes," Emily said from the door, "Has the world ended yet?" She smiled at Paul. "I need a strong arm to mash the potatoes." He heaved himself from the depths of the chair and followed her into the kitchen.

"I'll lay the table," Emma said hastily, before anyone could suggest a job for her in the kitchen.

"That boy looks as if he's lost half a crown and found sixpence," Janey said.

"Working too hard?" Bea suggested.

"He's staying in a house just outside Southampton while he's at the neurological unit and it isn't far from us. I really must get back to Alex, so when I go back the day after tomorrow, he can drive my car and see where we live, so that he can visit us." She shrugged. "I hope he uses my car. I don't need one when I'm at home as Alex has a better one. He can leave his here. I hate that car now that I know its history."

"Whatever is on his mind is more than yearning for you, Dewar," Bea said as they laid the table together. "Not that you don't look very inviting in the new frock! And he *did* notice," she added caustically. "For a girl who is immune to men, you still like to make an impression."

"It was the first thing to grab," Emma muttered and blushed.

"*Je crois*," Bea said with an irritating grin.

"I wish you wouldn't use that expression," Emma said. "It's becoming a habit."

"I only use it when you are lying," Bea said complacently. "It is very good for that."

"I agree that he looks tired," Emma said to change the subject.

"He's working with men back from the camps," Bea said. "That's all I know, but I can imagine it must be painful to try and get into the minds of men half-mad with fear and the memories of their sufferings. He will have to share their mental torture and try to be strong for them."

"Anyone who says they have a lump in their mashed potato will be given no pudding," Paul said. "Aunt Emily is a slave-driver."

"Stop fishing for compliments and take this in," Emily said.

"That's the dish Mother used when we had ducks for dinner," Janey said. "We needed three or four between us when we grew hearty appetites and this was the only dish big enough to take them all with a surround of baked apples."

"I haven't used it for years," Emily said. "It still looks good with the other blue and white china on the dresser, so it gets a wash and is put back for another few months."

She served the crisply fried fish and Janey added potatoes, carrots and mashed swedes.

Gradually Paul lost his haunted expression and ate all that he was given. By common consent, the war was not mentioned and the peaches from Dr Sutton's greenhouse were greeted with sighs of pleasure, with fresh cream and a sprinkling of raspberries.

Janey made tea and Emma found Paul by her side on the window-seat. "Good food solves many tangles," he said. "I think that it is more important than any medication when people have been deprived for a long time."

"It gives comfort as well as nourishment," she agreed.

"Company helps too," he said and smiled. "I've been moving about between London and Southampton, never really being in one place for long enough to take time off with friends, and when we do get together we talk shop, which is unhealthy." He looked apologetic. "I'd hoped to come here sooner, but work has been heavy."

She half-believed him. "Have you given up the idea of becoming a GP?"

"Not altogether. I could find more than enough work in psychiatry, but I also like the clinical side of medicine." He sipped his tea and made a wry face. "God, that's strong!"

Emma added hot water and handed him the sugar bowl. "The aunts like it strong with whisky," she said indulgently. "Some people hold their liquor, but they hold their tea and take stomach powder if they get indigestion."

"Coming here reminds me that I do love the Island and the quiet friendly pace here," he said. "But there's so much happening in hospital now, that I am torn. I'm in a painful kind of limbo with a strong pull of duty fighting a desire to do what I had convinced myself I really wanted. I can't see the future."

"I feel the same," she said, but wouldn't look at him. "A part of me wants to stay here, but I hear about Beatties and the busy wards and theatres and I feel guilty. Private nursing could be good or could be terrible, I have decided, so even if I take another case or so, I shall not make that my life's work."

There was an awkward pause and she knew that he was watching her. "We can't stay in limbo for ever," he said quietly. "There's more to life for both of us, Emma."

She glanced at his face, but now he was staring at the rose-bush outside the window and she couldn't read his thoughts. She wanted him to hold her close and let their loneliness seep away, but she was afraid to touch him. She took the coward's way and fetched him more coffee.

Chapter 13

"All the time I was in London I dreamed of hot weather and the time off to enjoy it, and now I'm too hot," Paul said. He dragged his deck-chair back into the shade of the pear tree.

"You'll get stung by wasps or be hit on the head by falling pears if you sit there," Bea said. "Oh, good! a cool drink."

Emma put down the tray and poured out glasses of lemonade. "Not the real thing," she apologised. "So don't grumble if it tastes of cream of tartar and lemon-flavoured sugar crystals, because that's what it is!"

"It's quite good," Bea said, sipping and then drinking with enjoyment. "I shall suggest to my father that he serves this as an economical substitute for champagne at the next reception for Heads of State. Where are the others? Not working in the hot kitchen, surely?"

"Aunt Janey is packing, as she wants to get away before lunch tomorrow."

"So soon?" said Bea with regret. "I do like her."

"There's a car ferry at twelve and I have to be in Southampton on Tuesday for a clinic, so I can see her safely across as she hates driving onto the ferry." Paul looked up at Emma. "I'm leaving my car here again as Janey insists that I'll be doing her a favour if I use hers. It's a very good car but she still feels guilty about buying it so cheaply when the widow really needed as much as she could get for it."

He seemed to be picking his words to make sure that Emma thought that he was doing her no favours, but was merely making sure that his car would be used and not left to rust.

"Aunt Emily does like to be collected from work," Emma said. They both nodded solemnly, as if that was the only reason for Emma taking care of the car.

"And it gives you an excuse to come back," Bea said, with her satisfied-cat smile.

"I need no excuse for that," Paul said. "This is one of my favourite places." He put his glass on the tray. "I've been lazy," he said and stretched. "I promised to call on a patient for Dr Sutton and I'm late." He grinned. "I heard the sirens singing and was led astray. See you later," he said carelessly.

"Not sirens of any kind," Bea said. "Listen! Isn't that a wonderful sound? Sunday morning in an English garden with church bells again. I never missed them in London, but here it's a sound of peace after they were banned for so long."

"I remember that night in Whitehall when we were in the thick of the VE crowds. All the bells in London rang out and it was magic." Paul's expression was tender.

Emma picked up the tray. "Yes, it was magic," she said softly, but when she looked at him by the kitchen door and he said his goodbyes to Emily, her eyes were pleading for understanding. "It was magic," she repeated. "But it was soon after that I had the news of Guy's death."

He kissed her cheek. "I know," he said and was gone.

"I'm still waiting for something to happen," Bea said as she turned on the wireless. "I listened earlier and they said again that if Japan doesn't surrender at once, it will be totally destroyed."

"They must know that," Emily said. "The Americans have bombed all their cities, and our ships have had more successes invading the islands that the Japanese held for so long. The war is nearly over for them as well as the Germans, and if they don't take notice, they will suffer even more badly. I blame their Emperor. He's a stubborn old devil who thinks he is a God. He doesn't care about human life even among his own people, so he'll deserve all he gets," Emily said fiercely.

The news consisted mostly of tragic details from the liberated Japanese prisoner of war camps and Emma went back into the garden to avoid hearing about the torture and starvation and gratuitous misery that the guards had inflicted on the weak and dying.

Bea joined her, looking very pensive. "All that was a kind of propaganda, almost an explanation and even a muted apology for something that hasn't happened yet but what they may do at any moment."

"If you don't watch out and be sensible and surrender, it will be your fault when it happens?" Emma suggested.

"Exactly. It means a big new effort and it could be terrible for everyone concerned, the Japs and us." Bea tried to contact her father, but twice the line was engaged and then the line was dead as if the phone was out of order. "Nobody wants to tell me what is going on. I haven't the courage to try the General, and the American Air Force office in London, who are usually very kind to me, gave me a firm brush-off yesterday, saying they had no news from the States and no news from my husband."

"It's like the security clamp-down we had over D-Day," Emma said. "We can't do anything about it, so why not take the aunts for a drive and try to forget it?"

But the day wasted away with nothing done; no drive

180

and no effort made to be cheerful, partly because Janey would be leaving the next day and partly because the heat was sultry and oppressive, and each of the women was lost in her own thoughts.

Salads were the only dishes acceptable and Emma drove to the ice-cream factory in Newport with a basin that they filled with good ice-cream of three flavours. They gave her a chunk of ice too, and she stored the ice-cream, on ice, in a haybox until after supper to keep it cold.

"We'll be over to cook breakfast," Emma said when dusk came and she convinced them that there was no point in making further efforts to be sociable. She was vaguely resentful. Paul hadn't returned and she had found herself looking along the road each time a car went by.

"Don't bother," Emily said. "I have to be in by nine to check incoming supplies, but I'll make some toast and if you'd drive me to work, I'd like that."

"What do you do when you have no car?" Bea asked.

"I walk or take the train to Newport station and walk from there. Or if it's fine, I go by bicycle." She laughed at Bea's horrified expression. "Emma left her bike here and I used to ride, so it wasn't hard to get the hang of it again. I manage the three-speed gear very well, and I can mend a puncture," she added with the air of being able to pilot a bomber.

"Now I've heard everything," Bea said and picked up her bag. "Good-night. See you about eight thirty?"

Back at the cottage, Bea twiddled knobs on the wireless set until she had a fairly good reception on the channel that gave the most detailed weather forecasts and the overseas news.

"It seems to work well," Emma said. "I'm glad we

brought it here. Have some cocoa while you find the news."

"Thanks." Bea took the mug of cocoa and then frowned. "It's the same old news, almost word for word that they gave us this afternoon."

She switched off and they drew back the curtains to let in what breeze there was, before going to bed. It was still difficult to get used to the idea that the blackout was over and they could let light from the house stream over the garden. Emma lay awake, thinking of George and trying not to think of Paul. She knew that it would be fun and exciting to fall in love with George. He could give her passion and laughter and a hint of danger, but he was her first cousin and somehow, even if it was legal to do so, an instinct as old as time told her that, for her, marriage to a cousin was out of the question. She turned over in bed and when she shut her eyes, she saw Paul's eyes, as they had been that morning when he kissed her cheek and said, "I know," and she wanted to weep.

Janey had given her a snapshot of George and when Emma had fetched her photograph album to add it to her collection, Janey had taken it and flicked through the pages. She had stopped at the selection of pictures of Guy, in RAF uniform, in slacks and jacket and an open-necked shirt, and one in gown and theatre cap that Emma had taken during a lull in the operating theatre after D-Day.

It had been the day after they first made love and she felt closer to that picture than to any of the others, but when Janey said, "Men look so different in uniform or working clothes: they could be several people mixed up into one," Emma wondered if Guy had been real.

"It's the same with us," Bea had said. "You wouldn't recognise us on duty when the pressures get tough."

She laughed. "Sometimes I didn't recognise myself after twelve hours slogging away over filthy wounds."

Which two people had fallen in love? wondered Emma. The RAF medic and the nurse in training? The serious surgeon and the dedicated operating theatre assistant, or the woman and the man, who had witnessed suffering and were worn out by work and more work, who needed physical love and bought a cottage so that they could abandon uniform and surface pretence and be themselves and find refuge in sex?

Emma sighed. "Darling Guy," she whispered, but he was not close even in her dreams now. "I'm a shallow bitch," she said, but she knew that her love for Guy had frayed a little long before his death, when he'd expected her to give up her training before taking her exams. He hadn't thought it strange that she should do as he wished; leave Beatties just so that she would be there when he wanted her. She'd known then that he could never have filled her life completely if she'd had to follow him wherever his work took him, regardless of her needs, while he led a full professional life with work that was his whole being.

Janey had said, "He has a good face; a very handsome man, but was it the camera that gave him that closed-in look?"

Bea looked over her shoulder. "It's Guy," she said simply.

The dawn chorus and the crowing rooster from the farm across the way made further sleep impossible. Emma showered and, while the water heated for coffee, she went out into the garden. Dew on the roses and silvering the spiders' webs on the grass was too delicate to last and the rising sun was already taking away the ethereal quality of the garden. Bea surfaced, after a deep sleep of only two hours. She accepted

183

her coffee with a muttered thank you and went to the wireless set.

Music filled the air and showed that they had the right station, then the announcer, sounding less formal than usual and slightly bemused, said that there was to be a special news flash.

Instinctively, Bea and Emma sat together on the settee, holding hands like children in trouble. Unprofessional murmurings came from the set and then a man coughed as if realising he was on air. He read a message from President Truman in the White House. The gist of it was that the Japanese had been warned many times that if they did not surrender at once they would face complete destruction.

"We've heard that so often over the past few days that we took it in, and so must the Japs," Bea said impatiently. "He makes it sound like the declaration of war all over again."

The now correct and disciplined voice continued. "At two forty-five a.m. today, our time, and eight-fifteen Japanese time Monday, August the sixth, nineteen forty-five, a B-29 bomber of the American Air Force dropped an atomic bomb on a town called Hiroshima in Japan, causing widespread and almost complete destruction of the town. It is estimated that many thousands were killed and it is impossible to say how many will die from the effects of the bomb."

"So that's it," Bea said flatly. "They'll have to give in now."

"They haven't said so," Emma replied more cautiously. "You know what the Japanese are like! They have this kamikaze mentality, so they might think they are still dying a glorious death for the Emperor and carry on."

"At least I know that Dwight wasn't involved," Bea said seriously. "He did his job well but I know that sometimes he thought about the people they had bombed. They never saw them, which helped a lot, but the thought was there, even though he was the pilot and not the navigator or the bombardier who had to release the bombs."

"War is terrible, but this might have prevented many more being killed on both sides. A shock like this must make the Japanese stop the war."

"Dwight told me just before he left that the Japanese had perfected a very nasty new aircraft which was almost ready to go into service. I think the Americans dropped this bomb before they could use those planes, so maybe now they will never be able to use them in battle."

"Come on, we'd better get to the house and make sure that the aunts know."

"Wait, Emma. They are saying more."

A message from President Truman was blunt and defensive, saying that if they hadn't dropped the bomb, the war might have gone on and killed many more Americans and British and others who defended liberty. If they had not dropped the bomb, and thousands more of American youth had been killed, every mother with a son in the forces would have wanted to know why something that could have saved them had not been used. Intelligence had shown that Japan had recruited the very young, the very old and many women to fill the gaps left by their own dead to make a final concerted push towards a hoped-for victory, and were ready to use new planes.

The announcer went into the background of the bombing. "The man who pressed the bomb release and the crew of the plane, which was called the 'Enola Gay', after the mother of the officer in charge of the operation, Colonel Paul W. Tibbets, CO of Composite Bombardment Group USAAF, have all been honoured."

"It must have been an enormous bomb," Emma said. "Heard enough? Let's go and see the others."

"Serves them right!" Emily said. "The First World War was terrible enough, but at least there was clean fighting. This lot take pleasure in torturing their prisoners and they kill innocent people in spite of the Geneva Convention."

Janey looked anxious. "I hope George is all right. They were saying just now that the warships that were put there to observe the results from the sea, were warned beforehand to sail further away to avoid the fall-out of debris and the radiation from the bomb. George said that they had been issued with special clothes as protection against something, so I suppose that was for this trip. I hope he wore them," she said as if telling a small boy to wear an extra pullover.

"What else did they say about observers?" Bea asked.

"There were two more B-29s following the 'Enola Gay,' Janey said. "They took films and came back to base safely."

"Thank God! I know that Dwight was in one of those planes."

"Are you going to telephone the Airbase?" asked Emma. "They'll be in touch by radio."

Bea turned away. "Not now. They'll have to analyse the results and develop the films before they release any information." There were tears in her eyes. "I wish I was with him," she said. "I think that this is the biggest thing that's happened to him in the war and he needs me."

"You could be right, but go easy." Bea felt Paul's hand on her shoulder. "I came over at once," he said.

"Why? Have you heard something that we haven't?"

He chose his words carefully. "No, but there are a few matters that might arise later," he said mildly.

"What do you mean?" Emily wanted to know, her face

186

set as if to prevent him saying anything that might harm her brood.

"When repatriated prisoners come home, they are scared and weak and need help in many ways. I don't say that the men on this mission will be the same, but they will suffer emotionally and the shock must have been terrific. Some will brush off the experience and manage to enjoy talking about it, but the rest will have something in common with the prisoners. They will need space and understanding. They may seem angry and unapproachable, and if they do, keep quiet for a while and let them make their own pace. The less you ask, the more they will tell you . . . eventually. That's when talking will be therapeutic."

"Must I keep quiet for ever?" Bea asked. "We share every thought and we need each other."

"When he comes back here, just act naturally, but don't swamp him with undue care until he comes to you. He isn't an invalid, but he might seem withdrawn even with you, Bea, and need to talk to a neutral person who will help him find his way back."

"I must fly out there," Bea said.

"Stay here, and when you talk to him on the phone, persuade him to come here after he's been debriefed, but don't ask him about the mission. He'll need a different scene and loving people who are not Air Force personnel, deeply impressed by men who had anything to do with the bomb. The Yanks are inclined to get hysterical over their heroes, and heroes who feel guilty are best kept in the quiet until they are healed."

"Guilty? When they have saved their country probably thousands of lives?" Bea's eyes were hot with anger.

Paul smiled gently. "We've all felt guilty at times in hospital when a patient died suddenly or we thought we could have diagnosed a condition earlier. It passes when we realise that it is not our fault, but, each time, it's acutely disturbing."

"You think he might need psychiatry," Emma asked. "How can we help?"

"Find out as much as you can about the mission, Bea. Listen to the news and the on-the-spot interviews that will come over each day, true or false, and be ready to discuss it with Dwight when he's ready, but not before."

"You really are serious? How can you think that my wonderful, happy and completely sane husband will feel guilty?"

"I saw the film they took of the Alamogordo test bomb explosion in the desert in New Mexico and the trial run over Bikini. Dwight will have seen them too as part of his briefing, but this bomb is out of hell, and for him was not just a film. He was there, watching high over a big city, while a terrible weapon was used deliberately on it. I think that many people will feel guilty in their inner souls, including the President of the United States of America and Oppenheimer, who invented it and said that he thought it would be no more lethal than a very big conventional bomb made of high explosives. We don't dare to guess at the damage it has done by radiation alone." He smiled to comfort her. "I may be talking through the top of my head, and he'll come home bursting with pride and energy, but it's as well to know what to look for if he isn't quite normal. It takes men in different ways just as shell-shock did in the First World War."

Emily appeared at the door. "Bomb or no bomb, I have work to do, so who is to take me there? It's done and can't be undone, as my mother used to say, so get on with what you have to do and don't look back, is what you ought to tell Dwight."

"I'll call you in for consultation," Paul said dryly.

"You will be here?" Bea asked in a quavering voice.

"I'll be here if you need me," Paul replied and he glanced at Emma.

Emily walked to the door. "The supplies will be there and so will a few itching hands." She sniffed. "I wonder what that woman feels like today?"

"Who?"

"The one who had a bomb called after her."

Paul gave her a hug which she didn't repulse. "Not the bomb. They called that 'Little Boy'. It was the plane they called 'Enola Gay'. Come on, I'll drive you then call in on Dr Sutton's surgery. A crisis makes everyone gather there to gossip and he'll be busy."

"I'll be ready by eleven if you can spare the time, Paul," Janey said.

"I've put my bag in the porch," he assured her.

"Don't desert me!" Bea wailed. "I feel safe here. I don't want to go back to London."

"Emma will stay," Paul said firmly. His eyes were serious.

"Unless you need the money, don't take another job yet. Stay here for a while and be with Bea and Dwight when he comes back."

"They may want to keep him in a military base in the States."

"That's what worries me," Paul said. "If he's there, he will have to talk to groups of people, who are longing to lap up details about the whole miserable tale from someone involved." He grinned. "I'm probably wrong and he'll come back triumphant, without a care in the world, but it's as well to look at every possibility. Even if he is untouched by this, he'll deserve a complete break from duty and the company of other flyers, and what better place and company could we choose for him?" Emily was already in the car and he followed and shut the passenger door.

The phone rang by Emma's elbow and she was startled. She picked up the receiver and tensed. "Yes, she's here." Bea and Janey both looked up enquiringly. "It's the General's aide. He said to hold the line for him to speak to Bea."

Bea grabbed the phone and Emma left her alone and closed the sitting-room door.

"Nobody had breakfast," Janey said. "I'll make toast and coffee." Her shoulders slumped. "I'm glad I'm leaving," she said. "I need Alex more than I ever thought I'd need anyone again."

"You love him very much?" Emma sounded sad.

"For me, he was a calm haven after I lost Clive. I didn't realise just how much he did for me at the time. I thought I needed a father for George and affectionate friendship, but I was healthy enough to need a man's body in my bed, and now, my love has grown over the years. The two men have merged in my heart and I feel tenderness and a really deep passion for him." She smiled. "At my age? Believe me, it gets better."

Emma cut bread and opened the door of the stove to toast it in front of the fire. When Bea came into the kitchen, the comforting smell of warm toast met her.

"Well?" Emma asked.

"What it is to have friends in high places," Bea said with an air of relief. "I told the General what Paul said and he agrees. He is sending a radio-message right away, stating that my husband has not finished his tour of duty in England, has not been completely signed off here as a casualty after his fractures, although he volunteered for this mission, and is due for leave of absence to join his wife immediately, where he can be treated for battle-fatigue, if necessary, by a consultant psychiatrist."

190

"Do you think it will work?"

"Yes. I think the top brass are still reeling over the massive impact of the bomb. They can't make up their minds if Truman is a very brave man or an impulsive idiot, and for the moment, until they test American public opinion, they want to play their cards close to their chests, as the General so succinctly put it, so if the men in those planes are not available for comment, so much the better."

"We'll get my room ready for you, Emma," Janey said. "Bea will need the cottage now."

"Leave that to us," Bea said. "I have to keep busy just now. That coffee smells good and I'm famished. Emma looked at her and smiled. They were both mentally rolling up their sleeves to get back on duty and to meet whatever challenge came their way.

"I'll stay long enough to know if you really need me," Emma said.

"We'll need you," Bea said. "Someone has to make the soda bread."

It was a relief to strip beds and wash the sheets and pillowcases, and as Bea held up a towel to peg it on the clothes-line, she was humming to herself.

Emma mixed knobbly lumps of starch with borax and boiling water as she had seen Emily do, and crisped the white valances and the linen mats on the dressing-tables in her room and the ones in the cottage.

Bea stretched and surveyed the long line of washing, billowing like the sails of yachts, and she breathed in the smell of clean wet linen as it dried in the open air.

"We've been so brainwashed into doing hard work that our poor tired brains tell us we like it," she said, and picked up a peg that had fallen from a tea towel.

"Janey watched with an amused smile as the elegant young woman slung the wicker clothes basket on one hip and danced into the house. "You seem happy," she said.

"We know what happened. That's important. Waiting in ignorance has never been right for me, and now I can cope with whatever it brings. I shall have Dwight back with me and I know that I am what he needs as a wife and friend and, if necessary, as a nurse, so all will be well." She added quietly. "I am practising my bright smile. Say it's good!"

"It's very good, because in an odd way, you *are* happy."

"What a pity you didn't do midwifery."

"What brought that on? You aren't pregnant are you?"

"Not yet, but I think I might be as soon as Dwight is demobbed and we make a real home together."

"No more Beatties? No more nursing agency?"

"No, but I shall do what they call *good works* in Texas and bear sons for Dwight."

"*Je crois*," Emma said and they laughed.

Chapter 14

"Why did they need to do that? And only three days after Hiroshima." Bea was white-faced and distraught. "Wasn't one bomb enough? It killed seventy-eight thousand people and injured far more."

"The bomb on Nagasaki has at last convinced the Japanese that there must be no more lives lost on either side, and they say that their surrender will soon be signed," Paul said. He had spent a lot of his spare time with Emma and Bea at the cottage, in the days after "Fat Boy" was dropped on Nagasaki, and he seemed to them to be a sane link with reality.

"At least Dwight was not involved this time," Emma said.

"Because he was undergoing tests for radiation," Bea said bitterly. "They've unleashed a monster and don't have any idea how to keep it under control."

"I think Truman was right when he said that two Japanese cities under a fanatical leadership were a small price to pay for half a million Allied men and women, with months of long drawn-out battles that would kill more on either side," he reminded her.

Emily walked in and sniffed the air. "I hope it's worth me walking over for Sunday dinner," she said. "I have my doubts about your oven."

"It will be very good, I assure you," Paul said. "Bea needed to test it before Dwight arrives and everything seems in fine working order. I peeped and the crackling is crisp, just as I like it. I shall eat at least half of it," he teased her, knowing her weakness for crisp pork skin. "If I am to carve, I have first choice, and it was *my* patient who happened to kill a pig and be grateful enough to give me a shoulder joint."

"If I don't get my crackling, I shall report you to the Ministry of Food about illegal rations," Emily said calmly.

"What would I do without you?" Bea said. "You are all so normal."

"Repeat after me, 'I am normal and Dwight is normal, and we don't talk about any other possibility'," Paul said briskly.

"Sorry," Bea said. "I just hate waiting."

"I'll tell you who isn't normal," Emily said. "Some Japanese general has disembowelled himself after they had that meeting when the Emperor told them the war was over. It said on the wireless that the Japanese people are more stunned about the Emperor telling them about the end of the war than they were about the bombs on Hiroshima and Nagasaki, as it means they lose face over defeat. Human life is not important to them. The Emperor speaks in a way that the ordinary people find difficult to understand, as it's Court dialect. They were not told of defeat as such, but just resignation that the war must end. That's the understatement of the year," she added.

"They must be in turmoil," Paul said. "There was an attempted mutiny which was put down. Suzuki resigned and Prince Higashikuni, Hirohito's younger brother has taken charge. They say that the surrender will be signed within days."

"So, when they sign, we'll really have Victory over Japan," Bea said brightly. "It will be wonderful. Dwight

194

arrives tomorrow and we can make it a double cel-
ebration; the end of the war and us being together for
good, and he won't have to take part in any boring
parades."

"Are you going back to London for it, Paul?" Emma
asked.

"No. We were together for VE night and it was
wonderful. Somehow I think that VJ will be different
and not have the same marvellous feeling of joy and
release we felt in Whitehall and by the Palace that night."
His eyes were dark and calm. "Even so, it will be a time
to celebrate and I'd like to be here, if that's all right with
you," he said.

"I'm glad," Emma said.

"Is everything ready for Dwight?" Emily asked. "You
will sleep in the small room here until he arrives and then
come back to me," she stated.

"And I have to work in Southampton until tomorrow.
Then I'll come back and celebrate VJ day," Paul said.

"I'd hoped you'd be here to meet Dwight and stay on
to see how he is," Bea said.

"He doesn't need a medic breathing down his neck
as soon as he sets foot on the Island," Paul said firmly.
"Just relax and I'll be on the phone if you need me. I'll
be over, casually as a friend, as soon as I can."

"When do you go?" Emma asked and felt suddenly
bereft.

"As soon as I've finished the apple tart," he replied.
"Will some kind lady give me a lift to the Cowes
ferry?"

"You go," Bea said. "I'll clear up here and bring in
fresh flowers for the hall. This is a very nice cottage,
Emma. I think you should buy it. Happy people have
lived here."

"Bert did say he'd like to know," Emily said. "I told

him to mind his own business until you've been here for the time you've leased it, but we did discuss a price and he'll let it go to you for next to nothing."

"What hold have you over that old man?" asked Bea.

"Emma is family," Emily said briefly.

"Your family, but not his," Bea persisted.

"It's all in the past, Bea, but he remembers and so do I. You needn't look so curious as I'm not telling," Emily said calmly. "Let's say that our two families were close and my mother did a lot for Bert and his wife."

"You should buy, Emma, if only to have that awful picture," Paul said, lightly.

"That's my picture and it isn't awful," Emily retorted. "I brought it here to make Emma feel she belongs." They gathered round the large picture of two dogs, a huge Great Dane and a tiny, white Maltese terrier lying in the mouth of a wooden kennel.

"Victorian sentimentality at its worst," Bea said when she read *Dignity and Impudence* at the bottom of the frame.

"If I'm to catch the ferry . . ." Paul hinted.

"You drive," Emma said. "If you go too fast, you'll be the one to be arrested." It was a relief to know that his attention would be on the road ahead and not on her. "It's funny," she mused. "I didn't even notice that the picture was in the cottage now and not in Aunt Emily's house. I suppose I've seen it so often that I took it for granted."

"Sometimes it's too easy to take for granted people and things that you imagine will be there for ever," Paul remarked as if casually, but she saw his mouth tighten. "Has it been in that house for years?"

"It belonged to my grandmother in the big house on the Mall, or I think so. I was a baby then, but whenever I saw the picture I was fascinated." She shrugged. "It

196

might have been in either house. I was too young to know, but I liked to see it and yet I've never talked about it in case it was taken away and I'd never see it again. Silly, wasn't it?" She laughed. "Aunt Emily reads my mind. She knew that it was a part of my childhood that would make me feel comfortable in the cottage."

"Did you have pets when you were a child?"

"Never. My mother said they made work and mess and I was better without them, but I longed for a puppy or a kitten to call my own as I was an only child. I envied Aunt Emily when she told me tales about my grandfather's animals and the big family and I suppose I thought of the picture as a substitute for the real thing."

"Aunt Emily doesn't need a degree in psychology," Paul said and chuckled. "Most of my work is applied common sense with a smattering of science."

"She has the edge on you," Emma said. "She has her psychic sense, too."

"And she knows your need for a firm base here, Emma. She's right, you know. Some day soon you'll have to make up your mind what you want to do with your future and who is to share it."

"But I might not work here."

"I don't mean that you have to be here all the time. For you, this is home, and you need it as a kind of haven where you can come when you need peace." He stopped the car by the pier entrance and they walked by the jetty, watching the ferry arrive and unload. "It has its dangers, of course," he went on.

"What do you mean?"

"You could buy your cottage, take a cosy little job and become a recluse, sheltering from the world. No, don't laugh, I've seen it happen to people."

"I needn't buy the cottage. I can go straight into the nunnery at Carisbrooke!" Emma said dryly.

He lifted his bag from the back of the car. "Not a nunnery," he said. "You might marry George . . . or me."

"It's too soon . . ." she began.

"The memory of Guy must never be your haven, Emma. Shrines to the dead are cold and empty places," he added brutally. "Guy is dead! This place and warmth and love must take his place, and soon, with whoever you choose to share it."

He took her in his arms and kissed her, with lips that were warm and deeply loving and vital. "Goodbye. If you'll meet my ferry I'll phone you tomorrow and be here as soon as possible. I'll have to go back the following day, but after that I'll come if Dwight needs me, if he ever does."

"And if he never needs you?"

"I'll come if you send for me," he said simply.

She could see him standing in the stern of the ferry as it churned the water to take the turn from the pier and leave for Southampton. On an impulse she drove the car to the Promenade by the Royal Yacht Squadron in Cowes and parked there.

Out at sea, small naval vessels were anchored, resting from the war, but on one barge there was activity. The trellises and racks that she recalled from Cowes Week fireworks nights in her childhood were being erected. Her pulse quickened. There would soon be Victory in Japan to celebrate and the now empty sea front would be teeming with revellers and servicemen and women eager for the real end of the war.

The fireworks had always been wonderful, with gigantic sprays of coloured balls of fire lifting and falling from the sky, and frightening rockets trying to reach the moon. The end of the display, marked by a set piece that outlined the figures of the king and queen and the words, "God

Bless our King", made everyone gasp at the cleverness of the people who had arranged it. Then the scuffle to leave for home began, with the train to Newport packed and the roads crowded with walkers and cyclists.

Emma gazed across at the sea and Southampton water, and she smiled. Paul would come for VJ Night even if he wasn't needed as a doctor. Southampton wasn't far away.

As she drove back to the cottage, her smile faded. Some men had seen enough fireworks to last a lifetime and, compared to the infernos of bombed cities, a few bangers and squibs would be insignificant.

"You took your time," Bea said and Emma told her where she'd been. "I had a call from the General," Bea said happily. "He'll organise a car for Dwight to bring him down to the coast from the American Air Force Base in Hampshire where he'll land, and then a launch to Cowes, where I shall meet him. He offered a jeep and driver over here, but I insisted that it would make Dwight too conspicuous and he agreed." She giggled. "What would Aunt Emily do with a laconic, gum-chewing American GI driver?"

"Feed him!" Emma said. "I'm glad he'll be here before the offical VJ Day celebrations." She told her about the preparations she'd seen in Cowes. "And it won't only be there. Newport will be full of soldiers as they still have two units at Albany barracks although the parachute regiment have left, which means the local girls will have no more parachute silk, and the fleet's in at Portsmouth, with many sailors whose families come from the Island, so they will have leave here. It might get a bit noisy."

Bea nodded. "I think we stay here quietly and drink some good wine and eat a splendid meal that we can cook, but avoid the fireworks."

"Worried?"

"Of course," Bea said. "I feel that so much depends on me, and I don't know if I can handle it." She picked a perfectly good carnation to pieces until Emma gently slapped her wrist "I wish that Paul hadn't gone back."

"So do I," Emma admitted.

"More than George?"

"Different, and yes, much more."

"Don't keep him waiting. Life is short and must be sweeter for those of us lucky enough to survive."

Emma looked at Bea's face. Her complexion was perfect, but her eyes showed a deep anxiety and she had lost her haughty assurance. "What are you going to do?" Emma asked.

"Whatever he wants me to do," Bea said with surprising humility. "If he wants me in a frilly apron making hominy grits and sluicing his bacon and pancakes in maple syrup, or if he wants a tart, I'm ready, and I shall follow wherever he leads me. I want to be by his side for ever."

Emma saw that she was weeping, softly and without grief, and she wished that her own feelings could let go as easily. "Can I do anything here?" she asked softly.

"Be here, Emma. I'm scared." She surveyed the spotless hallway and the polished floor with the beautiful, faded rugs. The flowers in the huge, brass bowl blended with the soft pastels of the drapes and she smiled. "If we can't find peace here, we can't anywhere. He'll love it."

"Let's go up to the house and see if there is anything we can do for Aunt Emily," Emma said. "She insists on cooking the first big meal for Dwight, so that you have no clearing away to do that night, but I can't believe that she'll have enough meat for many people."

"I wonder."

"What are you planning? When you have that crafty

expression, I know you are being devious," Emma said, welcoming Bea's recovering sparkle.

"I am expecting a parcel and it might be there now."

Emily was still at work and, as they opened the door, the telephone rang. It was for Bea, asking her to collect a parcel from the pier-head at Ryde. "We rang twice," the voice said reproachfully. "The goods are marked perishable so you'd better get down here fast."

"The General?"

Bea nodded. "You remember how he fed us when we were starving nurses at Heath Cross? Now he's convinced that, if Dwight has to exist on British rations, he'll expire, so he thought we could use a few bits and pieces."

"Why didn't I have a godfather who cared?" Emma wanted to know.

"Why didn't I have a godfather?" Bea remarked as they loaded several large parcels into the car.

There were canned vegetables and fruit, biscuits and the black pumpernikel that Dwight had enjoyed in Germany, bacon and smoked ham, tins of sausages and an enormous turkey. Bea sniffed at a pack of lemons and eyed the hand of bananas with pleasure.

"Might fill a gap," she said with an amused grin. "You fetch Aunt Emily and I'll pick some herbs from the garden for the stuffing."

"It's very fresh and will be just right by tomorrow evening, with plenty to have cold in the cottage after that," Emma said. "You can forget cooking for a day or so."

"I'll cut off the wing ends and put them with the giblets to make soup for tonight," Bea said. "No matter how hot the weather, I've noticed that Emily enjoys really thick home-made soup and there will be time to make it if I start now. Tell her that I have some bananas for her doctor friend."

201

"So, it's on with the frilly apron for a bit of practice?"

"I could get to like it. Makes a change from surgical gowns."

Emma drove to the British Restaurant and, as she was early, went into Emily Darwen's office. A grand name for such a small cubby-hole lined with shelves and with only a desk and two chairs, Emma thought. The war in Europe might be over but rationing remained and supplies of meat and imported fruit were as scarce as they had been in the middle of hostilities.

"I'll be with you in five minutes," Emily said. "I'm making out the menus for the next few days, so that I can leave a lot of the work to the others." She handed a packet to Emma. "That's dried eggs. They sent far too much and I don't like to use it after a week or so in case it grows something bad, so we'll use this for cooking at home. I thought that Dwight would like some real English pancakes."

"Everything revolves round his arrival," Emma remarked, as she loaded Emily and her bundles into the car. "Do you think there will be too many of us there waiting for him?"

"Only you and me apart from Bea and that will break any ice until they want to be alone. "We can't make up for her family, but she does need us here, Emma. Can't you see how frightened she is in case he has changed?"

"I wish she didn't love him quite so much," Emma said.

"Never wish that. She is one of the lucky ones and I think she knows it."

"We must stay with you until he phones from the mainland to say what time the launch will arrive at Ryde," Emma said. "I feel as nervous as Bea does, but

I'll have to drive the car to meet him. Bea might crash it in her state of mind."

"Remember what Paul said? Dwight isn't an invalid and he must be treated as one of the family just returned from abroad," Emily said bracingly.

"What if he hates it here and needs to go and stay with the General in his opulent house on Epsom Downs?"

"If he's how I picture him, he'll feel at home here," Emily said firmly. "I didn't leave much for supper," she added. "Since you came here, I've eaten more and enjoyed it, but I've let you down today."

"We have turkey giblet soup," Emma explained. "Roast turkey when Dwight comes and lots of cold meat for Bea to take to the cottage."

"It isn't Christmas!"

"The Yanks have turkey at Thanksgiving and what better time to give thanks than now, even if it isn't the right date," said Emma.

"See what Uncle Sam sent us," Bea called when she heard the car arrive. The savoury smell of giblet soup pervaded the kitchen and the kettle was simmering ready to make the tea. Bea looked flushed from the heat of the stove and she triumphantly produced a loaf of soda bread.

"That's a good one," Emily told her. "Make some more tomorrow and he'll be pleased."

After supper, Emma packed the things she'd left at the cottage except for her toilet bag and nightie. She transferred her case to the house as soon as breakfast was over the next morning. "I think I'll buy the cottage," she told Emily as she drove her to work. "Will you tell Bert?"

"I thought you would and he won't be surprised," Emily said. "Putting down roots, are you?"

"I have to start somewhere," Emma replied, but Paul's

words came back to her. I don't want to be a recluse, she thought, and could this be the beginning of loneliness when Bea goes to the States. "Even if I go back to London to work I shall need a real home. I can't stay with you for ever. You have Aunt Janey and George now, and they will want to stay with you."

"And you will need room for your own friends," Emily said.

"I have some furniture in store," Emma remembered, but couldn't find any spark of enthusiasm for the prospect of bringing it across to the cottage. "What I don't need, I can sell. The furniture here is better than anything I have stored and I want to forget the other cottage."

"I told Bert to find some nice bits," Emily said with satisfaction. "You should see the rubbish he puts in for holiday lets. He says that some peoples' children have no idea how to behave in other peoples' houses, so he puts in things that aren't valuable."

"You knew all the time that I would buy it!"

"I knew the time had come for you to have a place of your own and I gave Bert a rough time over it," she said laughing. "He wanted you to have a house in Totland but I said that you'd be lonely there as you weren't like one of his bits of fluff that he used to put out there in the old days."

"Uncle Bert?"

"He was a bit of a masher, believe it or not. I wanted you near but not to be in each other's pockets all the time, and when he saw you again he said you looked like your Gran, so you could have it for a song."

"Would he get rid of my other furniture?"

"I'll tell him." Emily said and looked pleased. "Cutting out dead wood never did any harm and you can get cluttered up with the past if you're not careful."

"And if the past doesn't go away?"

"It doesn't have to be forgotten. It's part of life just as the future is, and good memories never hurt the ones who come next unless they bring bitter thoughts. If you've learned from the past, keep the good and make it help you."

"I've learned," Emma said. "Why didn't you get married? Did you cling to the past and do all the things you tell me are wrong?"

Emily laughed. "I knew I'd never forget Arnold, but I was too busy for years after he died to think of courting, and then I valued my independence too much to do anything daft in middle age with someone I didn't really want. I was the youngest in the family and that meant I was expected to look after my parents and not marry."

"That's not fair!"

Emily shrugged. "It was expected and worked out well enough, but when I was alone again the men who sniffed after me wanted a good cook and a nurse! I'd been that for years and I enjoy working for others, but I like coming back to my own home in the evenings, making tea and putting my feet up if I want, having a game of bridge and not having dirty socks about the place. It was too late for me."

"So why bully me? I might want the same."

"You are just starting and you have complete independence now while you are young. You need to fill your life with something more than tending a cottage garden when you come off duty. You are like Janey and your Gran and you ought to marry and have children." She gave a gesture of annoyance. "There, I've said more than I ought and I never intended to do that, but it's true."

"Well, don't just sit in the car all the morning!" Emma said with a good imitation of Emily's more abrasive tone. "Get to work and I'll fetch you tonight in time to meet Dwight." She touched her aunt's hand. "Thank you, you old witch," she said. "It would save me a lot of time and bother if you just told me what else you have in store for me?"

"Not George!" was Emily's parting shot.

Emma drove slowly and when she came to Shide Railway Station she stopped the car. Bea would be almost glued to the phone at the house in case there was a call from Dwight and she wanted to prepare the evening meal all alone. Emma had been allowed to dig up potatoes and pick spinach and a large cabbage and Emily contributed redcurrant jelly, but Bea jealously wanted to take all credit for the roasted turkey, and the trimmings of bread sauce, good gravy and stuffing.

She parked the car in the driveway of the cottage and walked along the Blackwater road. The sun made bubbles in the tar at the edge of the road camber where not enough grit had been laid on the hot tar during road-mending, and she recalled popping the tar blisters on her way home from school and being in trouble when she returned home with her shoes sticky with tar.

She stopped by the open gates leading to a long, curving drive that led to the Hobart estate and remembered hanging on that gate, yearning for one of the Shetland ponies bred there.

The fields were empty now, the stubble golden after the hay had been stooked and taken in, and, at the top of the Down, it was black where the stubble had been burned. In the shade, she shivered. It felt as if it was nearly the end of summer, although it was only August. The trees were still in heavy green leaf, but the white candles of chestnut blossom had turned into prickly husks that would soon split and shower the drive with glossy, brown horse chestnuts.

I wonder if Paul ever played conkers, she thought, and turned back.

Bea was elated. "He rang as soon as he set foot in England," she said. "He slept on the plane, so he isn't tired, and he still loves me! He sounded just as I remember him."

"You are a ninny! Of course he loves you. When do we expect him? Maybe you should meet him alone, now that you know he's all right."

"No." Bea thrust a mug of coffee into her hand. "I'm still scared. "If we sit in the back of the car, he will hardly notice you, but I'll feel safe."

"Thanks very much," Emma said dryly. "Do you want me to wear a chauffeur's cap and call him 'Guv'?"

Bea giggled. "I shall make sure he has no time to notice the driver," she said. "Just to hear his voice made my thighs damp."

"Well, go easy in the car. The natives might object to an exhibition of uninhibited sex on the way down Ryde Pier!"

"You have the same acid turn of phrase as Emily. You need to be careful!" Bea said in mock reproach, but nothing could dim the wonder in her eyes.

They ate ripe pears and cheese under the shelter of the glass roof in the small conservatory and when Emma turned on the wireless, Bea begged her to turn it off. "Today, I want to hear no bad news," Bea said. "I want to think of us here and Dwight arriving soon." She stretched out on the canvas chair and sighed. "It's warm and bright in here and I feel as if nothing can spoil the day."

"It's cool in the shade," Emma said, but found it too warm in the heat of the conservatory.

Bea leaped up when the phone rang and ran to answer it, then called Emma.

"He's on his way," she said in a voice that trembled. "In half an hour, he'll be at the pier head."

Chapter 15

"We'll leave your luggage in the car and drive round to Aunt Emily's," Bea said. Emma glanced at Bea's reflection in the rear-view mirror and saw that she was tense.

"I could pick you up later from the cottage . . ." she began, but Bea shook her head.

"After all that travelling, you need a rest, darling," she said tenderly to Dwight. "I remember how I felt when I flew back from the States."

"Kinda empty," Dwight said. "I could do with a good cup of coffee and a deep armchair for an hour."

"The house would be best," Bea insisted. "I can keep an eye on you and convince myself that you are really here while I cook dinner."

Dwight gave a tired grin. "Now I've heard everything." he said and his smile blossomed as Emma remembered it. "Sure it'll be edible?"

Their greeting had been ecstatic and Bea had been radiant when they embraced as soon as he stepped ashore. They had watched the small vessel come out of the distance and saw it berthed with skill, and Emma was impressed yet again with the respect that Dwight inspired in the British services due to his rank in the American Air Force. It was true that his godfather, the General, had influence, but Dwight's war record spoke for itself and his many decorations, including the Purple Heart, could not have been earned by nepotism or wealth. Dwight was wearing civilian clothes and to the casual observer, could have been any fairly important visitor.

The motor torpedo boat that had been used as a launch to fetch him, sighed up to the jetty, Dwight stepped ashore and a smart Royal Navy rating saluted before the boat turned away again, threshing the water and glinting in the sunlight.

"Emma," he'd said as soon as he released his wife. He caught her up in a bear-hug. "How's my best girl?"

"Your what?" Bea said.

"I'm allowed a girlfriend. You are my wife. That's different, honey."

"She's the chauffeur and helps wash the dishes," Bea said briskly. "Let's get you home. You look so tired."

"I'll be just fine now I've got you," he said and put an arm round Bea's shoulders in the back of the car. "Is it far?"

He seemed exhausted under the veneer of humour and Emma drove as fast as she could, suddenly as anxious as she sensed Bea was feeling.

Bea snuggled close and said little, her usual ebullience muted as if she was with a tired child, and Emma knew that the discipline of her training was going to be tested. This was no time for passion or bright, trivial conversation and Bea was professional enough to know and accept it.

"Nice place," Dwight said when they came to the house. "Looks lived in."

"The cottage is even nicer," Bea said. "We sleep there, but first we eat with Aunt Emily and Emma."

"It's pleasant in the conservatory," Emma said. "There's a good chaise longue there and rugs."

"Dwight picked out a dressing-case from the luggage and followed Bea to the bathroom. Ten minutes later he appeared in the conservatory and eyed the bed chair with longing. "Brother! That looks real good," he said and was asleep before Bea brought the coffee.

"She tucked the rug round his feet and shut the door. "He's home with me. That's what matters," she whispered.

Emma saw that she was close to tears. "He'll be fine once he's had a good rest," she assured her. "After all he's been through we must expect him to be exhausted."

"Is that all? Just tiredness?" Bea looked bleak.

"What else?" Emma replied with caution.

"The General said that he wanted to get him here fast, away from people talking about the Bomb, as two of the men with him are suffering from what they now call "battle fatigue", which is similar to the shell-shock of the First World War. Already, the newshounds are gathering to catch a glimpse of anyone involved with the Bomb and clamouring for interviews. Some men have complained that they can't go to the jon without being spied on."

"The ones affected will be having treatment, won't they?"

"In an army psychiatric unit among other servicemen and women, with no chance to forget."

"Surely they are the experts who can see danger and treat it at once before it grows really serious?"

"The General said that Dwight had no symptoms when examined and debriefed and he wanted to get him away from the press before any delayed signs show up. He believes in good old-fashioned tender, loving care and a change of scene. I agree and I know I can make him forget."

"But there is a possibility that he'll need help?"

Bea moved restlessly and poured more coffee. "It's as well to be told the worst that could happen, but I know he'll be fine with me. Most of the men on that plane have suffered no ill effects, so I have no doubt that Dwight is just tired out and needs normal rest." She cleared her throat. "It's just that, seeing him now, makes me wonder if there is something more."

"We've seen men exhausted in hospital and they perked up wonderfully after a few days' rest and care."

"You're right." Bea picked up the coffee mugs and took them into the kitchen. "We can leave him asleep for at least five or six hours, then feed him." She paused with the tap running and said, "Try and get hold of Paul and explain. I know he's coming over tomorrow but he ought to be put in the picture." She sighed. "Thank God for sane and gentle men like him."

"Yes, Paul will be careful. He's never had an aggress-ively white-coat image even when I've seen him walking the wards in Bristol. He doesn't look like a psychiatrist and he'll be a great comfort to have around."

"About time you realised that," Bea said and dried the mugs.

Dwight was still asleep when Emma brought Emily back from the British Restaurant and the women crept about trying to be silent.

They had left the phone off the hook so that the bell couldn't disturb the sleeping man. Emma put the receiver back, then telephoned the unit in Southampton where she thought she might catch Paul at teatime.

"I'm glad you rang," Paul said. "I'm sure he'll be fine but if some of the observer team have been affected, he might not escape altogether. I'll bring a few things with me, like sedatives and maybe some thiopentone, but I hope that won't be necessary."

"He's exhausted, and has slept ever since he arrived, hours ago. Surely he doesn't need sedatives?"

"Sedation is often a good thing. It gives the patient time to recoup," Paul said, adding cheerfully, "Drugs don't eat anything in my case, so they can stay there until needed. Maybe Bea will be the one needing help."

"Bea? She's a tower of strength."

"Remember Ozymandias in the desert?" he said cryptically. "Even towers fall down. We're not very busy here, so I'll make over my cases to my deputy and be on the nine o'clock ferry. I'll stay with Dr Sutton for a few days more than I planned."

"Bless you," Emma said fervently.

"Just tell him I'm a friend or, better still, force yourself to say I'm your boyfriend," he said. "No talk of mind-bending."

"I'll meet the ferry," she promised.

"Well?" Bea asked.

"I meet the nine o'clock ferry tomorrow and he will make his visit open-ended until he sees if Dwight needs him."

"How do I introduce him?"

"It seems that I have acquired a boyfriend," Emma said. "Just for a day or so," she added hastily.

"Why stop there? OK! I won't tease you, but it does sound a good idea. Dwight has heard that Paul is your friend and it will seem natural for him to be here."

"What are you doing?" Bea asked, when they joined Emily in the kitchen.

Emily laughed. "I'm not interfering with your turkey. I'm making pancakes now that we have those nice lemons and I brought some egg back with me for the batter. She tipped a drop of oil into the frying-pan and swirled it round until it was smoking hot, then added batter from a teacup and let it flow over the hot surface. Bea watched the batter begin to bubble and Emily tossed the pancake over to cook the other side, then levered it free to join the growing pile that oozed lemon and sugar.

"They smell wonderful. Do I have to wait until dinner?"

"Certainly! I think we are ready whenever your husband wakes up," she said. "He's had a good few hours of deep sleep and I think we could wake him soon. I shall put these in the warming oven and they will be cut down in wedges when we are ready for pudding, so keep your hands to yourself! I can't spoil the shape now."

"This smells like my grandmother's kitchen in Kansas. I began to wonder if such places existed any more." Dwight came up behind Emily and hugged her.

"You'll make me spill the batter," she said sternly. "And did your grandmother let you loose in her kitchen to take liberties like that?" she asked, as if she had known the man for years and had the privilege of putting him in his place.

"Not often. She was sassy just like you," he said.

He had lost the deep lines round his mouth and his eyes were no longer tired. "Take a quick shower and change," Bea said, handing him a pair of flannel trousers and an open-necked shirt that she had taken from his suitcase. "Dinner in fifteen minutes, so stop flirting with Aunt Emily and get going," she said.

Emma made the "thumbs up" sign when he had gone and Bea smiled her relief. "What was I worrying about?" she asked the turkey as she transferred it to the huge blue and white dish that had been in the Darwen family for years.

"You'll love it," she said later when they sat at table and Dwight had carved the meat. He was pointing to the dish of bread sauce.

"Bread? No cranberry?"

"With onions, cloves, milk and butter, and the red

stuff is Aunt Emily's redcurrant jelly, much better than cranberries," Bea said.

Warily, he tasted it, then grinned. "It's great," he said and the three women watched, trying not to look like fussy mother hens, as he ate and asked for second helpings of everything.

"This ought to be VJ Night, not tomorrow," Emma said when she and Bea washed up and left Dwight to tell Emily all about his family back home, while Emily drank her laced tea and Dwight had whisky in his coffee.

"It's the one subject that Dwight hasn't mentioned," Bea said with a frown. "Not a word, as if the war had never happened."

"Remember what the General said? He wanted to keep Dwight away from everything to do with the war, and we have to give him time to get over any shock," Emma reminded her. "Aunt Emily has kept quiet at the restaurant about his visit and nobody here will know that he was on that plane."

"I'll keep quiet," Bea agreed. "Maybe tomorrow he'll say something. We all seem to have avoided any reference to VJ Day."

"He may talk to you tonight Bea, and say what he can't express before strangers."

"Strangers? What strangers? You know he's very fond of you, Emma. I couldn't wish for better company today as I was scared to be alone with him in case I said something wrong. With you here, I feel safe, and Aunt Emily and he are already so close that they are almost leaving us out! Should we knock before going in to join them? He loves her way of talking and I feel she will be very good for him."

"I think they'll allow us to take off our pinnies and drink coffee with them," Emma said and giggled.

It was odd to see how two completely different

214

people had slotted in together. Emily's home, though comfortable, could never compare with the background that Dwight was used to before he came to England and yet he seemed wonderfully relaxed and grateful to be included within her family.

Bea carved the rest of the turkey and packed most of it to take to the cottage with some of the other food in the parcels and lettuce from the garden.

"You take the car tonight as Dwight's luggage is in it, and I'll walk over to collect it tomorrow, before I fetch Paul. I shall have to leave here before eight-thirty, so just leave the key in the ignition and I'll not disturb you."

Bea smiled. "I feel better than I've been for days," she said. "I'll take him home soon. See you tomorrow sometime, and thank you for everything."

Dwight was telling Emily about the ranch and said that he would expect her out there for a holiday, but she said that like some really good wines, she didn't travel well and would want photographs instead.

At last Emma insisted that Bea must take him to the cottage. "You have a lot to talk over and a lot of sleep to make up," she said.

Bea looked back at the house, the stone walls and red brick softened in the dusk. The headlights swept over the rose-bushes and lit up the two women waving them away, before the car pointed towards the road and they were lost in darkness. A fox crossed the road ahead, his eyes iridescent in the headlights and his saffron brush heavy and thick.

"It's another planet," Dwight whispered. "Was all that real? I feel I've known this place for ever."

"As real as us now," Bea said tenderly. "We can stay in the cottage alone for a while, but go back to the house often, if that's what you want. I feel that they will belong to us for ever."

"Forever is a long time. Does anything last that long?"

She drove up to the cottage door, suddenly apprehensive at the leaden tone of his voice.

"You bring the cases while I light up. Do you want more coffee?" She had to tell herself that he was fine and could lift the heavy bags much better than she was able to do, although she wanted to do it all. She mustn't treat him like a patient. "Nothing but bed," he replied and Bea couldn't decide if he meant he needed more sleep, or her. Wearily, he heaved the biggest of the cases into the hall. She relaxed. It's going to be fine, she thought. He's dog-tired, that's all, then wondered why she had thought, however fleetingly, that anything between them could be less than perfect.

"You use the bathroom and I'll follow," she said and helped him carry his luggage into the spare room that Emma had vacated that morning. He unpacked his toilet bag and dressing-gown and put them in the larger room with the double bed. "I'll put the food in the cool larder and I'll be with you in ten minutes."

She blessed the fact that the larder was old-fashioned. It was chilly, with a thick slate shelf and ventilation out through the wall on the shady side of the house by means of a sheet of perforated zinc. The turkey would keep fresh for two or three days and there would be no need to cook anything except maybe bacon and dried egg omelettes.

She heard the water drain from the bathroom and went up the stairs. In the bathroom, she stripped and inserted her contraceptive diaphragm and put subtle perfume between her breasts, before slipping into a silk nightdress of pale blue that was almost dull compared to the lingerie she was used to wearing when Dwight came home. She

216

glimpsed her reflection and frowned. "I never wear this thing," she murmured, "But tonight, anything more tarty would be wrong."

The bedroom was dimly lit, with a rose-coloured lampshade softening the harsh glare of the light-bulb, and the patchwork quilt looked homely and welcoming.

Dwight lay back on the pillows and she saw with surprise that he was wearing pyjamas. He usually liked to sleep in the raw, at least when she shared his bed, but he liked to see her in a nightie and enjoyed peeling it off before making love, taking delight in whatever bizarre extravagance she wore for five minutes.

"Darling," she said softly. "It's so wonderful to have you home with me."

"You've no idea," he said and sighed. "I've dreamed of this moment and could almost smell the perfume you're wearing now."

Bea snuggled closer and he put this arms round her. She closed her eyes. He was being gentle and caring and she wanted to cry. His hands caressed her body and he buried his face in her breasts. She relaxed. Passion would come soon and she knew how much he loved her, so this pause was natural. He was very tired.

His kiss had an element of desperation and he clung to her, kissing her lips, her face and her breasts as if to generate passion. She was uneasy. Dwight was the perfect, virile lover, impulsive and sometimes almost too eager and hasty in his desire for her, but now, as she placed her hand over his taut stomach and down on to his thigh, she felt the limp organ and knew that he was unable to make love.

Consternation for his pride and her own frustration made her tense. This had never happened to them and she was at a loss what to do. She'd heard of women having to stimulate their lovers manually, but she'd laughed and thought that there would never be time enough for that to happen, as Dwight was impetuous and her needs matched his own. She had dismissed such practices as the working duties of whores paid to have sex with men unable to function without such help, but now she stroked him and pressed closer to make urgent bodily contact.

"I love you," he said brokenly. "I want you so much and I . . . can't."

Pyjamas and a virginal nightie, and now this, Bea thought, with a glimmer of wry humour. Are we now just an old married couple who will enjoy cocoa in bed, rather than sex?

Bea kissed him and held him in her arms while he sobbed uncontrollably. "Hush," she said. "You are tired and it's no wonder that this happened. Sleep now, and tomorrow, we'll be back to normal."

"Hold me," he pleaded. "Say you still love me, Bea."

"I adore you, stupid! Stop being sorry for yourself and go to sleep. You are worn out with work and travelling and excitement and I'm tired too."

"Disappointed?" he asked harshly.

"No," she lied. "Just glad to have you with me in my arms."

She stroked his hair and whispered to him and he went to sleep like a child spent after a storm of tears. Bea lay awake until dawn came and the birds defended their territory with song. She eased away from his heavy shoulder and went to put the kettle to boil.

She realised with a shock that she was wearing his thick dressing-gown and recalled the time when she had teased Janey and Emily about their masculine garments. Do I need comfort, as Janey did after Clive was drowned? For how long will this last? she thought, and shivered.

The air through the open window of the sitting-room

218

was sweet with the scent of nicotine flowers and the grass had the heavy dew of late summer. She wanted to call Dwight to share it with her, but instead she made coffee and showered while he was still fast asleep, and then dressed before going down for the coffee tray.

The car was parked a few yards along the driveway and she put a note on the driver's seat for Paul, hating herself for betraying Dwight's humiliation. It might not be relevant, but, if it was, Paul was the professional who must know how the situation could be approached. She thought of cases that Paul had described; the man who was paralysed from the waist down because his subconscious told his body not to function and so not to be sent back to the firing-line of the war.

I'm not the war! He doesn't have to escape from me! She tore up the note. I'm getting neurotic, she thought angrily. He's tired, and when he's rested he'll want me so very much.

Her thighs were sticky with mucus and she went to the lavatory to check. Not the result of lovemaking, she decided ruefully, but the more mundane sign of her coming period.

At any other time she would have said a few bad words about what a patient had once called "Eve's Burden", and then shrugged at the inevitable, but now she was secretly relieved. If she couldn't be available, it gave Dwight time to recover.

"Coffee, you lazy hound!" she called.

"Where were you?" he said sleepily. "You dressed!"

"Tired of waiting for you to surface, so I made coffee. It's too fine a day to wallow in bed all the time," she said briskly. "You've slept for twenty of the past twenty-four hours and it's time we went for a walk."

"A *walk*?" he said as if she had suggested hell. "What

219

happened to lying in bed until eleven and then staying until noon?"

"Feeling better?" she said and smiled.

His gaze focused on the wall and he bit his lip. "Did you get dressed to avoid . . . us?"

"Yes," she said calmly. "Remember 'The Lady of Shalott'?" She laughed as if everything was as it should be. "In school, we giggled about it as all numbskulls do when they first read it at the age of nine. It was like being made to read aloud anything with breasts in it."

"What the hell?"

"The curse has come upon me, cried the Lady of Shalott." Bea quoted in sepulchral tones. "So, Sir Lancelot, you'll have to wait for a while," she added as if she took it for granted that he was already feeling randy.

"Come here." They stayed close for five minutes and Bea knew that a new, deep tenderness enfolded them. "Know what? I could marry a girl like you," he said.

"Coffee," she said at last. "You hate it half-cold, so I'll heat it up again and we'll have bread and jam with it."

She left him dressing, and from the window she saw Emma open the door of the car and climb in, then look at the empty windows of the cottage. Bea stood back so that she was unseen and Emma smiled as she started the car.

"Little do you know, ducky," Bea whispered and went to get breakfast.

"Real apple preserve?" Dwight asked when he joined her.

"Emma never eats her sugar ration, so she gives it to her aunt to make jams and preserves. There are always apples in the country, so she makes a lot of jelly and apple curd. There's plum and some gooseberry, too, if you prefer it. It helps push down the awful

National Bread which the Ministry says is so good for us."

"That's not the grey loaf I've met up with over here."

"No, your devoted wife was up early and this is fresh soda bread."

He hugged her and she was aware of his physical strength and all that she loved about his body. Her mind refused to accept that he could possibly be impotent and that it might not be an isolated incident.

"Down, boy!" she said brightly and wondered if he felt safe now that she was not available to him.

They walked along the road past the mill and Dwight peered in through the slatted boards. "I'd like to see inside if the workings are still there."

"No chance," Bea said firmly. "The last man to do that fell through the floorboards. It's completely rotten in there."

He came back to the path. "Change and decay . . . and destruction," he said, too softly for her to hear, but she saw his face darken.

"I thought we'd have a picnic," she said hastily. "This way. I can hear the train whistle."

He laughed. "You have real trains here?"

"Not as big as your long-distance monsters, but much nicer," Bea said, as if she had a proprietorial right to all things on the Island. "I'll buy the tickets," she offered generously and took the green pieces of cardboard that the ticket collector gave her after punching each one for the outward journey to Sandown.

Dwight eyed the platform and the station-master's colourful garden with awe. "It's out of a story book," he said. "I never believed it but now it's true! Just get those white palings and that water tower." The steam train rounded the bend and hissed to a halt by the platform. "D'you think I could drive one?"

"Have you a licence? You only pilot boring planes. I don't think they'd let you take one of these." As soon as she said the words she regretted it."

"No," he said quietly. "I don't pilot planes any more. I have no control where they fly. I only sit in them and see what terrible things they do. I've given up flying."

The guard raised his green flag and Bea opened a carriage door and almost pushed Dwight inside the empty compartment. "Put the picnic basket on the seat and close the window or we'll be covered in smuts," she said as if she had noticed nothing amiss.

"No, I want to put my head out of the window," he replied and seemed to have recovered his humour.

"You'll get it blown off when we go under an arch," Bea said. She bit her lip. Why am I such an idiot, she thought, and pointed out a distant manor house and some very ordinary cows in a field as if they were rare animals.

"I can tell that you are a town girl," he said laughing. "We have cows, too, back home. At the last count about ten thousand head of steers."

She tucked his hand under her elbow and sat close to him. "Tell me more," she said. "I don't have to go near them, do I?"

"Only on a horse," he said, and pulled her closer to kiss her lips. "You'll love it," he said dreamily. "The space and the silence and the – I don't know," he finished lamely.

"I can endure cattle if we are together. We can take anything if we are together," she said slowly. "Enjoy today, darling. Relish the simple things. I love you and you love me and we have all the time in the world together. I shall give up nursing to be with you wherever you want to go."

"You will?" He was startled. "I thought it would take a revolution to make you give it up altogether."

"I think we've had that revolution," she said quietly. "It's time we assessed the true values. The war is over, really over, Dwight, and we have the future to sort out now."

"Yes." But the word seemed dragged out of him. "The future that some people will never know."

"Sandown Station," called the guard and Bea opened the door of the carriage. She was given back half the ticket for the return journey and they walked out into the sunshine and along the road towards the beach.

Chapter 16

"May we have dinner with you?" Bea asked humbly and Emily gave her a sharp glance.

"Why? Surely Dwight hasn't eaten all that turkey?"

"Please, Aunt Emily?" Bea glanced back to make sure that Dwight was still talking to Emma and Paul. "We brought fish from Sandown," she said placatingly.

Dwight appeared in the doorway.

"You know I haven't a fridge here, only at the restaurant, and I never eat fish over a day old," Emily said as if scolding Bea. She sighed. "Thought we'd seen the back of you for a while, but you'd better stay for supper and eat it here. You brought enough for a hungry football team," she added as if Bea was responsible for any hitch in her arrangements for the meal.

"My fault," Dwight said with a winning smile. "It all smelled so good. In fact, it didn't smell of fish, just smelled of the sea. That's one thing we can't have back home, living inland: really fresh fish like this."

Emily's sharp eyes glanced at Emma. "You'll have to lay up for two more," she said. "We can make a nice curry tomorrow to use up the turkey and you'd better come back for that, too, tomorrow evening," she added.

"Let me do the vegetables," Bea offered eagerly. Emma raised an eyebrow. Bea hated getting her hands dirty with the earth round the potatoes.

"You'll all have to help," Emily said. "Dwight can gut

the fish and wash them in the scullery, then dip the pieces in flour before Emma fries them. Paul, you know where the cutlery is, so you do the table. I'll make more soda bread as there isn't time to make yeast buns and we can eat in three-quarters of an hour."

"We'll need more vegetables from the shed," Emma said. "I'll show you, Bea. Bring that basket."

Dwight was tied into a rubber apron and given a small sharp knife for filleting the fish.

Paul laughed. "Rather you than me!" he said.

"You should do this. You're a sawbones." Dwight said, grinning and taking a stab at a fat sole.

"Not me! The sight of blood upsets me," Paul said. "I'm a physician, not a surgeon."

"Is that so?" Paul watched as Dwight expertly skinned the fish and reduced the pile into neat, manageable pieces. "You've done that more than once," he said in admiration. "You should have been a surgeon."

"I can flay a deer or an ox without making unwanted holes in the skin," Dwight said, modestly. With a vicious swipe, he beheaded a small hake. "Maybe I should have read medicine," he said and his eyes clouded with pain. "Healing instead of killing might have been better. You are one lucky guy," he said.

"Every profession has its pain," Paul said quietly. "We all face other peoples' deaths and think we are guilty."

A sliver of Dwight's left thumbnail joined the debris from the fish as the knife slipped.

"You have never watched seventy-eight thousand people die."

"Nor have you," Paul replied calmly.

"Hell, man, I was there!"

"You didn't drop the Bomb," Paul said. "You didn't invent it, or make it, load it or drop it and you had no idea that it would be so destructive."

"You think I didn't do all that? Then what you think is crap! What do you know about it?" His anger was intense and his eyes haunted. "It's Victory over Japan Day today, and nobody here has had the guts to mention it, as if it might upset me. They avoid it as if they are walking on broken glass because they daren't face my guilt."

"So why haven't you mentioned it, to set their minds at rest and let them know you haven't been affected by the mission?"

"Me?"

"Yes, you had more to do with the Pacific than anyone I know and are freshly back from it. You could say a lot, that is, if it really doesn't upset you to talk about it."

"I can't."

"And that's why they don't talk about it," Paul said. "Take your time and tomorrow we could go out together and you can tell me about it."

"Why should I? What is there to tell that the whole world will know soon? And why you?"

Paul shrugged. "We are almost strangers and it's often easier to talk to someone you might not see again. I'm a very good listener."

"I'll take a rain check," Dwight said. He called that he had finished the fish. "Where's the flour? Aunt Emily will have my guts for garters."

Bea surveyed her bowls of vegetables with the satisfaction of one who has done a good job with something she detested. She tipped them into boiling water and fitted the lids to the saucepans.

"That looked like a penance," Emma said softly and beckoned to her to go into the garden to pick parsley.

"It was awful," Bea said as soon as they were out of the house. "Dwight was fine until we got to Sandown. Remember what a lovely day we had, you and I?"

Emma nodded. "Did you swim?"

"No, we didn't take swimming-things as we had a picnic and no car, but the beach looked very inviting." She paused and looked unhappy. "I'd forgotten what day it is and when we reached the pier it was decked out with streamers and bright bunting and had 'Happy VJ Day' across a banner."

"Oh dear," Emma said. "Did it matter?"

"Dwight went white and I thought he'd throw up. Four sailors, already half-drunk, were singing rude versions of patriotic songs and shouting that the good old Yanks dropped the Bomb and finished the Japs for ever."

"What happened?"

"I got him to walk up to the cliffpath towards Shanklin and we ate our picnic overlooking the bay. It was so beautiful, with Culver Cliffs white in the distance and the waves washing the shore below, but we could have been eating sand for all I tasted of the food. Dwight told me he had finished with flying and that I might as well finish with him too as he was good-for-nothing."

"And then?" Emma's eyes were wide with horror.

Bea choked back the tears. "I think he's very disturbed. He went to the edge of the cliffpath and peered over between the gorse bushes. I think if I hadn't been there, he'd have jumped over."

"Why did he think he was good-for-nothing?" Emma asked cautiously

Bea smiled wearily. "To use an Americanism, he's a terrific stud and is proud of it, but last night he was impotent."

"Poor Dwight."

"Poor me, too! He left me up there and I couldn't sleep after we'd tried."

"He was tired."

"Never that tired," Bea said with conviction. "Today he said that we had no right to bring children into a wicked world and we must never try to have a baby."

"You don't like babies," Emma said mildly.

"I like sex and real love and in our most sentimental pillow talk we did agree that two might be nice if we could manage one of each and quite, quite beautiful," Bea admitted as if coming out with heresy.

"Did you quarrel?"

"No, he didn't want to know what I thought. It was so one-sided and dogmatic and riddled with guilt, as if he had the sins of the world on his shoulders. For the first time ever, I couldn't hug him and make him kiss me. We packed up the basket and walked down as if he had said nothing peculiar, and bought fish that I knew Aunt Emily didn't really need!"

"What about tonight?" Emma asked uneasily.

"That gives us a breathing space. I have the curse starting today and I told him so, as if apologising for no sex tonight and for a few other nights." She looked wistful. "He used to laugh at that and say we'd have to bundle like they did in the Middle Ages, when unmarried couples slept together with a bundling board down the centre of the bed to prevent any hanky-panky beyond kissing and the odd grope above the waist."

"That's enough parsley. You've picked off most of the heads and left all the stalks." Emma said. "Take it in and chop it for sauce. I'll see if everything is ready for me to start frying."

"Emma?" She turned and joined Paul by the shed where he was putting away a saw after reducing a branch into logs.

"I'm very glad you are here," she said.

"Why?" His eyes showed concern, then he smiled. "For you or the others?"

"Both," she said and their glances met in warm understanding.

"Good." He wiped the sawdust from his shirt and held her hand. "Dwight needs help, I think," he said. "Then I must talk to you."

"Yes to both. Bea is worried as he seems to have a guilt complex about the Bomb, and says they can never bring children into the world."

"Was he impotent last night?"

"How did you guess?"

"It makes sense. If he can't impregnate a woman, he will not be responsible for creating a child who would, in his opinion, be better off unborn." He frowned. "I'd like them to stay apart for a while, but that's tricky."

"Nature saw to that this morning," Emma said. "Bea told him and on the surface all is well, but she thought he seemed a bit suicidal when they were on the cliff walk in Sandown."

"Tomorrow, go shopping or something and leave us alone. I'm sure that Aunt Emily will find us something she wants done here." He grinned and hugged her. His kiss was warm and made her feel happy. "Thank you, nurse. I see that we shall work well together."

"Wash hands and sit up," Bea called. "I thought you were frying the fish! How come that I got the job while you and Paul whispered in the garden?"

Dwight laughed, with an edge of resentment. "Once, my dear, we were like that, young and in love."

There was a fraught silence, then Emily laughed. "So was I, but a girl can cool off when she finds out what a man is really like," she said, seeing that he was bordering on truculence. "Take that in and serve out the fish. I must say you can fillet almost as well as my father did and he was born to it."

"Sorry," he said. "Why doesn't someone bawl me

out?" He kissed Bea's cheek. "Sorry, honey. I'm all mixed up."

She shrugged and smiled. "Aren't we all?"

Good food and lively conversation around him made Dwight relax. Paul watched him and Bea, and Emma found herself watching Paul. I'll hate it if he goes out of my life, she admitted to herself, and when they had finished the stewed fruit and custard and were finishing the wine, she asked him what he intended doing in the future.

"I may not take up the option with Dr Sutton," he said slowly. "More and more, I find I'm interested in neurology and the attendant skills, and the locum GP is interested in the practice, so I feel that I'm not letting him down."

"You will leave the Island?" Her throat ached with a kind of sorrow.

"It will be here when I want to come back," he said.

"Come to Texas," Bea said eagerly.

"Later." Paul glanced at Emma as if her opinion mattered. "I'll finish at Southampton first and do a few weeks at Tommies. By Christmas I can make up my mind."

"You clear away while Dwight and I have our night-cap," Emily said and chuckled. "He takes away all the guilt I feel when I have a drop of whisky in my tea."

"Any coffee?" Dwight asked

"Of course." Bea bent to kiss him and he kissed her lips. "Fish face," she said.

"Speak for yourself. Get my coffee, honey, and leave the grown-ups to talk."

He settled in a big chair in the sitting-room and when Bea brought the tray, he was nodding his head while Emily told him more about her family. Bea brought the whisky from the cupboard, gave Dwight his coffee and and poured out the tea.

In a casually conversational voice, Emily said, "I heard from my sister Janey today. She used the telephone and I'm getting used to it now. You can say more on it than you can in a letter."

"That's what it's for," he agreed.

"She's heard from George." Emily paused and Bea seemed to be rooted to the spot. "You know he was on a frigate out at sea, watching them drop the Atomic Bomb?" she said.

"He watched *me*?"

"I doubt it, if you were in a plane, miles away up in the sky," she said dryly. "George said it was very dramatic and certainly saved a lot of lives by destroying two cities. They've said he isn't radioactive and the whole crew have been given leave, like you." She laughed. "I think Janey is more worried about his leave than about the effects of the Bomb. The American women are going mad over them and George likes women! She'd like him to marry Emma, but that's not possible as they are first cousins and we don't do things like that here," she added primly.

"Did he tell her what he saw?"

"No details, but he said there will be a lot of pictures released to the press soon. What a pity he can't come here now. You'd have such a lot to talk about," she said.

Dwight sat forward, his head in his hands, and Bea went to his side, but didn't touch him. "I can't talk about it," he said.

Paul appeared in the doorway. "You can't talk about the Bomb because you don't remember it," he said clearly.

"I did it!" The agony in his eyes made Bea want to cuddle him and tell him it was a good thing not to remember, but Paul gave her a warning look.

"You do remember," Paul said. "It's there, but you refuse to face it, Dwight. Tomorrow, you and I are going to talk and you will remember that you were not responsible for that terrible killing. Go to bed now and I'll come over tomorrow. I'll drive you to the cottage."

"Can you cope?" Emma whispered.

"Paul says he'll camp in your old room," Bea said with relief. "He said he'll fetch his bag and give Dwight a sedative tonight, so I think he'll be fine. I shall cuddle him and make him feel safe."

"I make a good poultice," Emily said with a note of satisfaction when they had gone.

"A poultice?"

"He's like a boil that hasn't come to a head. Everyone was poking round and not dealing with it so I thought it needed treating even if it hurt. Paul will get rid of what poison he's got in there and I shall have done my bit. Now I'll have another cup of tea and get to bed."

"Is George all right?"

"Fine. Janey said that he is staying with a family who have two lovely daughters, so he'll be in clover."

"And you won't have to worry about George and me?"

"That would never do. Apart from anything to do with blood, I can't see you as a naval wife. More a doctor's wife, if you've any sense and admit you want him."

"It might take me away from here."

"You'll have the cottage, and me as long as I last, which can't be for ever," Emily said more gently than usual, "You'll come back."

It seemed a long night for Bea. Dwight snored gently after he fell asleep, and of the three in the cottage, he woke fresher than any of them, and insisted on making the coffee for breakfast. "You came early," he said when he saw Paul, fully dressed, in the kitchen, and they said nothing about Paul staying the night and the anxious watch that Bea kept. "You look tired honey, but I suppose it's that time of the month."

"Coffee now and breakfast later?" suggested Paul. "I want to talk first."

"We can talk over scrambled eggs," Dwight said, half-defensively.

"Later." Paul's voice was firm. "We have some things to get clear, Dwight, and we're quiet now. There are things you must remember, and so get them out of your mind."

"I don't want to remember," he replied peevishly. "It's bad and I want to forget it all."

"So, Bea counts for nothing?" Paul said harshly.

"Bea? She knows how worthless I am as a man and in time she'll forget me."

"Just because you couldn't get an erection on one night, you think that's the end? Poor Bea! Maybe she does deserve someone better. Who do you suggest? There must be dozens of men aching for her and yet she chose you!"

"You don't understand! I dropped the Bomb and we must never bring more children into this world."

"If she leaves you, she may have a whole family of babies from another man," Paul said. "Looking like him, having his characteristics, and making her a good husband," he said brutally.

"*No!* Bea is my wife."

"Then stop making her suffer, if you love her. Come on, lie on the bed and I'll help you to get sorted out," he added more softly.

"Hell!" Dwight whispered. "What's happening to me?"

"Let's find out."

233

Paul drew up a syringe of thiopentone and pushed the needle into a vein in Dwight's arm, strapping it in position so that the drug would be adminstered slowly, as required. "I haven't perfected hypnosis without drugs, and we need him quiescent for a while," Paul explained quietly. "Hold his other hand and say nothing. You OK?" Bea nodded.

The room was very quiet and Bea wanted to switch off the intruding blackbird's song outside the open window, but she dared not move. I shall remember this wallpaper all my life, she thought as she forced herself to look away from her husband's face. That leaf design was never my favourite and now I shall shudder whenever I see it.

Dwight was relaxed and breathing softly and deeply, but was in the half-twilight between sleep and waking, when Paul asked him if he was comfortable and what he had done the day before.

Bea watched fascinated as Dwight replied, coherently and with no tension. Gradually, he was taken back to the day before the Bomb was exploded on Hiroshima.

"Tell me who prepared it all," Paul said. "They were your good friends?"

"I've known Bob Lewis since academy days." Dwight smiled. "He and Colonel Tibbet wondered if the plane would take off as it was seven tons heavier than the usual bomb-load, but they got it safely to Tinian for the flight out."

"Did you think it was a good idea?"

"No. It seemed a waste of time dropping one huge bomb when a strafing by a normal bomb-load would spread the damage and be easier to handle. Oppenheimer, who invented it, told President Truman that it would be just the same as a big load of explosive, but with greater force."

"So you didn't invent the Bomb?" asked Paul, as if surprised.

"Hell, no! That was the boffins."

"The bomb was loaded in 'Enola Gay', and you all drank the health of Oppenheimer and to the destruction of the Japanese?"

"Something like that. One or two of the men were really high and said it meant the end of the war; a final blessed clearing of filth."

"The next day? You were not in the 'Enola Gay', were you?"

Dwight shifted uneasily and Paul repeated the question more forcibly.

"No, I was in one of the two observation planes," Dwight said, as if surprised.

"So you had no power to put a warhead on, to arm the bomb, or to fire it."

"No, that was Tibbet and Major Ferebee, the bombardier. I saw him in the perspex nose cone of 'Enola Gay' by the Norden bombsight as we flew past her to take our stations about twelve miles away to the north-north-east and thirty thousand feet up. They armed the bomb at five thousand feet once they'd cleared Iwo Jima.'

"So you watched?"

"Two plane loads of officers and scientists flew there from Iwo Jima with powerful binoculars and cameras. We wore anti-contamination suits and mine was too narrow across the back and chafed a bit."

"What did you see?"

Dwight tore his hand away from Bea and she quickly clamped her hand on the arm with the needle in position, to stop him pulling it free. Paul gave him more thiopentone and let him go deeper, then asked him again what he saw from the observation plane.

"'Enola Gay' went over the city and at eight-fifteen

235

a.m. Hiroshima time, Ferebee was on schedule, and, on Tibbet's orders, got the bridge he was aiming for in his sights. He pressed the button and the Bomb fell."

"You were watching and did not release the Bomb," Paul said. "Is that true?"

"Yes."

"What did you see after the Bomb was released?"

"It had a delaying parachute to stabilise the fall and it took fifty-six seconds to drop thirty-one thousand feet. It was all in slow motion. 'Enola Gay' lifted as soon as she dropped her egg and made height and away, and our plane was shaken by the blast, eleven miles away. We turned and took pictures. A huge mass of cloud erupted in the shape of a gigantic mushroom, until it seemed it would never stop filling and rising, and under it, all the flames of hell broke loose. The noise was overwhelming."

Paul waited until Dwight was nearly back and repeated a lot of what he'd been told. Dwight moved restlessly, but as he regained his full consciousness, was made to accept that he had been an observer and was not responsible for the mission. All the time it took to return to normal, Paul relentlessly told him again and again that he need have no guilt over Hiroshima. "It was a final cleansing fire," he said. "The war is over now and you can go home."

Bea was crying and Paul hugged her. "Do you take confession and give absolution to anyone?" she asked brokenly, trying to hide her emotion.

Paul laughed. "That's not the first time I've been told I'm a priest." Dwight had slipped into a natural sleep. "What about my breakfast?" Paul demanded and Bea knew that he wanted to give her something constructive to do.

"Dried egg omelette as you have never dreamed it could be," she said. "Emma and I got this to a fine art form. Heat up the coffee, sit there and cut the bread and be ready! It has to be eaten straight from the pan or it goes a bit dry."

Suddenly they were both hungry and ate in near silence until Bea said, "Will he be all right, Paul? Really truly? I have to know."

"He may feel physically weak for a while and have bad dreams, but that's a catharsis. Let him decide what he can do and take the pace from him."

"You mean wait until he wants me," she said simply.

"He wants you for ever, Bea. It's just a little patience for a while, that's all you need."

"I'll try, but I doubt if I could ever be as patient as you."

"It's part of the job."

"You know exactly what I mean. Dwight suffered guilt in a dramatic form which you have exposed and it may be gone, but Emma has been guilt-ridden for most of her life in ways that she doesn't recognise. She needs a good priest." She smiled and he saw how Dwight must have fallen for her magic.

"So what must I do, Professor?"

"Bully her! You are so understanding that it makes me sick! You cure others and yet you fluff this."

"Guy . . ." he began.

"That's over and would have been if he'd lived long enough to show just how self-centred he was becoming." Her malicious cat smile showed at the corners of her mouth. "Hark at me telling *you* what to do! Tell her you are going away for good. Tell her that Tommies have offered you a job and it starts in six months, after you've been to the States with us."

"You must be psychic."

"What?"

"They have offered me a job, and I am going to take time off before I take it," he said. "I shall also take private patients in a shared clinic, using the money I would have needed to buy into the GP practice here."

"You'll need someone to run the clinic." He nodded. "Make her say yes to you before you tell her the good news," Bea said. "Make her want you in spite of that ghastly tie you're wearing and then tell her your plans."

"You drug me and flirt with my wife," Dwight said from the doorway.

"She's worth a second glance," Paul said.

"Brother! What was in that syringe? I feel as if I'm just recovering from the 'flu."

"I take it that you know now that you didn't win the war single-handed?" Paul asked lightly.

Dwight looked puzzled. "I can't think why I did," he said. "Must have been the shock." He frowned. "I think I was envious in a way that I wasn't in on it more, but it was a terrible thing for anyone to have to do." He yawned. "Any coffee? Then I'll go back to bed." He gave a one-sided grin. "If I'd known you were a shrink, I'd never have let you near me."

"I have a date," Paul said. "Work up an appetite for this evening. I was told we have curry and baked apples with cream and Aunt Emily doesn't like to be kept waiting."

Paul walked back to the house, the release of tension making his shoulders ache and his eyes heavy. Emma was alone and saw him walk up to the door.

"How is he?" she asked anxiously. Then she looked at him more closely. "And how are *you*? Come and sit in the conservatory. It's warm and out of the breeze, and I'll make coffee. Bad night?"

"Quite bad, but he is much better. He does admit that he was in no way responsible, and he's sleeping."

She stood behind him and kneaded his shoulders,

finding the tensed muscles and feeling a sweet sense of belonging. "Good?" she asked.

"Better," he said and turned to take her into his arms. "Better still, and I promise it will be better all the time."

He kissed her before her protest could be voiced, and she closed her eyes. "I don't know," she said, and he kissed her again until her body began to come alive and her mouth returned kiss for kiss.

"You do know that we must get married soon? I can't wait for ever," he asked as if the answer was purely academic.

"Yes, I know," she said.

"And after that? What do you want us to do? Where do you want to live?"

"Where will your work take us?"

"No, where will *our* work take us? Shall I take the share in the practice and you work at the hospital here, or do we go to America and start afresh near Bea and Dwight, or shall I take a consultancy and a private practice in London? The choice is yours. If it's to be the London job, I'll need someone to run the clinic, or you could go back to Beatties."

Emma smiled. "I can choose?" It was a strange feeling. With Guy there had been no choice for her, as he had taken it for granted she would follow him anywhere with no regrets for her personal sacrifices. Now she saw a different future, a different love and she liked the view. "Let's go to London and come here when we're tired," she said. "You'd be wasted away from the mainstream of medicine and we have a lot of friends there."

Chapter 17

"Are you turning us out?" Bea asked in mock reproach.

"Out of the cottage," Emily said firmly. "You and Dwight can come here for a few days until you leave and let Emma get organised in her own home."

"You have it all arranged," Bea said, amused by Emily's determination.

"Someone had to do it," Emily retorted. "The wedding is tomorrow and they'll want the place to themselves for a day or so. You can stay with them later if you are still in England, as there's the other big room."

"It isn't fully furnished. Do you think Emma would let us buy her some things?"

"No. Bert's son has got a nice few things for it, and I'm going over now to make sure everything is ready."

"Let's do that together before Emma comes back from Southampton."

"That's what I thought," Emily said complacently. "They insisted that they want to stay on the Island after the wedding and I think they're right. Everywhere is still in a state after the war and they will eat better with us! That parcel you had from Dwight's godfather will make a feast tomorrow. Where is your husband? We need his muscles for this."

"He's picking apples."

"Quite the country boy now." Emily said and called to him to start up the car. "Your room is ready here," she

240

added. "Use it whenever you want a bed for the night before you leave."

"Thank you, Aunt Emily. "Thank you for everything."

Emily saw the tears forming in Ben's eyes and said sharply, "We have a lot to do, so let's get your stuff out of the cottage and then you can leave Dwight and me to shift the furniture ready for you, if you go back there, and for Emma's other visitors."

Dwight carried a pair of shears to clip some overhanging roses by the cottage gate. "I hate to see it in a mess," he said. "When we go home, honey, I want a garden just like that, for you as well as me."

"Yes, darling," Bea said indulgently, and tried to recall just how often she'd said that over the past three weeks. He was so enthusiastic about everything that she wanted to shout for joy. She filled their cases and drove back to the house with them, leaving the small room empty of suitcases and ready for Paul's luggage.

Dwight heaved the chest of drawers into the position that Emily indicated in the other spare room, while she made up the bed in the main room with fresh sheets. The walnut table that had years of polish, giving it a gentle patina, sat under the window and an ottoman with a faint candy-striped cover matched the bedspread and curtains.

He went to find Emily. "Fit for a queen," he said. "It looks real pretty in there." He stepped into the main bedroom. "*Wow*! Get that! It must have cost a fortune. Is it a wedding present?'

"In a way it is but it's taken me years to make," Emily said, and twitched a corner of the window curtain as if she wasn't really concerned with what was on the bed.

"You made that?"

"I didn't sew it round the bedspread. Miss Caws did

that as the lace was too heavy for me to handle and she
has a huge table to spread it on evenly while she sewed,"
she added defensively as if that was the difficult part. "It
has come up well, I must say, and I promised Emma to
finish it when she got married." She smiled. "I didn't
bother to do that when Emma was with Guy, but now
it's finished."

Dwight raised a handful of the intricate and beautiful
lace that hung heavily round the double bedspread like
masses of creamy elderflowers in spring. "It's wonderful.
People back home would pay hundreds for this. Have you
any more?" he asked hopefully.

"Not like that, but you can take some doileys and
traycloths back for your mother if she uses them."

He laughed. "They won't get as far as my mother! Bea
will want them when she flaunts her very English afternoon tea parties for us ignorant ex-colonial peasants!"

"Help me fold it and put it in that chest," Emily said.
"Emma hasn't seen it and I want it to be here tomorrow
when they come back. I'll put it on the bed while you
are at the registrar's office."

"Why aren't you to be there?"

"It's best if no family goes. Paul has no family, as his
only relative is a brother in Australia, and Emma refused
to invite her mother, so if you and Bea are witnesses,
none of my family can accuse me of taking advantage
and leaving them out."

"Wise lady. I hate family politics," he said.

Bea returned to take them back to the house, and
Dwight insisted that she be shown the bedspread. "Don't
tell her," he warned, "Or you won't be given any lace to
take back home."

They argued happily and Emily knew that the crisis
between Dwight and Bea had passed. She kept quiet
about her phone call from Janey. George was due home

soon and Emily warned her that Emma was going to be married so it would be as well for him to stay away from the Island for a while.

"I'll come," Janey said at once. "If I can't have her for a daughter-in-law, at least she is my niece."

"No family," Emily said firmly. "Don't be hurt. Remember a girl in a yellow dress who went off and married a naval officer on the quiet, years ago?"

"So I did," Janey chuckled. "I'll keep George away and hope that he's fallen for one of those pretty Americans."

"It's as well we packed our clothes," Dwight said. "I have to report to the Airbase, so we might as well leave after lunch tomorrow. At least we can stay long enough to drink their health, but I want my discharge from the Air Force onto the reserve and can't wait to get back to Texas and ride a horse again."

Emily glanced at Bea who was smiling. "If he beats you, come back to me," she said.

"If *she* beats *me*, can I come back?" he asked, grinning.

"No, you will have enough on your plate looking after her," she said with a sly twitch of humour.

Bea saw the expression that said, I know something that you don't know, and she was thoughtful. When she drove to fetch Emma from the ferry, Emma wondered why Bea was so serious.

"Paul will be here tomorrow morning early, with his best man," she explained to Bea. She sighed. "It's a parting of the ways for us all. Paul has left Southampton and will go there only as a consultant later, when invited, and we shall have a flat in London as well as here, for our work there. Thank God for this place. It gives us roots, Bea."

"We go soon after lunch tomorrow," Bea said. "Never

fancied playing gooseberry and we have to go to the base and then to another wedding."

"Your father?"

"Yes, Pa has finally convinced Miranda that he will care for her and love her madly, just like Dwight and me."

"As you are? Really?"

"You've been almost too tactful about us, and I appreciate it, but there's no need now. Paul is delighted with him and he can sign any document to let the powers-that-be know that Dwight is mentally A1.

Emma blushed. "What about sex?"

"She mentioned the word! My, how that child grows up fast," Bea teased her.

"Stop trying out your American voice and tell me!"

"We avoided the subject until I thought we had lost it for ever," Bea said. "I hated sitting up in bed at night, reading!"

"Good books?"

"I was tempted to leave a few Girly magazines about, but I hadn't the courage to buy them, and if it hadn't worked, we would have felt sordid and cheap."

"You look happy and so does he," Emma ventured.

"Dwight is fine," Bea said flatly.

"And you are not?"

"I think I am." Bea looked out of the window of the car. "It was wonderful. One night, we kissed and held each other as we had done on each night after he . . . couldn't, and when he kissed me, something happened. He said in a low voice, "Boy, oh Boy, let's go!" I was puzzled, then helpless with laughter, as he was so relieved to know that everything was in fine working order again. But what a way to tell a girl he was better and he loved her!"

"So, it was all right?"

Dreamily, Bea smiled. "It was wonderful and he made

244

up for lost time until we were both exhausted, but so very happy."

"So what's wrong?"

"Is it wrong? I have yet to decide. He took me by surprise and I had no time or inclination to take precautions. I'm sure I'm pregnant."

Emma drew into the side of the road and stopped the car, her shoulders shaking with laughter.

"It isn't a bit funny," Bea began and then began to laugh too, until they were both convulsed.

"The girl who knew all the answers and educated me about birth control," Emma spluttered.

"I know. I even mentioned the subject to Miranda in my best possible nursing sister manner, as she's a lot younger than Pa."

"Diabetics have very pretty babies, if they are well stabilised," Emma reminded her.

"I don't want a half-sister or brother who is young enough to be my child," Bea said. "Fortunately, Miranda values her figure as an essential for her work, so she'll be OK."

Emma drove on slowly. "Tomorrow, everything will change," she said sadly. "Some things for the better and some will break my heart. I know that Paul and I will be happy. I had no idea he could be so wonderful. It's quite overwhelming." She glanced at Bea. "No, we haven't slept together. Do you know, I feel like a bride."

"You are. Guy was a lover during times of stress in the war and now you can look forward to a fresh beginning. I can, too. That blip in Dwight's health did us good. There are no areas of tension left." She managed a feline smile of sheer anticipation and Emma relaxed. "That doesn't mean I shall be very meek and mild. I think I might even enjoy being pregnant." She laughed with glee. "I shall demand everything

245

unobtainable and be a pain! Dwight will have to be my slave."

"What's new?" Emma asked dryly, and drove back to the house.

"You took your time," Dwight said. He was waiting at the gate, sitting on the wall with the careless ease of the very fit. He jumped down and kissed Bea as if they had been parted for hours and took Emma's bag into the house.

"What's for lunch," Bea asked and looked pale.

"Pork and beans that I showed Aunt Emily how to make just as they do back home."

"Lovely," Bea said faintly, and took three very deep breaths.

"I'll bring in the apples," Dwight said. "See you soon, honey."

"There's a letter from Bristol," Emily said and pursed her lips. "You'd best read it now and get it over. You don't want anything hanging over you tomorrow."

"I wrote to say I was getting married," Emma said. "I thought I must do that, but I didn't actually invite her."

"Read it."

Emma opened the letter. It was short, but not sweet. Clare Dewar was far too busy to travel all the way to the Island and she supposed that now she would never have a daughter to look after her in her old age, as Emma was as selfish as her father, so she washed her hands of her. She was going to stay with friends from the Chapel who were going to the Lake District.

"Bad?" Emily asked gently, and Emma gave her the letter.

"A relief. Now I feel really free," Emma said and smiled. "Tear it up and throw it on the fire. I've only one regret."

"What is that?"

"A long time ago you said you'd finish that bedspread lace for me when I got married. I wanted to treasure it as it was from you. When I was with Guy, you never mentioned it and now I suppose it's gone? It made me think of you as my mother, caring about me."

"It's finished and will be there tomorrow," Emily said quietly. Emma went quickly from the room and Bea raised questioning eyebrows. "Is she upset?"

"A little bit sad as she has never had a happy time with her mother, but I'm glad it happened now, before she and Paul set up house together. He'll be strong if Clare tries to interfere in the future, but I doubt if Emma will hear from her again."

"She has you," Bea said, simply. "That's enough. What's that?"

Emily uncovered the tray. "Your lunch," she said and laughed. "When Dwight made me soak all those haricot beans last night I had to smile, as I knew it wouldn't suit you. Been sick yet?"

"Only once, a little bit this morning, but the thought of pork gives me the shudders. How did you know before I did?"

"My mother could tell and so could most of her friends. There's a slight pinching in of the nose and a softness of the skin as if it's extra fine, almost transparent, that means only one thing to me."

"And obstetricians spend hours doing tests and examinations! They need witches."

"I shall help Dr Sutton with that. I use the telephone now and he's persuaded me to leave the Restaurant and sit in his clinic to advise on homely measures and diets and answer the telephone."

Bea said shrewdly, "You are doing this so that Emma will feel you aren't lonely."

"No, I was content before she came and, although I'll

miss her, I know she'll come back often. I shall enjoy talking to people at the surgery, and I can play more bridge."

"With Dr Sutton?"

"And others," Emily said firmly. "Janey will visit me and we shall have a nice time as we always got on well."

"May I eat in here? I'm hungry for dry things and something bitter."

"You've started early! My mother had cravings for lemons eaten without sugar, dry toast and swede turnips mashed with salt."

"Sounds heavenly," Bea said.

"Go and tell Dwight or he'll be the only one who doesn't know and that would hurt his pride. I promise to sound surprised when he breaks the news!"

"Hide the tray or he'll know that you guessed. Mashed potato and dry toast aren't his idea of fun eating."

"He's bringing in the apples. Go out there now," Emily suggested.

"Where's Bea?" Emma asked.

"Telling Dwight that he is to become a father," Emily chuckled. "I think she's told him. Listen to that. I think that's the way he'd call the hogs, as I've heard they do in America."

Bea came in looking demure, with Dwight holding her hand as if she were Dresden china. "We're having a baby," he announced.

"Not before lunch," Emily said. "I thought Bea looked peaky but it's early yet isn't it?"

"A bit off my food," Bea said solemnly. "I think a little mashed potato and dry toast might be what I really need." She managed to look satisfyingly fragile and dependent.

"What a good idea," Emily said and went to prepare the tray for the second time.

248